◆

30 APRIL 1945

WITHDRAWN

THE GERMAN LIST

ALSO AVAILABLE

December

Alexander Kluge, Gerhard Richter

TRANSLATED BY MARTIN CHALMERS

Air Raid

Alexander Kluge, Gerhard Richter

TRANSLATED BY MARTIN CHALMERS

WITH AN AFTERWORD BY W. G. SEBALD

◆

30 APRIL 1945

The Day Hitler Shot Himself
and Germany's Integration with the West Began

ALEXANDER KLUGE

TRANSLATED BY WIELAND HOBAN

Assisted by Thomas Combrink

With Guest Contributions by REINHARD JIRGL

TRANSLATED BY IAIN GALBRAITH

LONDON NEW YORK CALCUTTA

This publication was supported by a
grant from the Goethe Institut, India.

Seagull Books, 2015

Originally published as Alexander Kluge, *30. April 1945. Der Tag, an dem Hitler
sich erschoß und die Westbindung der Deutschen begann*
© Suhrkamp Verlag Berlin 2014.

English translations of Alexander Kluge © Wieland Hoban, 2015
English translations of Reinhard Jirgl © Iain Galbraith, 2015

First published in English by Seagull Books, 2015

ISBN 978 0 8574 2 298 9

British Library Cataloguing-in-Publication Data
A catalogue record for this book is available from the British Library

Typeset by Seagull Books, Calcutta, India
Printed and bound by Maple Press, York, Pennsylvania, USA

Contents

ALEXANDER KLUGE

Arrival at the Endpoint

◆

FIGURE 1. Europa. Anselm Kiefer

◆

I experienced that day in a town north of the Harz Mountains. At the age of 13. Our town has been occupied by the Americans since 11 April. At this point, I know nothing about the rest of the world from direct experience (what I hear and what I read should be considered indirect). No one has a real idea of the whole, says the architect Uri Bircher in Zurich. He reads the Neue Zürcher Zeitung.

This whole doesn't even exist, a doctor replies. They are sitting in a cafe. The collapse of a large-scale organization like Germany produces debris. And that debris, the architect adds, is not just from the buildings, trains and roads that have been destroyed; the soul-sack of every human being there contains pieces of different realities muddled together. I imagine, says the doctor, that in the enclaves where the organization of the previous years exists, that is to say, in Oslo, on Rhodes, in Breslau, in the fortresses on the Atlantic coast or in Prague, flags are still being raised.

As a reader in 2014, says the educator Böhmler from Bielefeld, it is actually difficult to empathize with what one knows (or thinks one knows) from those who experienced 30 April 1945. Everything that fills the senses in the cellars of embattled Berlin is so blatantly different from what is happening in an already-new state of reality under the rule of the Allies in the West.

Sluggishness: the hit songs of 1939 still playing in a person's head. The eye sees the brutal grey of explosions. The soul withdraws: Erwin Brinkmeier saw a group of Red Army soldiers at work, driving women into a cellar. Although he had buried a rocket launcher in his garden, he and his comrade, Block Leader Fred Schüller, did not leave their hiding place.

FIGURE 2. Refugees climb over the detonated bridge over the Elbe at Tangermünde to reach the western bank, and thus the Americans. (Photograph by Fred Ramage.)

'Galloping Daybreak'

The red sky of daybreak passed over the Reich capital which lay beneath a low-lying cloud cover, with the grey dust of battle and fires underneath. The light could barely find any footing in the debris and the streets. By contrast, the day cast itself expansively across the land to the west of Brandenburg up to the Harz. There, a rain front quickly sucked up all the power of morning, for example, on the border between Dingelstedt and Zilly. US Army supply convoys pushed along the avenues from the west in the hope of reaching the tank units, which were waiting there idly, by breakfast.

Death in Confusion

The von Voss family made for the woods. They wanted to flee. The bridge leading westwards across the river seemed impassable. Russian troops were approaching from Anklam. The landlord of the estate decided on suicide. He shot his wife, then his daughter. He killed the estate secretary, who came running out of the village, at her own request. Then he shot himself. The five were buried in the woods. Von Voss was not a large landowner but, rather, the overseer of a relatively small estate; the Russians would have called him a kulak. He was not a party member. It is far from certain that the Russian front troops would have done the refugees any harm; yet still this death. Von Voss considered his life over; he believed he had fallen out of reality.

The Weapon of Disregard

Still drunk on victory one and a half years later, the FRIEDRICH-WILHELM MÜLLER COMBAT GROUP in their quarters on the island of Crete. Mountain troopers, paratroopers, members of the 'Brandenburg Regiment' (secret service) and units of the 22nd infantry division. In November 1943, they had forced the British soldiers who had landed on the island of Leros to capitulate.

Once the German troops had left Athens and the northern mainland, the occupying forces on the Aegean islands and Crete were isolated. They were spoken of as an 'armed prison camp'. But in reality, they told themselves, they were capable of defending themselves against any of their local opponents.

The food situation was critical, especially for the Cretan population. A ship chartered by the Swiss Red Cross brought provisions and medication to Heraklion. The delivery was accompanied by British officers who had to be allowed on land and back on the ship again, and who were meant to supervise the proper use of the supplies for the population. As if the German troops would have stolen the goods! There was something disrespectful about the way the British envoys strode through the vicinity of the heavily armed Germans. They were the last intact Axis forces in the south. Once again they were condemned to wait. There is nothing more enervating than being ignored by the enemy. In the end, the German cadre wished that someone would pick them up there. On Monday, 30 April, they radioed the Allied headquarters in Alexandria and Naples to make an urgent enquiry about what was supposed to happen to them.

The Way to the West

He was considered the best shock-troop leader of his division. He was a headmaster, one of the youngest in the Reich, a classicist. Knowledge of the ancient languages helps one to distinguish between trees, bushes, soil conditions and the enemy, which almost constitute grammatical relationships when someone wants to creep through the terrain unseen. In this way he found a boat when he reached the Elbe from the east. He crossed the front on the western bank unrecognized and marched on west. In this way he got as far as the Rhine, where he surrendered to a rearguard post of the Americans.

He had raised suspicion with his long march. Was he a Werwolf belatedly surrendering? The German soldiers had already been taken prisoner months ago in this part of the country. The prison camps were soon to be dissolved. The description of his path to the West that he put on record sounded rather improbable. But he had achieved what he wanted—to get so far away from the front facing the Red Army that it would have been inconvenient for the Americans to hand him over to them.

The Most Dangerous Weapon of the Second World War
En Route Further Westwards

At night along the Danube, trucks drove up to riverboats that lay hidden in the undergrowth on the riverbank. Barrels were loaded onto the barges. The barrels were unmarked. Even in the darkness, the captains of the six river vehicles were still advancing kilometre after kilometre on the Danube, going upstream. They were ensuring distance from the eastern enemy.

Only years later did those involved find out that their task had been to prevent the enemy from getting their hands on the nerve gas, tabun, on the river. By day they were meant to look for shelter under overhanging branches on a distributary of the Danube. Before morning had broken, a motorboat caught up with them and gave the command to unload the containers once more onto pioneer barges.

—Extremely dangerous.

—This was one of the wonder weapons that people were talking so much about. The insidious gas was unknown to the Allies. It affected the nerves and could kill millions of people within seconds.

—If one had known of an effective way to spray it.

—It wasn't clear how one should spray it. For a while, people were saying that the gas was supposed to be sprayed over London by aeroplanes with converted lawn sprinklers, so to speak. One could have murdered the population of that metropolis.

—And the air crew too?

—That stuff is dangerous.

—The most likely contamination occurs in an accident when the gas is being transported.

—Terrible. That's why shipping it around at night was so dangerous.

—The point was to prevent the enemy from discovering the combat agent, because people would have said, 'That's the sort of thing the Germans want to use.' So it was a 'mobile escape'. The idea of stowing the containers in barges on the Danube and the Elbe came from Hitler himself. He was a man of the First World War; gas was a matter for the boss.

—It was moving the stores around that exponentially increased the risk of discovery.

—Ordered by the Führer. He still felt a secret horror at the mention of gas.

—But it wasn't a gas like they used in the First World War, it was an infernal new stuff.

What Is a Born Fighter?

It was 1958. Driving at night was relaxing for my employer, Hellmut Becker. The trees illuminated by the headlights which marked the limits of the country road, lulled him to sleep with their rhythm, the prospect of returning home to the house in Kressbronn. I noticed this from the fact that before he really started dreaming, he would grab the steering wheel and adjust the position of the car in relation to the middle of the road just in time. He 'played' with risk. He generally drove with the upper beams on in the expectation that oncoming vehicles would be dazzled by them and then switch on their own upper beams, thus warning him—even if he were only half awake. This way of driving was not without its dangers.

When he was in this sort of mood which reduced the day's tensions (we had had eight meetings in different places between Frankfurt and Ulm), he liked to attack my naivety which he presumed to recognize in my accounts of scenes from stories I was working on. One of these dealt with the reactions of a general in the Second World War, which I considered rash and unworthy of such a senior officer's position because they brought misfortune on others.

—And that surprises you?

—I would have expected something different.

—What do you imagine these generals were like?

I hesitated. Except for one senior officer in my family, whom I did not consider typical, my impressions came from hearsay during my childhood, as well as books, 'war magazines' and the accounts of adults who were interested in wars that were already in the past by the time of the Second World War. They spoke about historical commanders: negatively about officers during the Prussian collapse after Jena and Auerstedt, positively about officers in the Seven Years' War. I was also thinking of hussars and Pandurs, some of whom had risen to become commanders.

'But you know Döhner, Schuricke and Heckel,' Hellmut Becker continued insistently. These were senior officials in the Hessian education authority whom we both knew. 'Or Dr Schliephake and Director Rothe,' Becker went on. They espoused the ideology of the German Philologists' Association and were considered conservative and bureaucratic naysayers when it came to educational reforms. Becker claimed that the teachers associated with the Stuttgart Waldorf School, on the other hand, were inconceivable as generals. But it was precisely they (in my view) who were 'self-confident', 'determined', 'responsible' and 'boldly inclined'—heroes at the education front.

—You have to imagine a colonel like the headmaster of a state school, and a commanding general like the head of a ministry department.

—But those are civil servants.

—Career officers are civil servants.

Becker was winding me up, probably because he assumed that I didn't consider officers in the Second World War civil servants. 'An army group looks and acts like a ministry,' he said. Schlieffen was in charge of the archive in the historical department of the Prussian general staff before he became a war planner. Becker zeroed in on my ignorance. A further anticipation of the well-earned night's sleep that came closer with every kilometre we travelled through the night.

He had observed a great deal. Unlike myself, whose impressions relied on the eyes of others, he had experienced every phase of the Third Reich with the status of a 'man without qualities'. The concern of his mother, a lady from the Augsburg aristocracy, the director of her children's futures, was that he had no interest in committing to any existence, a profession, a commitment or a resolve in his present surroundings, instead moving along the periphery of his time, so to speak, as an observer. After the war, the circumstances seemed to have entangled him more in the realities of life. His mother remained suspicious. Even when he had acquired a wife, children and a lawyer's office, his mother still wondered whether he was living that life provisionally. Someone who concentrates on perception has a rich store of experience; they are INDEPENDENT. Indeed, Hellmut Becker struck me not as unable to commit but, rather, unwilling to commit, as if he was awaiting the arrival of a different reality that would demand a higher level of respect from him.

His mother's worldview was class-oriented. The Augsburg patrician was chosen to inject her husband's old, Flemish family with a touch of vitality and practical sense. It seemed to me that she had passed on contradictory impulses to her son: a high degree of ambition (which failed to reach her son because of the second kind of signals) and a quantum of haughtiness. Thus such words as 'teacher', 'headmaster' or 'civil servant' had a mocking undertone in the diction of this mother. How would she have characterized an enthusiastic type? I suspect that Becker would refrain from speaking about a type whose stance he might respect, in order not to damage such an image. I knew him well enough to know that in his tired state at the wheel, with a route full of twists and the headlights tracing every bend in the road, he would not have answered any questions. One cannot speak of what a born fighter or a hero is without chasing away its image.

No Securing of Property at the Sudden Dawn of a New Age

When I left my house in the expectation that I would never set foot in it again—perhaps I would still get as far as the border river which, rumour has it, the American vanguards have already reached—I pondered whether I should lock the front door or leave it open. Along the avenue, of which one could see a few kilometres from beside the village, Red Army units were advancing towards us. I hurried. It was as futile to lock the house as it was to leave it unlocked. I never saw the house again. When we looked for it after the reunification, we found that it had been replaced by a different building.

The Ways of Money

In the town of Schneidemühl, far behind the Red Army fronts, as if on an island, a telephone exchange was still operating, as was a consultant from the Deutsche Bank, geographically separate in an outbuilding of the financial institution. Thus 300,000 Reichsmark were transferred telegraphically from the account of a wood wholesaler to Minden, which was already occupied by the British, to the account of the account holder's brother, who was likewise a wood wholesaler. The capital flowed immaterially, electrically crossing seven zones of military power (as Soviet columns that had advanced far alternated with nests of German army resistance and Allied groupings) without any weapon effect through wires from peacetime that ran along railway lines.

A Future Fortune

As soon as he arrived on the western bank of the Elbe, a man carrying two suitcases was stopped by the GIs controlling the refugee crossing. The Americans suspected the civilian of being a German officer in disguise. Both suitcases, which they were able to open, were filled with shares (Siemens, Deutsche Bank, AEG, IG Farben). They were not worth the paper they were written on, said the German interpreter in his translation of the civilian's answer to the American guards' questions. Hence the GIs let this 'fool with the paper-filled suitcases' carry on along the road to the west. The papers were pressed tightly on top of one another and bound with clips.

At Least for a Glance

American convoys had advanced towards Gröningen, Oschersleben and further to Magdeburg. The old woman left her farm in Langenstein on 12 April after seeing to her cows and cycled in the direction of Ballenstedt. What she really wanted was to take her grandson out of the National Political Institute of Education and bring him home.

Three years before that, she had viewed the chance to be educated at the Napola[1] as something positive. She had approved of farmers' children from the primary school being chosen for grammar school, then transferred from there to the Napola. That would have led to a good career for a farmer's son. But now she felt that such 'selection' was dangerous. She could not bear the thought of a front of enemy soldiers between her and her grandson (who was all she had been left with after his father fell and his mother left the farm). She did not want to lose her grandson.

She imagined how she would approach him and speak to him. He would be standing with his schoolmates, she assumed. She would go up to him and urge him to come with her. At the same time, she realized that such an attempt would turn out to be an impossible

---

1 *Napola* is an abbreviated form of *Nationalpolitische Lehranstalt* (National Political Teaching Institution). These were secondary boarding schools with a focus on instilling National Socialist ideology and training military skills. [Trans.]

undertaking. An old woman cannot bring a boy who is standing around with his schoolmates back home; her grandson was not a mummy's boy. She hesitated inwardly while riding along her way.

In Ballenstedt she went around the building which was situated on an elevation. She had already advanced to the anteroom of the school administration. What should she say to them? She heard from the porter that her grandson's class was training in a high-lying woodland area. She appeared there, pushing her bicycle, the rucksack fastened to her narrow shoulders, observing the line of armed boys at the edge of a forest. The vantage point she had chosen kept her out of view of the group. Now she had at least seen her boy. She got back to the farm late at night. She had crossed the front twice.

On Imagined Roads

A convoy of military trucks, loaded with packs of duplicated planning documents concerning the defence of the Reich in the west, was driving towards the Elbe along a country road in the Uckermark. The papers were stamped 'Top secret! Delivery by officers only!' They were being driven across the country by non-commissioned officers. They contained the assessment of a war plan from 1924, only just declassified, in which von Stülpnagel, the head of the troop office at the time, had planned and described the manoeuvres for a defence of the terrain from the Rhine via the Weser up to the middle of the German Reich for every little river, every bridge, every hill and the majority of localities, based on the reduced forces of the 100,000-man army. Back in January, that would have been a valuable contribution to the current western defence.

The units still available now, in 1945, had more modern weapons and were more numerous than the troops supposed in the plan's model. They were, however (aside from a few experienced veterans of battles in Russia), less well-trained and lacked motivation; the troop was determined to stay together because the soldiers feared the end more alone than as a group. In addition, most of the terrain to be defended was already in the hands of the western enemy. This conceptual reinforcement, therefore, came too late. Since the autumn of 1944, every operation planned by the general staff had lacked 12 to 24 weeks for its realization. The plans were made in a space with negative time from which neither the leadership nor the defenders could escape. One could say that the trucks with their cargo, which was delivered versus receipt to a few scattered staff units that same evening, were driving beside realities, on 'imagined roads', while the wheels of the vehicles were still wearing themselves down on real avenues from the days of Napoleon. Petrol was excessively scarce.

Undertaking in the Manner of a 'Scouting Game',
Simply Because There Was Petrol Available

As there was still a Hungarian-delivered fuel depot in the southern Harz, having so far been protected from Wehrmacht access by the priority level of the subterranean arms cave project MITTELBAU-DORA, some assault guns and a few captured Czech tanks from 1938 standing in a shed came together for an elegantly led flank advance that, for a short while, gave an American supply unit something of a fright. The operation would have been praised in a 1934 Reichswehr manoeuvre, and now too, it gave those involved a last moment of happiness. Then, because no one could have said what purpose this military exercise served, and there were hence no guidelines for concluding it, they were ambushed by a US tank division and shot up by their artillery fire.

A Practice Flight out of Recklessness

The night before 1 May 1945, a British training squadron flew up the Rhine up to Mainz. The young pilots, who were to be trained first for deployment over the Reich, but now already for combat operations in the Pacific, and who already had some idea of how to fly the heavy machines, were practising night flying and orientation in the airspace via radar. As in the days when pilots had to fly by sight (that was the world of their instructors), the turnaround point for this practice flight, which was already going unnoticed by the enemy, was over Mainz, where the Rhine takes a distinctive bend. The glittering of the Rhine's tides in the moonlight made this bend a fixed landmark on night flights by sight, which had meanwhile become the stuff of legend. Squadrons that had lost their way in the expanse of the night looked for this Rhine knee almost habitually and dropped their bombs on Mainz which, in the dark, pilots could always presume to be at the edge of the great river in the dark. It then flared up, however, and was clearly visible to the observers in the rear after the drawn-out turn taken by the flying formation. An excess of orientation after every errant flight.

For the commander, this practice flight was a sort of 'farewell to the enemy'. With a parade like this he was paying tribute to the comrades who had been shot down. The training exercise itself did not correspond to any situation in which the crews could ever find themselves in the future. Nor were the bombers carrying any bombs. Had there been an accident or losses, it would have been difficult to explain the deployment to the superior officers. It was an excursion for luxury reasons, undertaken simply because the commanders, pilots and machines were able to.

Aftershocks of Wartime

Three large hotels flank the forecourt of the federal state capital's train station. The middle one was called the Station Hotel during the war and was only later renamed after the family that owned and managed it from the mid-1950s until 2008. Visitors from the periphery of the state who have business in the capital provide the hotel with custom. There are also hurried meetings for amorous reasons between extramaritally connected persons living far from each other. The advantage is proximity to the station—someone falls straight from the train into one of the beds. In the war, the centre of this state capital was lastingly demolished. By 1945, only two of the lower floors and the facade of the middle hotel (which continued to be family-owned after 2008, a well-functioning guest-accommodating machine but not 'modernized' by any corporate headquarters) still survived. The building was then reconstructed and furnished with what was available and using private means.

The marks of the wartime tremors are still visible in the interior, in the geological warping of the furnishings. There is a prevailing DISTURBANCE that can, after some acclimatization, feel 'cosy'. Objects are moved together by the guest and thus obey the guest's spirit. From the window one can see the side wing of the hotel, where window openings have been walled up. This would be unnoticeable looking at the papered wall inside; it is simply misshapenly larger than the opposite walls. Each room saw the later addition of a wooden frame comprising a bar, a clothes rail and a shelf. A second piece of carpentry 'refreshed' the wild, bare wall which, here too, suggested a bricked-up window. A lamp is built into the installation. Recently a 16:9 screen was fastened to the upper edge of the woodwork with a hinge.

Next to the chipboard door from the 1950s, which jams when opened and can therefore only be opened by jerking it towards the inside of the room, is a narrow mirror with a broad frame made of gold and silver. The mirror's reflection makes the space of the narrow room seem larger by a sliver. The bathroom displays dark violet wallpaper with large flower-shaped structures from a design period that lies in the past and is no longer common in the city. Above the modern ceramic sink is an 'antique' mirror with a broad golden frame that was already part of the furnishings before the outbreak of war (meaning that it survived the bombardments). It was never valuable, but it points to values (unnecessary in a washroom) that are actually found in palaces. It wandered from one of the salons or entrance halls of the former Station Hotel to this bathroom.

The blankets, half polyester and half cotton on the top and bottom as well as 100 per cent polyester in the filling, met a need in the years of reconstruction after 1950. At the time, the big chemical works that filled out the terrain between the state capital and large neighbouring cities provided large parts of the region with such cheap and cuddly blankets.

Guests and staff from many years paved the WAYS TO COSINESS in this incongruent accumulation of furniture and rooms. In the lift cabin, whose shaft was an empty cave for a long time after the bombing and was then renewed in its function through the installation of a used lift, there is a picture on the wall bought in 1926 by the original owning family, bearing the inscription: 'Give every day the chance to become the most beautiful day of your life. Mark Twain.'

The phases of reconstruction and the disastrous history of the city's destruction jumbled up the interior fittings. One also finds this mixture of shabby and precious in Parisian hotels. But those are homogeneous and well rounded. A situation where the objects in a hotel do not go together, as if an earthquake had shifted them to where they now stand, is only found in bombarded cities and formerly middle-class houses or palaces used by workers' organizations before 1989.

Film Scene in the Park

We are walking through the park. Do you want to get through? Then please go this way quickly. The area is cordoned off due to a film scene whose shooting is being secured by young helpers. Tracks have been laid. Please, you can go through here! The members of the film crew are asked not to obstruct the 'public traffic' in the park.

When I see a forest at night I do not think of robbers but of rapes in 1945 that I heard about. It doesn't help that I know; we are in our own present, not in those days. I found the efforts made to imitate 'forest' for the camera unnerving.

As we pass by again somewhat later on our next round, there are five-kilowatt lights shining on the trees. This creates a certain depth of impression that now means 'forest at night', not 'park'. It is 9 p.m. An actress wearing a rucksack over a red anorak is waiting for her cue. A rain machine is connected by fire hoses to large barrels standing in the undergrowth, and will produce 'dense rain' as soon as the unit manager gives the word. And within a radius of six square metres, the cameraman, controlling the rail ride in the seat of his dolly, has to adjust the squaring of his image to this rain. 'Please!' The camera dolly starts. The actress hastily strides over to the camera and 'stops with a dismayed expression' (which is difficult to act, and follows precise instructions, with a piece of tape stuck to the ground to mark where she is meant to stop).

The darkness thickened. As a result, the lights that had been set up behind the camera and were presumably being used to prepare for the next scene became more present. They illuminated the tips of the trees, setting them off against the dark in a bright green that vaguely recalled the light on young trees in May—though here, instead of coming from the sky, it reached the trunks and leaves from below. The contrast to the black of the park's other trees would later, in the film, create the impression of a forest that does not exist anywhere in the world. In the present case, however, this was not the intention of the film team, and would only have stood out to a future viewer as a 'strange effect' if the complete picture had been shown without any plot, not as a background to the realistic scene prepared in the script which advanced the plot.

In the meantime we, my sister and I, had completed a few more rounds of the park. We stood curiously next to the script and saw that the scene with the girl who 'quickly approaches, then suddenly stops with a fright, carrying a rucksack over a red anorak' had now been shot 16 times. The clapperboard for Take 17 was being prepared. The director, who was sitting in front of his monitor and saw neither the 'forest' nor the interesting rain machine, nor anything else outside the picture's limits, was impatient and dissatisfied. It seemed to me that he was watching the scene with the eyes of the editor who would, some 8 to 12 weeks later, devote herself to cutting these images on the studio monitor. He thought he could make out a little inconsistency in how the picture was filled out with 'downpour'; he pointed to the upper left side, where the thickness of the water (he saw this on replaying the picture) seemed to decrease. The unit manager responsible for this rain machine came over. The technician producing the rain was a specialist; perhaps it would have been worthwhile to develop 14 variations on 'rain with orchestra' with him (as an entertaining intermission in the occurrence of the criminal events). The way the scene was being shot, little of the rainmaker's expertise was being captured on film. And by now the actress was no longer as 'nimble' as at first; her performance seemed exhausted. Her glance towards Slate 22 had also become routine which meant that her facial expression in the close-up (exactly registered by the camera which moved towards this face on the dolly) could also be read as that of a young innkeeper looking at a guest in surprise at an unusual order.

We walked around the events on the park path another 12 times without any noteworthy change in the series of repetitions. Only late at night did the convoy of lighting and camera vehicles leave the grounds. The following evening, the place where the rain machine had released its watery loads was still marked as a mud desert limited to six square metres, a park ruin (micro-image of a destroyed city). In roughly one month, this ground surface will become a park again. The collective of earth and vegetation, 200 years old, is resilient. The 'healing process of a piece of ground after technological interference' would be worth capturing on film as a motif. The shooting requires patience and a sure sense of timing—a translation of the drawn-out process into a 'snapshot in front of an audience'. Perhaps also a bribe for the viewer in the form of an interesting noise or a comforting music, for watching such a film costs the viewer energy because they have to redirect their channel-trained interest towards a process that will only give them enjoyment after watching—an enjoyment of which they are unaware when they start watching the film. Better to offer them (as a confidence-building measure) a short introductory film to win their tolerance.

End of an Epoch

In Graz, in the days when the city was waiting for the Russians to march in (early April), there was a single tram that drove in a circle around the centre. 'I observed,' wrote a senior army doctor, 'an elderly officer entering the tram, and recognized him as Field Marshal List, who had commanded the Greek campaign four years previously. The fact that this man was using the free tram without any entourage,' the doctor continued, 'indicated to me that it was the end of the epoch.'

Processing the Spoils

In the north of Germany. With a trained hand, the British sergeant (he was a locksmith by profession) broke the marshal's baton of his prisoner, who attempted to behave like a figure of respect; but the young Briton would have none of it. This expert fiddled the gold moulding that decorated the baton at each end out of its fastening and pocketed the loot. Then he turned his attention towards the diamond embedded in the baton. The leather coat of this commander, who was now vigorously demanding something to eat, was of no use to the victorious non-commissioned officer because it was too wide; nonetheless, he laid the coat aside in the hope that he would still think of a good use for it. He did not expect any reward for handing over a high-ranking prisoner to his superiors. He left the appalled German behind in the house, unguarded.

It served that pompous ass right, felt the young London officer, who—in his native dialect, the jargon of the London docks—added the thought 'if one doesn't even think he's up to getting away.' The field marshal was no longer important. That was what the treatment the sergeant had chosen was meant to express. This disregard shocked the National Socialist, decorated with his embroidered and star-studded epaulettes, even more than the defeat of his country, to which he was gradually becoming accustomed.

Overcome by the Front

The files of the army's general staff, the memory of the army, were kept at the headquarters in Zossen, south of Berlin. Marshal Konew's troops had passed through this place and continued towards the capital without leaving a guard behind. One of the archive's administrators had been left behind to serve that function by the rest of the staff, who had fled to southern Germany, because he could not decide on the spur of the moment to leave his habitual field of work. He was also an invalid. Someone was needed who would look after the old stores—extinguish the flames if they caught fire but, equally, destroy them to prevent them falling into enemy hands. He had a great deal of time now. No chance of getting away on foot. Where could he go anyway? On the other hand, he was also attached to his documentary treasures. Every war plan written between 1881 and 1943 was kept there. The files were still tied up with string in those days. All of that was stacked on shelves in the cellars and on the ground floor.

One Disaster among Millions

When the trek came under fire, a mother sent her three children towards the forest, led by her eldest, an eight-year-old. They were to run up to a woodpile they had passed the previous day and wait for their mother. The children could not find the right place, and wandered through the forest from one woodpile to the next. Soon they had lost their way, and kept going in the direction they assumed would lead them back home, to their home town from which they had set off. Their mother looked for them in vain at the arranged meeting place, then proceeded in large circles. She had already fallen too far behind the column to catch up. As far as she went, she found no trace of the children. Even after the war, the mother's search remained fruitless. Where had the children run? Had they starved to death? Had they been met by someone? Were they lost without a trace?

No Enemy Was Needed to End the War

The soldier Köstritz (a roofer in peacetime) had survived four war zones unscathed and was now only a few kilometres from his home town. On his night march, he was shot in the stomach from a thicket by a young member of a Volkssturm or Hitler Youth unit. He wept, imagining the state in which his wife might still see him, a dying man with an open belly. The unfortunate shooter stepped towards him and saw the man weeping. Then the pain had already defeated the soldier. For Köstritz, no enemy was needed to end the war.

A Fatal Encounter between Two Jurisdictions

The roads leading from the southern slopes of the Thuringian forest to Franconia, sophisticatedly designed by the cameralists of the time to meet the needs of the eighteenth century, were jammed by vehicles from authorities that would never have encountered one another in such high concentration at any previous time. The convoy of the earlier administration of Zamość district was stranded in a little forest. Vehicles damaged, fuel used up. Another group of former officials from the east, still in full possession of their vehicles' mobility, encountered these colleagues. Immediately an argument broke out that dated back to 1943—at that time, the currently immobile civil servants had attempted to carry out a trial phase of Generalplan Ost locally, while the new arrivals in the forest had obstructed the decision together with other neighbouring districts. The feud between the authorities had ended with career setbacks and threats of duels.

Now the stranded group advanced towards the vehicles of the hated enemy with their service pistols, took over the parked cars and chased their colleagues into the woods. They began draining the opposing vehicles. But the rival authority had already mobilized a bivouacking unit of the military police (as stated earlier, all manner of ranks and organizations came together within a very small space that night, protected from the enemy's fighter bombers). The police with the gorgets arrested their institutional opponents, those who had been robbed of their vehicles. A military court was set up on the spot;

the officials for eastward expansion, who were of no use to the Reich anyway, were convicted of stealing the Reich's property and shot at dawn. Thus, a dispute over jurisdictions in 1943 revealed the murderous nature it had essentially always had.

An Anti-Bolshevik Prague for One Day

Too late to play a relevant part in the Second World War, the anti-Bolshevik army of the Russian General Vlasov had been set up and armed: three army corps, each consisting of three divisions, which meant three times 17,000 Russians. Two-thirds of this army marched through Southern Germany in late April 1945 with commandeering and threatening gestures. The German Reich no longer had any reservists that could have tamed this monster which felt betrayed as an ally of the Reich and saw no way out as an enemy of the victorious enemy. Left behind by the main forces, the First Army Corps, which included the elite regiments and was equipped with better weapons, stood in the environs of Prague, occupying almost the same positions from which Frederick the Great of Prussia had besieged Prague.

The commander of this unit, without authorization from his superior Vlasov whom he could not reach by radio or telephone, made an agreement with the Czech National Committee which was preparing a revolt against the German occupation. The Russians were to help shake off German rule; as a reward, officers and soldiers from the anti-Bolshevik army corps would be taken up into the new Czech National Army. Thus the German occupants and authorities scattered across the city and only weakly entrenched were surrounded, captured and, in certain cases, liquidated immediately. This was primarily the work of the disciplined First Army Corps which proved itself like a Praetorian Guard. After starting at five in the morning, the action was over by early afternoon—a day of hope and glory.

Representatives of the Czech National Committee were sitting together with anti-Bolshevik officers in one of the halls of Prague Castle. In the subsequent hours, however, it transpired that the US tank vanguards from the allied high command had been stopped near Cheb. Surrounded by Soviet units, the Russian troops were locked in; some of the battalions were decimated on the spot while others were deported in trucks to eastern camps where they were interrogated, arbitrarily split up into different degrees of guilt, and almost all killed. The National Committee in Prague, now without a military power base, was unable to keep its power and was deposed by the authorities installed by the Red Army.

Much That Had Been Left Unfinished
Was Still Meant to Be Taken Care of

The carriages shunted together at a railway junction between Pilsen and Prague on the night before 30 April were loaded with large crates of candles. The delivery was a delayed response to a request from the winter of 1941/42. At the time, as the defence officer von Gersdorff reported, there had been a crisis of confidence about the command at the eastern front because the supply lines had broken down and the soldiers felt they had been left in the lurch. In the middle of winter, the worst aspect was that the front was in darkness for 16 hours a day. The supply machinery, which had gradually returned to operation in February, responded to the November and December requests according to the terms they were used to: ammunition, rations, human reinforcements, construction materials, supplies for the horses, medication, bridge material, mail, propaganda and leaflets. The demand for lighting equipment vigorously made by the Army Group Centre went unanswered. The Hindenburg lights brought along for the attack on the Soviet Union and the few aggregates for generating electricity had been lost in the hasty retreats before Moscow. In the spring and summer, it was impossible to give priority to the demand for candles and petroleum lamps. Then, in the winter of 1942/43, there were other concerns and the troops (now in the Russian south) were no longer lying static in the winter desert but were, rather, in a state of excited regrouping until the muddy period began.

In the meantime, however, the requested candles had been produced by various firms back home and been taken up into the Reichsbahn's transport plan without precise dating. The eastern front no longer existed. The railway officials responsible for transporting the crates were planning a delivery to the Slovak border, where the Army Group Schörner had kept a line of defence occupied only three months earlier. Bringing the carriages together on 30 April was an implementation of that three-month-old plan.

When asked whether the rail transport of the candles (the train was already lying burnt-out on the rails by that afternoon, having been destroyed by fighter bombers) had been a case of bad planning, the British historian John Röhl replied that this should not be decided purely by the result. Providing light for the winter front in 1941 had been a psycho-strategic priority. Such an aim does not lose its validity because it has been imperfectly pursued.

The railway carriages then burnt up on the tracks, though this did not reduce the mass of candle wax. Candle wax is a combustive agent, unlike the wick. The wood of the carriages and the wicks fell victim to the fire. The wax mass lay inert on the tracks, under the destroyed freight train.

—What could have been the reason why they didn't send enough candles to the eastern front in December 1941?

—The rail system broke down. Candles weren't available.

—But there were enough candle reserves in the Reich in the lead-up to Christmas.

—Not in the organizational sector of the army procurement office.

—One should have had civilian institutions hand over their candle reserves.

—Then tell me, who would have been authorized to give such a command in a reserve army?

—But it was a dictatorship.

—The highest authorities that were running the dictatorship were in a state of constant and escalating agitation. In a dictatorship in particular, not everyone can command.

—So a lot of things piled up on the last working day of the Third Reich?

—Much that had been left unfinished was still meant to be taken care of.

The Last Days of 'Eternal France'

Well into April: radio contact with a few bases of the Vichy government that were still reporting to Hohenzollern-Sigmaringen. The German ambassador had taken President Pétain across the Swiss border in a convoy. This ensured physical invulnerability. For functional reasons, he stayed in the empty rooms of the South German palace where a number of prefects and secretaries, because there was nothing else to do (and they did not want to wait idly for their arrest by the advance troops of the so-called FREE FRANCE), were confirming administrative decisions, promotions and death sentences— an authority that had real consequences abroad and which, in the unreal nights of the regime's end times (coming in a direct line from the Merovingian ruler MEROVECH, born of Quinotaurus, half bull and half man), was entirely remote from any stirring of the heart.

A Provisional Life

An émigré from the old France, the doctor and writer Céline, for whom an arrest warrant had been issued by an examining magistrate of the 'free France', had been taken from his residence in Sigmaringen to Denmark by women who were protecting him (just as Sarah Harrison is guarding Edward Snowden today). What was he supposed to write, and for whom? Can a writer be transplanted? Until then, he had run his medical practice underneath Sigmaringen Castle. A Danish lawyer managed to obtain a provisional residence permit for Denmark from the department of internal affairs.

The Trains East of the Brenner Pass Were Running at Full Tilt

The American aerial-warfare planners called the procedure that became increasingly refined towards the end 'interdiction'. The railway tracks that filled out the gorge-like terrain of the Brenner Pass had been mangled by air strikes. The trains stood there on the rails which were interrupted by funnel-shaped holes; some of them had burnt-out flak stands. But the locomotives and carriages had also been jack-knifed by the force of the explosions. The passage through the valley was blocked by a mass of iron parts. 'No traffic can pass through here for some time,' said Chief Rail Official Schmitt, who still had a radio team at his disposal and could thus inform the subordinate branches on the way to Italy and Innsbruck, but did not know how he was to leave this 'place of devastation'. Even on foot it seemed a difficult task.

The return transports of the army group in Italy came to a halt after Fortezza and Brixen. The personnel explored routes and secondary lines to get machinery and men (or only the men, if need be) out of the neck of the valley to be transported to the Reich via the Carinthian route.

—What difference did it make whether the troops were taken captive in northern Italy or on the territory of the Reich?

—There was still the notion that the comrades wanted to go home. It was a matter of saving people's faith in their leaders. The trains east of the Brenner Pass were running at full tilt.

Three Russian Offensives in the Eastern Alps and up the Danube

The special correspondent of the *Neue Zürcher Zeitung* had travelled through Southern Germany before returning to Zurich, where he gathered information from Austria by telephone. In his report he wrote:

Marshall Tolbuchin achieved the encirclement of Vienna with the same tactic he had used to enclose Budapest 15 weeks earlier. After a deployment in the south, his troops went around the city in the west until they reached the Danube. The last people who managed to leave Vienna by automobile fled east across the Danube, then escaping to Linz or Budweis on detours.

One of Tolbuchin's remarkable achievements was the rapid crossing of the Vienna Woods west of Baden. Now the advance is following in three directions. North of the Danube, Malinovsky's army is heading directly west in order to reach the hill country on the Bohemian border. South of the Danube, Tolbuchin's army, marching towards the Enns via the rivers Traisen and Ybbs, has a substantial headstart. Between the rivers Leitha and Salzach there are several camps, where many of the Hungarian Jews deported by the Germans were kept in the autumn.

[. . .]

The Royal Hungarian Army, which Hitler had to withdraw from the front because, after the Miklós cabinet's declaration of war on Germany, it was only waiting for an opportunity to go over to the Allied camp, is stationed in Upper Austria and Bavaria. This means there may be great surprises when they encounter American and French troops.

Although the mountains on the border between Lower Austria and Styria constitute an obstacle, especially the Hochschwab massif (2,277 metres), there is an easy route into the Mürz valley via Mariazell. As all attempts to advance to Mürzzuschlag south of the Semmering Pass have so far failed, the third Russian route follows the upper Rába and the railway from Steinamanger after the central Mur. But the 'iron ring of the SS around Berchtesgaden' only starts at the Dachstein (2,995 metres) and the Hochalmspitze (3,360 metres).

[. . .]

While Carinthia, where the United States have had major capital interests for over 30 years, supposedly belongs to the British or American zone, the Yalta plan assigns Lower Austria and northern Styria to the Russian occupation zone. Russian interest in a new Austria is undoubtedly also supported by industrial-political considerations.

'But this one is called the Ister. It dwells in beauty.'

Yet the river almost seems
To flow backwards, and I
Think it must come
From the East.

Friedrich Hölderlin, 'The Ister'

Like ships, unnoticed by the battlefronts, they had advanced *eastwards* with the river. They could have reached the Black Sea like that. They got as far as Budapest. It was a test advance of the navy. The special diving unit had been rubbed with grease and wrapped in cold-repellent suits. The divers were really only meant to enter Red Army–occupied Budapest to prove that it was possible. Then the besieged city would be supplied via the Danube using containers of ordnance (guided by a few people steering these containers on converted one-man torpedoes).

In the meantime, the direction of movement had reversed. Lieutenant Bernd Ullrich, director of a community college in peacetime, had already been moving upstream in parallel with the Danube for four days and nights on his bicycle, taking a mountain path. It was the thrust of the fear of being overtaken by his Russian pursuers that impelled the young commander, far more strongly than the river with the swimmers could ever have done. He had lost all his people on this return march. He did not feel drawn to the river's source. But with all his power he pushed on towards the only enemy he still trusted—the tank vanguards of General Patton far to the west.

Down in the valley, leftovers of the rearguard were racing away in flight. In the night, Ullrich had seen the flashes from exploding Russian tank shells on the horizon in the east, not far off now. Here, the river was already narrowing. Ullrich rode upstream 'as if out of his mind' (from fatigue and overexertion). The Romans called the Danube the ISTER. Hölderlin used this name to refer to the river in his hymn. This was not a direct help to the passionate teacher Ullrich in these decisive moments of his backwards advance (with more energy than the one that had taken him to Budapest).

The End of Hostility, Experienced at the Vienna Burgtheater

In October 1944, as a consequence of the total war, all theatres in the Reich had been closed and the staff made available to the Wehrkreisersatzkommandos [military district replacement troops]. Five soubrettes from the Gau of Saxony-Anhalt were given a crash course in radio communications and deployed behind the front in

Hungary. For as long as possible, they stayed in radio contact with a tank division that had blown up their tanks on the retreat, owing to petrol shortage, and were searching for an escape route to Vienna. At every step of this fiasco, they, the soubrettes, telephoned and radioed in just the same way they would have completed every performance at home (even if several singers had cancelled). In the meantime, this was happening more by telephone than radio, because the robust telephone and telegraph lines remained operational for longer than the sensitive radio devices which also had the disadvantage that the enemy could listen in.

And so the five had reached Vienna and there, put up by artist colleagues and dressed in mufti, been overrun by the Red Army. On 30 April they arrived at the canteen of the Burgtheater. That was the first day of rehearsals for the first premiere after the war, Grillparzer's SAPPHO. They were put in the chorus, even though they were singers and would have had more to offer than declaiming choral songs. They were so happy to have returned to a temple of art from the bitter war that when the rehearsals were over, the five of them combined Grillparzer's words with melodies by Ferdinand Raimund and sang them, with members of the theatre chorus joining in. This created a comedic mood, a burlesque that—in the midst of devastated Vienna—gave artistic expression to the end of hostilities.

A Hotel in No Man's Land

On 30 April, the Grand Hotel Adlon is running almost as smoothly as in peacetime. It has its own electricity supply. Well stocked, partly because the deliveries for the Foreign Office's traditional Wednesday dinner, which is no longer taking place, have not been used up.

There is fighting a thousand metres away. A fire in the roof truss this morning was put out by the staff and some of the guests. Since yesterday, the hotel has no longer been billing guests. No change in the rhythm of meals throughout the day. Guests from Hungary and Sweden, and Austria which no longer belongs to Germany. There are wounded lying in the foyer and on the bottom two floors.

The head waiter has been doing his job since 1925. Instructions are made and carried out with no problems. No nervousness.

FIGURE 3 (LEFT). The head waiter at the Hotel Adlon, which was still intact at the time, 100 metres from the Brandenburg Gate.

FIGURE 4 (BELOW). The Brandenburg Gate on 30 April 1945. The molecules of this monument are the same ones as in 1945.

FIGURE 5. Behind the four flags, to the right of the Chancellor: one of the pillars of the Brandenburg Gate. In front of Obama, the bulletproof wall of armoured glass.

The 'Black Hand' of 1914

Would Not Have a Chance against the President of the USA

For security reasons, the US President's motorcade took a detour on its approach. The sun was coming down hard on the exposed guests sitting in the stands without suit jackets, and on the thick pane of bullet-proof glass behind which President Obama was giving his address. To the back of him, a 600-metre area behind the Brandenburg Gate that was guarded and cordoned off. None of those present could imagine this historic monument in the state it had been in during April 1945.

The president's immediate and long-term safety is the concern of his own security staff. German security measures are only of an auxiliary nature and relate to the wider region. But just as a conspiracy killed the heir to the Austro-Hungarian throne in Sarajevo, an attempt on the president's life would only trigger a world war if a major power could be found guilty of the deed.

We, the security administrators of the Federal State of Berlin, will be glad when the president is back on board his aeroplane. It seems to me that his speaking time is coming out of the time needed for the solution of world problems, for finding mines and defusing conflicts that is the duty of the leading power's president. If one adds up all the interruptions in a US president's term of office, like this detour from the G8 summit in Ireland to the German capital, it becomes apparent that a US president's term of office is too short for his task.

Outrageous Decisions in So Short a Time

On a June day in 2013, within some 20 minutes, the President of the USA had to decide in real time between seven options, modified by lectures at the conference, whether and to what extent (and above all, to which individual organizations in the armed Syrian opposition) light weapons should be delivered. Four assistants watched like guardian angels over his papers and what he said; the president was not to act hastily or do the wrong thing. But his helpers could not simply say to him, 'Mister President, you seem muddled at the moment—calm down, your hands are shaking.' Or: 'Please think twice about that.' There would not have been any time to go over everything more than once within the 20 minutes (divided into minutes and seconds for the individual fragments that combined to form the 'decision'). After the 20th minute, once the resolution had been recorded, there would either be a further escalation in the Middle

FIGURE 6. The wall of glass protecting the US President from possible attackers also separates him from anyone who would fall to their knees before him in surrender (Snowden, for example); indeed, it separates rulers from ordinary reality as a whole.

East or the limited arms shipment would have a de-escalating effect. What happened here can only be judged years later. In the case of a spiral of escalation, the consequences of the president's morning decision could extend to a period of 10 years or more, or be completely irreversible.

More Waste than Ever Before

From the president's arrival until Air Force One had closed its doors for take-off, the detour to Berlin cost one and a half days. Punched out of the time budget of the 'most powerful man in the world'. But he is not *powerful*, because he has no time. US time, represented by a wealth of urgent messages, was lagging seven hours behind the local time. In that sense, the moment in which the aeroplane doors shut and the moment in which he arrives at the White House airfield are (according to the global average time) one and the same. As it happens, however, irreplaceable decision-making time was wasted all day long—on being transported back and forth, radiating friendliness, marching past lined-up troops, waiting times and times for leaving.

Intense concentration between all that, because every word of the speech had to be delivered with no mistakes and with pauses between sentences. Thinking a little, making decisions, internalizing information, looking back on the course of two years—none of that is possible during the activities of the state visit. The result is a long-standing deficit in the time budget of the great hope with regard to the gradual production of a better world by not speaking.

Deadline Pressure for the Führer

I am often overlooked. I organize the Führer's diary when his secretaries do not. In addition, as his manservant's assistant, I put out his shirts for him in the morning. Many of the Führer's decisions, which ultimately led us to disaster, were based on the special value (and thus deficiency) held by the time of a man who combines so many areas of responsibility, and is the object of so many expectations that one individual does not have enough hours in the day for everything. He was always worried about his health. He did not believe he had a long life ahead of him. (Though he did reckon with a longer one than that which he brought to a close this afternoon.)

As a result, everything happened too hectically. One could have waited before declaring war on the USA, a disastrous act, until our submarines had actually gathered out on the Atlantic. Then one would have had time to consider and perhaps refrain from declaring war, just as our Japanese ally never entered the war against the Soviet Union. And certainly a whole week, not two days, would have been the right time frame for Molotov's visit. The conference was over before those participating in it had even warmed up. The attack on the Soviet Union would also have needed to take place either three months earlier (with mud-equipped tanks, if such things exist) or not before 1952. For all these decisions, too little time and no time at the right moment. My Führer did not like predictions about his resilience in the years to come. Hence the rush. We also saved too little of the head of state's precious time. Six handshakes already take up a minute of living time. But now, in the last days since his last birthday, the value of 'Führer time' has dropped. I often saw him sitting around on the few seats in the bunker. It seemed to me that he was waiting. In fact, barely anyone spoke to him. For the first time in over 12 years he had a surplus of time, but there was no longer anything in the national interest for which he could have used it. Going by his diary entries, the appointments and the record of his activities, he had already been dead for some time by the time he died (if I knew my boss, he saw the end coming).

Venus Plus Mars in Square Relation to Saturn:
The Constellation of Death

I am writing my expert's report in anticipation of the anniversary of Hitler's death, and the Conference for Astrological Research which will take place in Hawaii in August 2015, owing to public interest in the facts concerning the end of the war in 1945 (which, because of the conference's location, includes events in the Pacific). I am less concerned with Hitler's death (which is a trivial matter for any astrologer as soon as they compare, even superficially, the constellation at his birth with that on 30 April 1945); rather, I am interested in the splendour of the Assyrian school of astrology which examines the details more precisely than any other.

We 'Assyrians'—unlike those in the occident—count 52 planets, and can therefore measure the Führer's signs of paralysis, the death of his bitch and the constancy of his strictly negative posthumous fame, and explain more clearly why he cannot have experienced the progression of Jupiter which gave world events in general a brighter disposition almost simultaneously with his death. It was a matter of hours.

We show the concentration of energy in the horoscope. It is characterized astrophysically and psychophysically by the inversions of above and below, as these are mirror-symmetrical. This strikes me as instructive concerning Hitler's already weakened body, because the spiritual potential of this fragile carrier rises before death. We Assyrians say that it emanates. That is the only explanation for the insistently undying significance of this man, especially in the media of the Anglo-Saxon world, but also sporadically in Africa, as well as the great popularity of all Hitler films which make him a figure never matched by actors. In astrology, positive and negative portents are of equal value. So I need not even begin to speak of fame and counter-fame, as negative fame postulates the same energetic attention as the positive kind, and indeed persists for longer than affirmative distinc-tion, which requires a height from which something can fall, whereas a consistently negative position, that of lying on the ground, proves the more resilient form of life. According to his birth horoscope, that is what he always wanted—to become famous.

Survivors of near-death experiences who returned from comas and recounted what they had witnessed allegedly stated that they did not see Hitler in Elysium, yet did find Robespierre and Napoleon there. These witnesses are unreliable. What person, returning from death, could have seen the entire hereafter during such a brief experience? Then it is more realistic to analyse the movements of the 52 relevant heavenly bodies, not merely the nine planets, the Moon and the Sun. Therein lies the thoroughness of the Assyrian method—it takes into account spiritual, yet high-mass stellar bodies such as Lilith (of the 52 Aristotelian planets, 12 are real and 40 imaginary). In this way, the discipline I represent differs from all competing ones except that of Dr Fludd, who can himself be considered Assyrian-Syrian and, therefore, congenial.

The Threshold for Violent Killing in a Stone Age Tribe

The ethnologist Erwin Zumsteg, like all those of his age, had received a draft notice via a post office box in the northernmost Australian city in September 1939. He had not interrupted his research work (he was integrated into a tribe continuing a Stone Age culture on one of the islands of New Guinea). One cannot arrive or leave at short notice in such a context. Later he did not enquire again, living here in a temporal structure far removed from the present and beyond reach for the enforcement measures of the German Reich authorities. He was a conscientious objector, as it were, a deserter from the now for important reasons but a front soldier of prehistory.

He had adequately documented the rituals and everyday habits of this tribe, as well as their vocabulary, as far as he could understand it, and recorded the rudimentary structures of this indigenous people's elaborate grammar, until the spring of 1945 when a meteorological disaster destroyed his documents, forcing him to write them down again from memory. Thus he continued his residence here, fed by his hosts like a 'white god', though he doubted that they considered him anything extraordinary. He attributed the tolerance shown towards him by the presumably warlike tribe to a tradition of hospitality rights that protected refugees, oddballs and fools from violence. In Europe he would presumably have been shot dead by now, he told himself. Thanks to a primitive radio that enabled him to listen passively to distant transmissions but not to make any of his own, he had received sufficient news on his island to be certain that a return to the homeland was currently impossible. He did not dare venture into British-controlled territory. A journey via Japan and Siberia seemed out of the question to him that April 1945.

The Stone Age tribe whose life he documented was in a state of permanent conflict with neighbouring tribes. Internally, however—aside from battle-like rituals that evidently served to stabilize the memory and reinforce the establishment of social distinctions—there did not seem to be any killings or violent exclusions. In the six years of his research he had not known of any theft, nor any concealment of facts or lies. The 'savages' were heavily armed. They had a suitable physique for confrontations (indeed, they could bite or strangle like wild animals, but only directed such violent force at objects).

Zumsteg, who was going by a native name with which the researched addressed him, noted a high potential for attack, yet also a clear threshold for the violent deployment of these powers. If other Stone Age peoples were similar, he thought, then the early beginnings of humanity were not based on aggression, as Sigmund Freud had assumed. Cannibalistic fantasies were reported in the myths of the tribe. But certainly not in practice! Neither with their own nor with prisoners from different tribes. They had disarmed the enemy and sent them away. After his return to 'civilization' in 1952, Zumsteg (who had meanwhile become a Swiss citizen through marriage) attempted in vain to achieve the recognition of the Stone Age people he had studied as an *autonomous* nation by the United Nations. Land, defensive capacity, a community and (as he documented) a culture of writing, as well as a form of judiciary—these are the requirements of a nation—could be found in the little tribe which consisted of no more than 120 people and did not feel subject to any power on the globe.

'Everyone Approved of the Killing'

The Werwolf members in a village in the Inn Valley, located between Rosenheim and Kufstein, included the 17-year-old son of a carpenter. He had signed and sworn by the certificate that made him a Werwolf. Now he wanted to leave the Werwolf. The leader of the local Werwolf group went to the apostate's father and reproachfully confronted him with his son's behaviour. One could not revoke a sacred oath like that of the Werwolf pact in the same way one terminates an employment contract.

The carpenter disagreed. There was an exchange of words, made all the more heated by the fact that they knew each other as neighbours. The father seized a pistol and shot. The Werwolf leader was injured, but not fatally. He was now lying in one of the rooms of the house. The pain caused by the wound seemed to have tempered his motivation.

The incident was reported to the local commander, a major general from far away in the east who had ended up here. The situation was unstable. The village was prepared for defence by one company each of the Waffen-SS, the Reich Labour Service and the army. The Werwolf base had been set up in a nearby wooded area. With such differences of background and training among the three defence companies, tensions arose between them.

The village's opinion leaders arrived at the conclusion that the half-killed man groaning in his room should be done away with entirely. Everyone assumed that were was little time to carry out their decisions. An army officer born in the village then killed the wounded Werwolf with a hammer. All of this happened on 30 April 1945.

Many years later, the public prosecution department of Traunstein investigated the case. The army officer who was interrogated as a suspect referred to the major general's orders. The latter, who had meanwhile become a resident, denied given any such orders but confirmed that he had approved of the killing. The danger was too great, he explained, that knowledge about the attack on the Werwolf would have triggered a reprisal from the SS unit against the locals. The respected master carpenter was in danger, at any rate. And why, the prosecutor demanded of the defendant and the witness, was the Werwolf not shot with the pistol which was after all within reach? The jurist had to ascertain whether the killing of the injured man, defenceless at the time, with a hammer met the legal prerequisites of 'maliciousness' and 'particular cruelty'. Those involved replied that the only way to prevent the incident from becoming known was to eliminate the victim noiselessly. The bang of a shot would not have been appropriate in the actual situation. But the earlier pistol shot

that had wounded him had also been audible, countered the prosecutor. One should not tempt fate twice, responded the apparently
calm major general.

The outcome was that after consulting the president of the responsible criminal chamber, the prosecuting authority (also confused by the
execution of an executor who was sworn to murder, and had
demanded the master carpenter's support for such activities with a certain verbal threat) decided to close the proceedings on grounds of
EXCESSIVE SELF-DEFENCE. In extreme situations, the district
court's director stated in his conversation with the prosecutor, the law
is 'bent'—like space and time when a star explodes. The modern-
thinking jurist had only recently read an article about stellar disasters
in the science and technology section of the *Frankfurter Allgemeine Zeitung*.

How Small a Number of Military Predictions Survive a Quarter-Century

A series of lectures that took place in one of the large hotels near
Wilhelmstrasse in the autumn of 1929—only for invited guests, who
had to sign a statement that they would treat the content of the pres-
entation as secret—dealt with the modern conception of war that
could be expected in 25 years. The cities of the Ruhr region and
those along the Rhine would then be encased in a gas bubble. 'Fogged
in' by us? No, set up by enemy air squadrons as a gas bubble. The
towns could not be entered either by the enemy or by their own residents. It was unclear where the populations would go. Would they
survive in sealed basements?

The notification system would be revolutionized, the speaker continued. But he did not describe the ultra-short-wave technology that
would genuinely be available after 25 years which would allow tank

crews to communicate while at full speed but, rather, assumed that radio transmissions would use ready-made abbreviations ensuring that no harm could follow if the enemy listened in. The air squadrons would be rivalled by immense flak-proof zeppelins, floating artillery platforms, as it were. The Reich's flying machines would be set up far in the east, he claimed, hidden in wooded areas. They would be used as a surprise weapon as soon as the enemy had advanced far into the Reich. Then, between 1944 and the first quarter of 1945, there would be a counteroffensive progressing gradually from the north to the south-west, with cannons mounted on motor vehicles accompanying the vanguard of the infantry attack—as practised, but carried out with insufficient determination in May 1918.

It was assumed that the enemy would rush forwards with armoured cars which would be equipped with mounted floodlights at night. These would turn night into day and initially startle the German troops with the dazzling beams of light. All these modern methods could be faced with the necessary training which would have to make soldiers immune to such terrors. Rockets, it was assumed, would be there to make the vehicles faster. They were useless as long-range weapons.

In the 26 years between then and 1945, the picture of war had arrived at entirely different sceneries. No gas warfare at all, amazingly enough, although the troops always carried gas masks with them. Rockets as long-range weapons that could decide a war, if used on a sufficiently massive scale, could have been developed as a globally effective means of destruction by 1952, especially in the form of a V4 which 'rides' on the stratosphere like a stone bouncing on a water surface, its effect increased by the rebound. No zeppelins anywhere. A popular uprising in the east to defeat the western enemy at the last minute, the final piece of the 1929 prophecy, was obsolete there in 1945, both geographically and on account of the Red Army's presence.

Arrival at the Endpoint

The leftovers of my heavy battery of 15-cm cannons got as far as Harsleben. Reported for duty in 1939, and reached a place in April 1945 that we could not consider the end of our odyssey. We saw to the horses in the local stables. We concealed the cannons. The surrounding villages seemed to have been occupied by US troops.

My superiors never understood what exactly they could do with a unit like ours. We artillerists are the same as our limbers, the cannons and the horses, and they are like us. The 15-cm cannon is too heavy to be transported in one piece on a cart pulled by the four horses. So the barrel is removed and carried on a separate cart. The assembly of this industrial device designed for long-range shots takes 20 minutes. But then we are ready to fire. In the 20 minutes leading up to that, any Indian can capture us.

At the start of the eastern war, we were still gaining ground; the command had the idea of setting up artillery bases with heavy weapons. Certainly such a concentration of several departments would have had enormous firepower. In reality, we spent hours and days in such cases going back and forth behind the front, and almost always arrived late. The planners never learnt that we could not move the heavy machinery and the Belgian horses so quickly. If we go uphill, the horses are out of breath by the time we get halfway, and they have to rest—often overnight. It would have been better if we had not moved and simply shot.

We who were stuck in Harsleben had gathered ample experience of this kind. We were waiting to be captured. We had a retreat of over a thousand kilometres behind us, taken at a trot. Would the horses be taken care of properly if we were not here?

Then, that afternoon, a US patrol came driving through the village in their jeeps. They were amazed by our cannons and the genuinely excellent horse material we showed them. They then symbolically 'captured' us by taking away our bayonets. They realized that they needed us to tend to the machines and the horses. They came from the Midwest, and had experience of their own with horses and tractors. Late in the evening they also brought supplies (biscuits, canned meat, ice cream). They had taken a shine to us.

On Side Paths

North of Hanover, on side paths that already belonged to the heath, a herd of high-quality horses was being driven along. The team driving them belonged to the manor of the aristocratic family who owned the thoroughbreds, and wanted to bring them to safety at a large farming estate they owned near the Danish border (they feared the covetousness of the occupying power). Field Marshals Fedor von Bock and Erich von Manstein had joined the group. Each had a cart for himself and his luggage, drawn by horses that were not comparable to those from the stud farm (though they were more suitable for drawing a cart, and patient). The caravan proceeded slowly along sandy paths. Here, so far from the main roads, there were no British patrols. On one occasion they came by a German artillery post, still ready for fire. The commanding officer reported the number and assignment of his people to the marshals, whom he knew from the propaganda postcards made for them.

He Wished He Could Come Home

Still the old arrogance. Wrapped up in his military coat, physically intact, even chubby cheeked. He also had a car with a driver at his disposal. There was no visible sign of the guilt he carried inside him.

He moved carefully and approached the property, his own house, from the edge of the forest. When he could see all of it he paused. He waited for a long time. Now the children came out, they played in the yard and the garden. He watched them for a long time. He also saw his wife, who was setting out for town. He would have liked to take a shower, change his clothes, embrace his wife and children. He could not show himself. His presence would contaminate the family, and he could not rule out the possibility that the property was a trap and there would already be men waiting to catch him. Perhaps he and they were watching the same house. When he returned to the vehicle, he had a strong feeling that he would not see this place again. Even if he made his escape alive, using the route prepared by his comrades, there would be an ocean separating him indefinitely from what had once again attracted him so violently.

'Guilt, the Oldest Marble'

It is a misinterpretation to say that guilt is 'as hard as stone', Ezra Pound remarks. One cannot hew guilt with a chisel, and it is nothing that can be rolled along. It is no obstacle to vehicles, of whatever kind. Nor does guilt flow (and it cannot be drained from the guilty body through bloodletting). Rather, in its obsessively defended ETERNAL

LIVELINESS—like an old woman who refuses to die—it is comparable to a breath, or a storm or sudden temperature drop. In keeping with this, Pound heard a loud hooting sound at midnight on the accounting date of the Axis, 30 April, that was unlike any alarm siren. He could not find anyone to confirm this impression.

The Intertwinement of the Spiritual World with the Real

In the spiritual world, which is after all unaffected by the country's victory or defeat, the essences from the 52 realities that correspond to the Aristotelian planets and enclose our own, merely imagined static reality, drifting over unavenged from various pasts, moved through the villages and countryside in microscopic tunnels on 30 April—as on every other date. The leaders of these drifting entities stated that they were on the way to the Reich's day of judgement. It was clear, however, that the wild hunt of the transmigrating souls, which is what they turned out to be in the night-time, came from many other parts of the world—for example, Tasmania and the Mexico of the Aztecs, and by no means only Central Europe. And the trains too, on their high-speed journeys, shot about among one another like bullets. This created little flashes when they collided, but these were one dimension too small to be perceived by the human senses. They were enough of an event for the emotions.

A Ghostly Celestial Phenomenon over the Brocken

In the months leading up to his death, in which he already felt very weak (he staged a revue based on Alfred Döblin's NOVEMBER 1918 at the Deutsches Theater in Berlin), Einar Schleef developed his SKETCHES FOR NEW MUSIC THEATRE in the breaks at work.

He had already compiled music by Bach, Wagner, Gluck, Purcell, Rihm and Nono on tapes for the project. Imposing choral passages, not theatre scenes, were a means of expression for him.

He was preoccupied by the vision of his (presumably 'possessed') piano teacher in Sangerhausen, who claimed to have seen a light phenomenon mostly in the east during the night of 30 April—Walpurgis Night—that she had described as a 'wild hunt': an 'unusual, luminous storm formation' over the Brocken. 'It is out of the question that I am mistaken' was her answer to any further enquiries. She was already fleeing to the west in a cart, but this intense impression caused her to interrupt her journey and return to Sangerhausen.

Now Schleef drew on Goethe's early sketches for WALPURGIS NIGHT IN THE HARZ. He considered it possible that a faulty circuit had caused the political propaganda phrase 'Now, people, rise, and let storm break loose' to turn up in the FIELD LINES OF SPIRITUALITY of that night. Subsequently, for one historical moment, the annual gathering of witches and their followers in the last night of April relinquished its being-for-itself. It was also possible, according to Schleef, that the sudden arrival of so many FRESH DEAD had caused a form of short circuit among the spirits.

Schleef had understood the piano teacher's words to mean that witches, abused women from all over Europe, and the entire swarm of spirits had taken the propaganda literally, viewed themselves as the last array of troops and gathered to unleash a storm of destruction. In Schleef's sketch, they were seized by a lust for vengeance that made no distinction between the fleeing columns of German troops, the tanks of the Red Army and the advancing western Allies—that is to say, between nationalities. For a few hours, this storm wind annihilated everything it encountered. The losses from this explosion of all the WRONGFULLY BURNT OF THIS EARTH are not adequately included in any list of the warring powers, Schleef argued.

Schleef's sketch closes with the last of the seven moving choruses, video-supported music entitled 'Shining Storm and Thunder Clouds', hummed by the chorus. The symphonic mumbling and groaning gives way to the popular song, 'Lenore woke at the break of day, and when she finished, she had passed away'. Schleef called the new revue sketch FUNERAL ODE FOR CHORUS AND MUSIC. In his view, the work was destined to replace the final movement of the Ninth Symphony as the official music for ceremonial occasions in Europe, as Beethoven's respectable work 'is unsuitable to reproduce the vision of the Sangerhausen piano teacher whose name was Miss Bülow'. For one must distinguish between the unreal reality in which we all live and the original words of the LOST HISTORY that expresses itself unusually and sublimely—there, the burnt and murdered do not die but rise at the end and break loose as a storm.

HEINER MÜLLER:

THE IRON CROSS*

In April 1945, a stationer at Stargard in Mecklenburg decided to shoot his wife, his 14-year-old daughter and himself. He had heard from customers about Hitler's wedding and suicide.

* English translation in *A Heiner Muller Reader: Plays, Poetry, Prose* (Carl Weber ed. and trans.) (Baltimore, 2001), pp. 5f (translation modified). [Trans.]

A reserve corps officer in the First World War, he still owned a revolver and two rounds of ammunition.

When his wife brought in the dinner from the kitchen, he stood at the table and cleaned his gun. He had pinned the Iron Cross to his lapel, as he usually did only on national holidays.

The Führer had chosen suicide, he stated in reply to her question, and he would be loyal to him. Would she, his wedded wife, be ready to follow him in this too? He had no doubt that his daughter preferred an honourable death by her father's hand to a life without honour.

He called her. She did not disappoint him.

Without waiting for his wife's answer, he asked both to put on their coats, since he was going to lead them to a suitable place outside town. They obeyed. He then loaded the revolver, had his daughter help him into his coat, locked the apartment and threw the key through the slit of the mailbox.

It was raining as they walked through the darkened streets and out of town, the man in front, without ever looking back at the women who followed at some distance. He heard their steps on the asphalt.

After he had left the road and taken the path to the beech grove, he turned to them and urged them to hurry. Because of the night wind, which blew more strongly across the treeless plain, their steps made no noise on the rain-drenched ground.

He yelled to them that they should walk ahead. As he followed them, he was unsure—was he afraid they could run away, or did he himself wish to run? It did not take long and they were far ahead. When he could no longer see them, he realized that he was much too afraid to simply run away, and he very much wished they would do so. He stopped and passed water. He carried the revolver in his trouser pocket, feeling it cold through the thin fabric. As he walked faster to catch up with the women, the weapon knocked against his leg with each step. He walked more slowly but when he reached into the pocket to throw the revolver away, he saw his wife and daughter. They were standing in the middle of the path and waiting for him.

He had intended to do it in the grove, but the danger that the shots would be heard was no greater here.

When he took the revolver in his hand and released the safety catch, his wife threw her arms around him, sobbing. She was heavy and he had difficulty in shaking her off. He stepped towards his daughter, who was staring at him, pressed the revolver against her temple and pulled the trigger with his eyes closed. He had hoped the gun would not fire, but he heard the shot and saw the girl stagger and fall.

His wife trembled and screamed. He had to hold her. Only after the third shot was she still.

He was alone.

There was no one who ordered him to put the revolver's muzzle against his own temple. The dead did not see him; no one saw him.

He pocketed the revolver and bent over his daughter. Then he began to run.

He ran all the way back to the road and then along the road, though not in the direction of the town but westwards.

Then he sat down at the roadside, his back against a tree, and considered his situation, breathing heavily. He thought there was some hope in it.

He had only to keep running, always to the west, and avoid the nearest villages. Then he could disappear somewhere, best of all in a larger city, under another name, an unknown refugee, ordinary and hard-working.

He threw the revolver in the roadside ditch and got up.

As he walked, he remembered that he had forgotten to throw away the Iron Cross. He did so.

IN THE WESTERWALD AFTER WINTER, BRITISH PRISONERS UNDER GERMAN SUPERVISION WERE DRIVEN EASTWARDS, FREEZING. THE SMALL COLUMNS MARCHED UNDISTURBED FROM THE LARGE PINCER ARMS OF THE ALLIED ADVANCE WHICH THEY HAD LONG SINCE OVERTAKEN. AT THE HEAD OF THE COLUMN: ALFRED KRUGK.

FIG. 7 Alfred Krugk

The Last Meteorologist of Pillau

The cyclonic turning point of the main stationary Scandinavian low-pressure area lies in the eastern Baltic Sea. In this eastern part of the European continent, the treks and the German ships heading for Copenhagen enjoyed stable weather at that time. Warmer than in other years, favourable for rescue.

The meteorologist Dr Erwin von Freitag, who knew the 'cyclonic turning point' (roughly 70 kilometres north-east of Bornholm), had put on his warmest winter coat on leaving the weather station in Pillau, carrying a bag with important measuring instruments of the weather service, and headed eastwards with several thousand prisoners of war in a long column. None of the guards asked him, the knowledge carrier, anything. None of the comrades, who after all saw what the weather was like here, wanted to find out anything from the expert. And yet, aside from the little fat that had remained on his body (as with the other marching comrades), he possessed a special self-confidence that would ultimately prove life-saving (and protects the body as the blubber protects the whale's innards). For he was able, even without renewed use of the instruments he carried with him, to predict what would happen in the heavens over an area of 2,000 square kilometres. This was a result of his experience. There was no thunderbolt of Zeus or meteorological singularity in these climes; even if the entire Reich fell to pieces, the sluggishness of the weather in north-eastern Europe would remain.

2

REINHARD JIRGL

◆

War Births

In the column marching from the Westerwald was German-sergeant Alfred Krugk (born in 1914 during the first autumn of the 1st-World-War), whose superiors had assigned him to desk-duties.

The meteorologist Dr Erwin von Freitag, whose downright pedantry & brimming arrogance were widely known, brooked no interference in his own=pet-subject=the-weather—. His research in peacetime had been into weather-modification, schemes to influence so-called natural weather conditions by artificial means. This had entailed the use of certain chemicals—silver=iodide, for instance— which, sealed=in-shells, were shot into the troposphere & detonated, causing clouds to rain over precisely=defined areas. Similarly, other chemicals were successfully deployed to artificially induce mists hail or their reversal: the breakup of fog-banks, prevention of rain hail blizzards. Much of this had barely progressed beyond a theoretical stage, its realization stymied by slashed budgets. Be that as it may, von Freitag's meteorological work had been promoted to the highest level of Strategic Importance, for the Führer=himself had under-taken a thorough study of Napoleon's campaigns & was therefore apprised of The Invisible Hand-of-the-Weather...... a decisive factor in the outcome-of battles. If von Freitag's calculations proved correct & the-weather, that hitherto wayward & unreasonable variable, could be artificially generated & altered, then the fortunes-of-war would henceforth be decided in the troposphere.—Cognizant of his=own impOrtance—he had been promoted from civilian *stat*us to the rank of a Lieutenant-Colonel (without military authority) and unceremoniously incorporated into the-army—Erwin von Freitag hoped his work would give him *reserved-status*, exempting him from service on the dreaded Eastern-Front. He therefore permitted !no 1, not -even his closest assistants, insight-into his=research-documents.— To-Army-Command, for the day&hour of The-Ardennes-Offensive, he had predicted a cloudless sky, which, from a meteorological point-of-view, would have doomed any attack to failure (amongst other things there would be no cover for bombers), but not-1 of the top-brass in the Supreme Command of the Army=OKH or: Supreme Command of All Armed Forces=OKW had believed him; !they were not going to let some !wretched weather-*crackpot* spoil their Final-Victory.—Now, however, this Bearer-of-Knowledge and Doyen-of-the-Weather was marching=east, a course which must have seemed his final-resort.

Quite unlike Sergeant Alfred Krugk. His prescribed task=of recording Official Army Business & other matters of a military nature had brought forth a different-sort-of-writing: secretly, our-sergeant had begun to write a diary. Initially, his language betrayed the austere grasp=of-the-soldier, marshalling words as precise as they were soulless to dutifully depict the horrors as-well-as the unbearable nightly&daily drudgery=of=war. It was as if his-pen were the spade with which the-soldier, hacking into an earthy=realm of language, digs in against: impending assault : short sharp jottings logging the humdrum grind of Operational Procedure (for military-campaigns consisted above all of marching & waiting, the boredom-of it punctuated only by boozing-sprees & fits of fretful apathy in which finally even 1's own demise holds out the prospect of a welcome diversion; a wartime human=routine......). Our clandestine scribe was unaware of those fundamental distinctions=in-language that distinguish the-cartographer of a landscape from the rambler walking through=it.— But the mere activity of writing, much as speaking can aid the composition of thoughts, prompted a rapid !change in his use of words; it was not long before the persistence of his=writing hand had coaxed from the rudeStone of the workaday vernacular an *idiom-of-his=own*, and it was as if he were a sculptor who, chiselling at The Block, were al*one* capable of seeing the sculpture that lies hidden= within-it. For writing tells the born writer !where it wants to go.—It was thus during the final-days=of the-war that Sergeant Alfred Krugk, who had seen much in the course-of his various Deployments In The Field, realized something that may have *saved his bacon*: cap-tured=in-words *terror cannot touch me; the horror I write about cannot happen again.* Such was undoubtedly the tenor of Sergeant Alfred Krugk's thoughts as he began to write as-much & as-hard-as a Machine—a Machine that must 1 day break apart. The 'Ahasver-of-war' had become a writer. After his physical birth during the 1st-World-War, here was his 2nd birth in a different war.

At the-same-time our new=born writer had a discovery to make: the commanding=heights of a writer Marshalling his=words are not the same as Hegemony in a political, economic or material sense, where mechanistic controls extend solely to flesh & materials. On-the-contrary, the one is often the enemy of the other: *whenever I see Top Brass I imagine what he'd look like topped.* A writer must be a master-of=stealth—Epicure's 'lathe biosas' should be his motto.

Many of Alfred Krugk's papers—among them notes beginnings (fragments of poetry too, those short-winded nocturnal word-emissions of-all=budding-writers)—went missing in the last days of the war & in its immediate aftermath. Indeed he=himself, after escaping the maelstrom of fire that was The War, sank without trace in the quicksands that followed. According to Seneca the vanished and the forgotten are always the happiest. On Alfred Krugk's disappearance a fellow soldier (who prefers to remain anonymous) took=charge of his papers &, after years of indecision, finally handed them over to us. It is thus to this voluntarily=nameless person that we owe some of the texts notes and other items which are collected in this book. The whereabouts of the Army Clerk chronicler and writer Alfred Krugk remain unknown.

The first, albeit markedly soiled A5-size page of his writings, its lettering in office ink partially dissolved, is dated 30th April 1945.

(Scene, written by Alfred Krugk)
Afterpiece. Lucky Shadow.

Unfit-for-service, K-O on our feet: *1 Reich 1 people*, around your neck the dependant's=noose = the umbilical-cord that helps you stand in your=platoon-of mighty-masters. Every-man's a master, women too, all the mightier since our Lord & Master came down to=Earth, the dog that doesn't exist. World=doom=iNation, grounded on 3 words: Born. Crucified. Interred. That's good for 3 thousand years or more of war hatred & slaughter. All boats all brains on=fire and yet: nothing is consumed. Rage stays rage, hatred stays hatred. All else = the world for you or some-1 else like you. What's left is taken by the-rats and other functionaries. A New Age with New Heroes : heads bowed, not looking at anyone-or-anything. Guilt, the oldest marble, hewn from the Rock of Ages, onto which these Prometheides' heads & souls are shackled, their hope The Crow-Bar for mass-murder (?what vulture would stop at liver these days). Dull & worn deathly thin by guilt is the traveller = 1 who is forgotten even unto death. Dying =a life=too-long. Death, why-of-course, but not now, and now is always. Stupid joke. The beginning of Always is always in=the-family. In-the-end it's !your turn. So you might-as-well change !everything : name, origin, language, handwriting, body. Above-all: change your smile. What I want is to go deep down under the language, buried alive—like you, my friend of bygone years, who bit=the-dust before your time, & before me for that matter, for being older I ought to have gone-before—so-deeply=buried that I am able to forget it by finding a way to speak of this Grand Oblivion. A language of-strangers following the Insurrection of-Words. Every uprising is beautiful if your knife is in=the throat of-your torturer or your bullet in=the heart of-the oppressor. The-cry giving vent to-hope engenders the war-birth. And again: a world full=of-promise, bespeaking all-manner-of-things.

Bespeaking as a way of bespeaking=myself. In order to speak: misspeaking. Misspeaking: not to bespeak *myself*. In order to speak: not misspeaking. Bespeaking: as a way of not *bespeaking* myself. In order to speak: not, *myself*, misspeaking.

The Ego that is capable of laughing super-Ego. Albeit too loud and with a twisted mouth. You were friendly. Says the Ego. You were always friendlier to others than they were to you. It's always the friendliest who pay-the-piper. Surplus-value begotten for society. But when coarseness=takes over, the friendly have no friends. The Ego, a filthy soldier in Wehrmacht rags standing in the middle of the road, sticks a pistol in his mouth & squeezes the trigger. A felled scarecrow hits-the-dust. What remains is a star-shaped stain of blood & an real figure. The dead man's head lying in the middle of the bloody star of his own spilled brain : the Unsung Icon of all Futility. 1 of the British prisoners nearby glances at the corpse lying in=the mud and murmurs (& only I can hear him):—*Lucky shadow.*

3

ALEXANDER KLUGE

In a Different Country

◆

◆

He knows the area. At night he sets sail for Switzerland. The search boats of the German and Swiss customs authorities give themselves away by tiny lights on the bow, even before one can hear them. He has to let them past. He only has a little over a thousand metres to go until the saving shore.

He flew transport planes on the eastern front for a long time. Then his entire unit was (for lack of planes and fuel) supposed to be taken over by the Waffen-SS. He was half-Jewish. So far, the family had cleverly concealed this (against all odds) in all registrations and official documents. They had still managed to change their surname as late as 1928. He expected a more thorough review upon being taken up into the Waffen-SS. Would his plea to be accepted onto Swiss soil have a chance? He could only describe the situation, not prove anything.

Through a wooded area. Finally reported to one of the country's authorities. It is already late in the war. Switzerland does not want to risk any suspicion of violating its neutrality at the last minute. The Argus-eyed Allied inspectors take note of every trifle. Since the balance of pressure between the warring parties broke down as a result of the destruction of the Axis, the influence of the Allies on the sovereign country has been increasing. As soon as the refugee sets foot on Swiss soil, he feels as if he is in a DIFFERENT REALITY. The restlessness he has brought with him still makes him doubt whether he is already in safety.

The Large-Scale Celestial Events,

Neutral towards the Turbulently Changing Fronts on the Ground

The weather observer at the Jungfraujoch Station (throwing a snow-ball south from this Swiss col will add a quantum of water to the Mediterranean, and the same will happen to the North Sea if one throws the snowball north) noted down that the outside instruments had measured -40° Celsius last night which was too cold in comparison to the preceding years. The first 20 days of April, on the other hand, had been too warm by 4.5° Celsius. Since Wednesday, 25 April, there had been two cold spells. The Swiss meteorologist wrote in Sütterlin script.

> Like the first, the second (yesterday's) cold front had come from the Atlantic. There one finds Arctic air masses at the ready over the East Greenland Sea every year. They flow south behind low pressure areas, up to the edge of the trade wind zone. On the eastern decline of the North Atlantic anticyclones, the pressure-drop areas drifting southwards and south-eastwards constantly give the immense accumulation of Atlantic air over Greenland new stimuli to leak out. These drop areas (over 400 kilometres long, like the descent of a continental shelf of air) form swirling vortices that advance towards Europe.

One such advance had abruptly extinguished the blue sky over Central Europe, after it had helped the bomber commandos for three weeks. The man on the Jungfraujoch was in unprotected radio contact with the sister office in Bern. Only a short time ago, such measurements had been of interest to the intelligence agencies of both the

Allies and the German Reich. Now the military staff there were too excited to be interested in predicting the weather any more.

When the cold spells return in late April, the meteorologist went on, the North Atlantic Subtropical High first turns rapidly to the north, up to the polar region—a high-pressure tent that sustains the cold nights over the ice for a long time. In the sea area around Iceland, this maximum air pressure remains stationary for weeks.

Here convoys of merchant vessels, coming from the American continent, were steaming to the gathering place north of the island and then on towards Murmansk. These supplies did not manage to reach the Red Army before the war ended in Europe; US controllers had therefore advised aborting the shipments. In the responsible organizations of the western Allies whose task it was to decide this, however, certain confidants who had infiltrated them saw to it that (making use of the inertia that characterizes all institutions) as many recoverable products as possible still reached the workers' home country. The ship owners also had an interest in continuing the shipments—the building contractors of Liberty ships needed a reason to build new ones. So a fleet of cargo ships with a high commissioning and asset value sailed eastwards north of Bear Island. The storm circling the polar high like a pack of wolves collided with these steamers. Six ships were lost owing to ignorance about the weather activity that was frequent in the area.

A patrol of Swiss border guards guarding some woodland between Lake Constance and Basel was camping in seven tents on the night of 29 April 1945. After the reveille, they went outside and found hoarfrost. Twenty minutes later, with their rigid limbs, the soldiers were unable to stop a group of German armed customs officials who ran onto Swiss soil and disappeared into the woods (they had been giants in 1943, but now they were people seeking rescue). Swiss warning shots were returned by the armed colleagues—a twofold violation of law, namely, the crossing of the border and the use of German service weapons on Swiss soil. Even if these were untargeted shots intended to delay pursuit. The damp limbs of the border guards, which would perhaps have been in a state for continuous running by eleven o'clock, could not be effectively activated by the unit leader's orders so early in the morning.

Judgement at Dawn

Dr von Dach, extraordinary presiding judge at the Bern Criminal Court, entered the miserably illuminated courtroom. His fat body could still not get used to beginning sessions at eight in the morning. The Swiss judicial system had exhibited a foible for early starts since the first days of the war. It corresponded to the notion that all authorities had to be prepared for a state of emergency and therefore hurry (even though there were enough court employees with whom one could have scheduled appointments at a more civil time, such as eleven o'clock).

The following were charged here: a 35-year-old businessman, a 46-year-old bookkeeper and the president of a private company from Geneva. The first two were employees of the Swiss War Transport Authority. While giving the opening speech for the main trial, Dr von Dach scribbled on the red lid of the file (which is actually forbidden, because it is an official document, though one could also argue that the document only begins on page 1, under the lid): 'Seduction by war'. It was a case of unfaithful administration of office.

The employee Olbers was responsible for the ocean freights of import and export companies. For no apparent reason, he had promised refunds to a private firm in Geneva totalling 83,999 Swiss francs. For example, 24,463 francs merely for a deck loading onto a Caribbean steamer, supposedly ordered by British controllers, instead of loading the cargo with a crane. In return, the firm's president Gérald Moulin had granted him a non-refundable loan of 5,500 francs. He was also provided with 6,000 francs to bribe the book-keeper Hermann Inken who, likewise, worked for the War Transport Authority. This made him guilty of aiding and abetting, bribery and forgery of documents.

Dr von Dach had already reached and announced the verdict by ten o'clock. Now he was sitting around idly in the canteen until lunch at one o'clock, simply because the judicial administration and the schematicism of wartime dictated it. There was no place to lie down for a nap.

The War Transport Authority had worked wonders of reliability and balancing of interests during the Allied BLOCKADE and the German COUNTER-BLOCKADE. Switzerland had no port for international trading. All road and rail traffic of Swiss goods was subject to a tangle of regulations that was hostile to trading. Switzerland has no machete to clear a path through such a jungle. Thus everything depends on the intelligent sensitivity of employees of the War Transport Authority which constitutes the alternative to the Allies or the Germans controlling things themselves.

That, according to Dr von Dach, makes the authority's employees susceptible to fits of imagination—and the imagination is hard to stop once it reaches the threshold of disloyalty. In the sleepiness of morning, Dr von Dach had announced a mild, empathetic verdict. Colleagues scolded him for this. For the whole of 30 April, Dr von Dach had nothing else to do.

FIGURE 8. Railway track at the border crossing between
Switzerland and occupied France.

Metaphor of a Refugee Who Ended up in the Neutral Country

Harald Welzer relates the following story:

A Jew in Berlin who managed to escape the deportation train to Riga,
but saw no possibility of escape from the Reich at that point, decided
not to save himself by hiding (they would have searched for him in
every hiding place) but, rather, to appear in public in an elegant white
suit, in the best company. His barefacedness concealed him. A graphic
artist by profession, he used his art to create all manner of documents
and proofs of his existence, none of which would have stood up to
closer scrutiny; in the outfit he had chosen, however, no one checked.
In this role he gained new friends and had relationships with officers'
wives. He often found himself in dire straits, but always mastered the
situation—Welzer calls him a *player*—by insisting on his lucky streak.

Finally he cycled to the Swiss border (his fabricated papers were accepted by the country constables), where he entered the neutral country in a quite densely populated zone where no one would ever have suspected a border crossing from Germany to Switzerland. He revealed himself to the Swiss authorities. He was granted asylum. He had been under constant pressure during his open appearances in Berlin society—he compared it to the pressure in ocean trenches. Accordingly, when asked how he felt in Switzerland, he replied: 'Like a deep-sea fish in a village pond.' Swiss bystanders who did not understand the metaphor reacted with irritation. Switzerland was no village pond, they said; the guest was speaking impolitely.

Will You Be Emigrating in the Foreseeable Future?

> Will you be
> ## EMIGRATING
> in the foreseeable future?
>
> I would be very keen to join you as your companion. I would like to provide a kind, cultivated gentleman of initiative and a reliable character with a comfortable, sunny home of his own abroad. I am a young, charming Swiss lady, amiable and from a very good family. Suitable gentlemen should send their replies with a photograph to the classifieds department of the *Neue Zürcher Zeitung*, Box Number K6535.

This newspaper advertisement received a response from a young German doctor, on the way up both as a talented young surgeon and a party member, previously adjutant to Prof. Max de Crinis, who, as

Reich Head Doctor, was responsible for sinister deeds and killed himself. His final order to his adjutant had been to flee from Berlin to Graz and escape abroad from there. The young man had performed a life-saving operation on a prominent member of Schellenberg's spy organization, so the adjutant, who was considering a future abroad, had a great array of passports and travel papers no longer needed by military intelligence which had meanwhile been taken over by the SS. Because of his letter (with a photo in civvies), he and the Swiss lady 'from a very good family' conducted a lively correspondence, first via a post office box in Zurich, then in Lisbon.

The 'future lovers' connected through an advertisement, it transpired later, were an astoundingly good match. After some communication they met in Porto, from where a crossing to Uruguay was relatively unproblematic for a married couple. The advertiser's Swiss status was helpful for the necessary checks. Thus they reached Montevideo. The man escaped the nemesis that descended also on the medical leadership of the German Reich, thanks to the bright idea of replying to an advertisement in the *NZZ* at the beginning of his escape, thus deciding quickly on a shared happy future with a Swiss woman. They had five children together. Later they moved to Tierra del Fuego.

A Current Advertisement for Life Insurance

On 30 April 1945, the general agency of the 'Vita' life insurance corporation published the following half-page advertisement:

> ### Cases from Real Life
>
> B., commercial director of an industrial firm, unexpectedly had to travel abroad on business. It was no harmless undertaking,

however, for the journey took him to an area that was constantly being subjected to the terror of aerial warfare at that time. Before his departure, Director B. had taken out a short-term life insurance for 80,000 francs payable at death.

He returned from his trip after two and a half months, tired but safe and sound. Two weeks later the life insurance expired, and our insurance salesman went to him to enquire if he wished to renew the contract. Director B. declined. He had, he said experienced six heavy bombings, had helped put out a hotel fire, travelled hundreds of kilometres on endangered routes . . . How, he added with a smile, could anything happen to him during his peaceful office work after all that! . . . In an irony of fate, barely a week later, a bakery delivery man cycled into him as he was making his way to the office. The edge of the mudguard scratched his leg. It was a tiny little cut, and he paid no attention to it. A severe case of blood poisoning followed. It took eight weeks before he was able to return to work. Today, Director B. has a 'Vita' policy for 60,000 francs.

Newspaper Report on a Tragic Detail

Near Münster in Upper Valais, some children wanted to go to the landing site to see an aeroplane going down. On the way there, the little son of the stationmaster Erich Bader fell down a gorge some 200 metres deep. The boy could only be recovered as a body.

Every day, since his time in Küsnacht, Thomas Mann had read a Swiss newspaper to which he had grown accustomed (even though it always reached him in the US a few days late). That a detail such as a child's accident should find its way into such an international newspaper struck him as revealing the fundamental difference between peaceful Switzerland and the countless deaths in Germany, which, as Thomas Mann noted in his diary, were entirely absent from the news partly because 'the immense number of deaths caused by the authorities and the unauthorized attract all the attention'.

Transfer of Migrant Workers to Their Home Countries through Switzerland

There are three evacuated German steamboats at Romanshorn harbour. With their dirty-grey camouflage paint, they form a bleak contrast to the friendly and inviting ships of the Swiss Federal Railways. More ships from Lindau had arrived in Romanshorn over the last few days. They brought a contingent of migrant workers.

Refugees that could not be sent on to their home countries immediately enter a transit camp—the civilians to Adliswil and the members of the military to Gyrenbad. Upon arrival, thorough disinfection with neocide and hot air. The concern was to avoid the introduction of diseases.

On the race course at Oerlikon, where bicycle races had recently taken place, those who had not yet been cleaned were waiting in the straw. Many got across the border with bacon, margarine or tinned food. On 30 April, the main contingent consisted of French, Italians and Poles; between them, Greeks, Czechs and Dutch. In the intermediate gallery for the clean, namely, those who have already been disinfected themselves, had their clothes and baggage disinfected and been given fresh laundry, smoking is allowed. A card table has been set up for playing poker with French banknotes and German Rentenmark.

A Military Hospital Crosses the Border with Heavily Wounded Patients

A convoy of 46 German ambulances, followed by a few motorcycles with sidecars, some trucks and cars, parked in front of the border checkpoint at Chiasso. It was a mobile army hospital with heavily wounded patients. The head doctor commanding the convoy had applied to the Swiss border authorities for internment. The way back, he argued, would lead into the hands of the partisans. Who could be sure what they would get up to with the heavily wounded patients?

Heinz Huttiger, colonel of the Swiss border troops, crossed the border to Italy and inspected each of the waiting vehicles. He liked the orderly state in which this elite medical unit had appeared here at the Swiss border, and in such neat ambulances too. He also checked the authenticity of a few bandaged wounds. He found it implausible that a Nazi functionary, whose passage he would have had to refuse, could have had such wounds inflicted on himself merely to get to Switzerland under a pretext. One could not drive the heavily wounded around the country and make them wait. It was advised that the ambulances, which had been kept in excellent condition, be confiscated for the Swiss army. And so this army hospital and its head doctor were granted asylum on Swiss soil. The wounded were sent to various military hospitals.

Free Time

She rushed in that very minute. Now there were 10 minutes of 'free time' before the film. Twice a week, the nanny for the Faber family in Zurich had this leisure time which she always spent at the cinema. Taken as a whole, the films she had already experienced in those seats had gained a credibility that made it irrelevant which particular film was on. She no longer even checked the titles.

She felt young. She was living an intermediate existence here, far from her home in Grisons, yet not settled for good in Zurich. But nothing was as rich as the life in the many films she had watched so far. Her blood pulsed. The brown-tinged light in the auditorium produced a twilight that was not frightening. She had waited for this afternoon showing since the previous day. That neutral existence before the film had even begun! The state of limbo between times gave her a feeling of 'openness', 'bliss'. Unlike the prospect of an actual future life with a husband and children that was awaiting her. For here, in the cinema, many side paths and adventures were still possible, dark depths and joyrides (often in carriages). She was over-come with worry when she thought of the family she worked for. For the mistress, she 'managed' a secret stash in the kitchen where the lady received her lover's letters. The dreamy nanny had the duty of taking them from the postman as soon as they arrived, then depositing them there. The mistress was planning to separate from her husband. If this marriage broke apart, her time as a nanny would also be over. A gong and the very slow dimming of the lights announced the start of the opening film.

The Weekly Film Schedule at Zurich Cinemas

Apollo	*Love Is Stronger than Death (L'éternel retour)*
Rex	*Random Harvest*
Orient	*The Magic Violin*
	Premiere. With Paul Hörbiger, Gisela Uhlen,
	Eugen Klöpfer
Pallas	*Arabian Nights*
	America's latest million-dollar film

Bellevue	Premiere! *Escape from Hell*
	One of Our Aircraft Is Missing
Seefeld	Big laughs week! (1) *Charley's Aunt* (2) *The Three Merry Musketeers*
Walche	*Hell, Where Is Thy Victory*
Cinébref	(1) Newsreel (2) Berlin during the first days of bombing by the USA (3) *Doctors on Call* (4) A newly arrived DISNEY

FIGURES 9A (above), 9B (left) and 9C (right)

FIGURE **9D**

The Explosive Device in the Gotthard Tunnel

During the German military attaché's visit to the Gotthard Tunnel, Colonel Flierz, director of the Swiss Technical Armaments Authority, offered him a glance at the explosive device in one of the side tunnels which was to be detonated in case of a German occupation of Switzerland. The fact that Germany could be sure the confederation would destroy the transit tunnel if attacked prevented an occupation and, after 1943, an economic war waged on Switzerland by the Reich—which would have been a promising move, as all of Switzerland's external borders (that is, those with Italy and Vichy France too) were controlled by Germany.

—Would Gotthard and Simplon really have been detonated?

—Maybe not.

—Because one wouldn't have been able to repair the damage afterwards?

—Such a massive detonation would be unknown territory, technically speaking. Maybe we should have tried it out on a smaller object first.

—It was enough for the Germans to believe in Switzerland's determination?

—Evidently that was enough.

The danger of such an explosive device was that a chain of coincidences could have set it off at the wrong time. The conversation with Colonel Flierz was confidential, and could now, in late April 1945, be had more openly in the Zurich hotel because it would scarcely have been relevant any more for the Reich to see through Swiss secrets. The colonel, who had kept all manner of information to himself for so long, seemed to be somehow blocked—he finally wanted to talk about the skill he had commanded in the form of his diligent staff. One problem, he related, was that the colonel of the army engineers who had set up and wired the explosive marvel died shortly afterwards. The matter was so secret that no notes had been made. Thus, for a long time (even up to this moment at the war's end, Flierz added), no one could have removed and destroyed this 'hidden treasure' that guaranteed the country's security. One could, the colonel continued, wall up the 12 rooms from which the detonation was supposed to be triggered. His successor would have to decide that, as he would be giving up his post at the end of the year.

On the 'Black List'

The life of the Swiss chief negotiator in London, Minister Dr Sulzer, owner of the Sulzer Works, was in immediate danger during his negotiations in 1943. A manoeuvre by his British conversational partners, whose insolence appalled him, put his cells and veins in a state of turmoil. Against whom? Against himself, the understanding and reasonable chief negotiator. His face red. No digestion any more. That same night, red pustules on his neck and chest. Fever.

The British negotiating partners had viewed their gambit—the news that the Sulzer company had been placed on the BLACK LIST of 'bad neutral' parties—as a tactical aid. They wanted to increase pressure on the Swiss envoys. Dr Sulzer's vital spirits had taken this disregard for the sovereignty of his fatherland as a personal attack

FIGURE 10. In 1940, General Guisan gathers the senior officer corps of Switzerland on the Rütli meadow to swear to defend the confederation unconditionally.

(while he, as his own SELF, attempted to maintain diplomatic equilibrium and struggled to answer)—a stranglehold. Who are these vital spirits? Everything that lies beneath his upbringing, his rehearsed tolerance and will power. Is there something resembling a 'second will'? That of the spirits which do not obey the mind? No—Dr Sulzer's mind also felt injured.

The open contempt of this move lay primarily in the fact that the Sulzer company had followed the rules of the agreed neutral equilibrium between blockade and counter-blockade in exemplary fashion. Inclusion in the 'black list' was considered disastrous, as its effects continued even after the name was removed (just as Internet shaming today cannot be taken back). The BLACK LISTS of the British had a lasting effect in the US.

Dr Sulzer just managed to reach Bern on the morning of 24 December, after a seemingly endless series of customs inspections, ship and rail journeys via Portugal and occupied France. He had barely brought the leftovers of his body home before the chickenpox from his childhood aggressively seized control of Dr Sulzer's body— shingles. He was already unable to report to the Federal Council. After four weeks, this hero was ready for battle again. Fighting on the neutrality front is as life- threatening as any battle in war.

Background Conversation in 1983

The defence plans of the Swiss Confederation must (without attracting attention) address possible scenarios, even if these are considered remote in the current awareness of the time. Thus the escalating tension between the western and eastern superpowers in 1982 led to an inspection, by a military and planning committee, of all facilities that had been set up to defend the Confederation in the Second World War.

—You have to develop a defence plan using the planning ruins of an already ancient war, as well as whatever current armament the budget will allow?

—In case of emergency.

—What's the difference between a case of emergency and a case of defence?

—No difference. It isn't the Swiss who determine whether the emergency occurs, after all.

—Does the federal government believe that Swiss neutrality would be respected by the putative conflicting parties in case of emergency? If a shooting war broke out?

—The federal government will not make any explicit comments on this. We, the field commanders, assume that in such a scenario (which we hope, of course, will never take place and will remain a train of thought) neither of the two parties would still be able to control the hostilities in any way. No one governs the kind of powers deployed in such a conflict. Facts cannot distinguish between neutral and enemy soil.

—A retreat to the National Redoubt?

—What good would that do? If nuclear bombs fall, staying in the Gotthard Tunnel might protect the troops. If they step into the open, they will have to deal with the fact that the falling bombs make no distinction between the mountains and the plains.

—What can the border guards learn from the experiences as a neutral country in the Second World War?

—One can almost never learn anything for the next war from the last.

This was a background conversation with one of the responsible Swiss military leaders. The authority of the NEUE ZÜRCHER ZEITUNG lies in the fact that it has never revealed the results of such conversations to third parties or published them without authorization. The paper's correspondent had quickly established that the content of the background conversation would not lead to any current article, which is why he refrained from asking further questions. The field commander and the journalist got on well.

Laconic Reply

Before the end of the Cold War, new preparations were made to detonate the north–south railway lines in case of danger? Did the thought of the Redoubt and closing off central Switzerland play a part? In a destroyed Europe (in the Third World War), replied the military expert Hürzinger, the north–south transfer through Switzerland would have been obsolete. The freight tracks would have sufficed for a long time during the reconstruction of Europe.

A Straggler

On the tracks extending from the Ruhr region to Lombardy, a single coal train arrived at the Swiss border station on 30 April, 14 weeks late; this was due to contracts with the Reich going back to December 1943. The train was allowed into the country. The locomotive crew and the driver, given the choice of being taken back to the border or retaining responsibility, under the authority of the Swiss railway service, for the train, which was now confiscated and had no destination, chose the latter. The relationship between Swiss railway workers and their colleagues at the Reichsbahn—respectful, as is the norm among experts.

The Grave of Stefan George

In April 1945, as in every spring, a flower arrangement was placed at the grave of the poet Stefan George in Minusio, owing to a standing order from the German Embassy. It is unclear whether such a decoration, which always, after all, constitutes an intervention in the appearance of the resting place, is permissible at this grave. Corrections were made to the arrangement by order of a Swiss chemical company in Basel. The payment of the standing order came, like the funds for sanatorium stays in Davos by tuberculosis sufferers from the Reich, from a clearing account supplied by the frozen Reichsbank assets.

There are reports of nocturnal visitors to the grave. A note was found under one plant:

The face of my beloved
served as my grammar

Heinrich Heine, *Book of Songs*

4

REINHARD JIRGL

◆

(From the papers of Alfred Krugk)

The Great March

I am not-i. The other I, who, as long as I write, will always die for me. Whoever kills themselves in times like=these shows Human Greatness & Character. *(Sergeant Alfred Krugk noted in hurried, jittery handwriting under his scene about the Lucky Shadow. Continuing:)* Unfortunately my own lowness lacks the necessary size for character. Creation is not only cleverer than the Creator, it is also better.—Today's=prisoners, guarded by tomorrow's=prisoners, continue their eastward-march on the last escape-route to the finish. ?What else can a marching-column do but ?march.

And onward they march, further-and-further on their=long-way-east...... —a squad of German soldiers &: their throng of British prisoners.—The Westerwald, bleak and desolate in winter, lies far behind-them, and they have now passed=east though the 'Pincer-Mouth', the only way-out (for some reason the-Allied-troops have not crushed this Enemy Column; it can hardly have escaped their notice)—and on—past Kassel northward to Göttingen, leaving the Harz to the north, crossing the Elbe between Dessau and Wittenberg—and no peace for !them, for despite exhaustion and sickness the column must keep-marching, with those of-its=number who still possess intact=greatcoats now weighed down by carapaces of muck&soddenFelt, and with layers of rust & verdigris covering their every weapon, their rifle-butts rotting—and !still they march—Death is at=work among-the-ranks of soldiers &: prisoners, but still they

march past Dessau and on to Frankfurt, and=East across the-Oder—
and into Poland once again, the skies above the-column heavy with
clouds, and the searing eastern winter's rearguard assault of Freezing
Rain hurling its projectiles in their faces (the weather throughout
recorded with fastidious attention to=detail by the meteorologist Dr
Erwin von Freitag, who is only sorry not to have his Chemical Bombs
to deploy against rain hail and wind).—Those who were 1st-to die
are also 1st-to=rot, conspicuous by the bagginess of the capes & man-
tles smacking like waterlogged flags against their scrawny frames, as
in the lunging swing of their marching steps: cloth lasts longer than
flesh. Politeness prevails among-the-Rotting: as flesh falls from the
bone it is gathered up by the-next-man & proffered with a gracious
smile to his comrade-at-arms. Distinctions between guard &: prisoner
have long dissolved; the marching-column has assumed the appearance of an ensemble of puppets in-transit to some burlesque revue
on The Front.—Under tin-hats that totter from side-to-side as
they march, their fleshless skulls stare=straight-ahead with expressions of raw-boned resolve—south of Moscow they march—avoiding
marshes—marching=onward through the-Urals, and ever-forward
through the vast-expanses of Siberia, a marching-column of skeletons, and not 1 of=them, whether German=guard or: British=pris-
oner, stands fast in his flesh.—In the easternmost extremity of Siberia
on the Chukchi Peninsula by the Bering Strait, near the small town
of Uelen, the marching skeletons come to=a-halt. !No conqueror has
ever come this !far: the march of the-dead is the-longest.

It is said the last painting will be the-General Staff Map; the last
song—the sound of a squall blowing through skeletons. Our last crys-
tal ball will be the latest weather report.

The Smile of a Family Man

I secretly observe my Father. As=always He is sitting opposite me at the big table in our living-room, the white damask tablecloth casting a pale shimmer across His Face. He has straight grey backcombed hair, tiny tufts of hair protruding from His ears and a short grey strand sticking out above the right earpiece of His spectacles. As=always. And as=always the eyes behind the lenses of His glasses contain a subdued smile, while His lips, as He raises a silver spoonful of soup, are pursed. The hair; the pearl-grey waistcoat (with the lace border of a hand-kerchief showing above His breast pocket), worn at=home no less than to university; His continuously smiling eyes (which strangers often misinterpret as a sign of kindliness or goodwill)—:it is this triad of traits that defines Father's identity. If I close my eyes and try to imagine Him, my mind's-eye cannot conjure Him in any other way. I have not heard Him speak this evening; since getting back a little under 2 hours ago He hasn't said a thing—His eyes as ever silently smiling. Father cannot stand it when I, His daughter, am the 1st to talk to Him when He gets home. Nor does Mother ever speak at-table; there is only the sound of silver spoons clinking softly in=time on porcelain plates. Ilonka, our Russian housemaid, serves the rest of the evening meal, placing dishes on the table and clearing the empty soup plates. Lately I have noticed a change in her bearing, a change too in the way she looks at us: the docility of her dark, submissive eyes has given way to a rebellious gleam, an almost Feverish Glow, and when a spoon drops to the carpet from 1 of the dishes she is clearing away, she does not stoop to pick it up. Instead: with firm-step & upright posture she steps (in triumph, as it seems to me, as in the-pictures of Caesar crossing the Rubicon) over the obstacle of the fallen silver spoon. Mother keeps mum, Father's unremittingly smiling eyes say nothing, and the leisurely walnut pendulum clock in the corner of the room drops seconds as viscous as golden treacle into the growing silence. Gazing from a photograph set at an angle on the dresser behind Father's back is my smiling brother. The smile on his lips resembles the smile in Father's eyes. My brother fell on-the-Eastern=Front 3 years ago...... (:!East: not-1=of-us has ever been there. But when I hear the word I hear theSuffering, feel theEnormousPressure bearingDown out of leadenSkies, theFrost, smell the blood&mud, and am horrified by the rumours of woebegone squalor & the relentless savagery of the-inhabitants). Mother's silk dress makes a faint rustle, as if she were sighing. 30th April: another quiet evening in Heidelberg.

The lines are evidently still=working; the hall telephone interrupts= dinner, its strident ring piercing the-house like an acoustic bolt-of-lightning. Before the maid can get there, Father has the receiver in His hand. I leap up from the dinner-table too, but hold back in the living-room doorway. From here I watch Father=on-the-telephone. He is looking directly=at-me, but nothing in His face tells me He sees me, or rather: !what He sees is a stranger, some-1 who is even a little threatening. Meanwhile, a voice crackles excitedly in the receiver and Father gives the appearance of listening, although without responding. I cannot take my eyes off this tall man who is supposed to be my=Father and: who suddenly seems so strange, so different, standing there talking on the telephone just 3 steps away. Just as a person's breathing is measurable in the rise-&-fall of his breast, Father's constant smiling breathes in his eyes, and what my=gaze meets now is a blank space, a deep depression, the nameless absence of the smile in his eyes, the smile he will no=longer be able to maintain. And I know it will not be the-news he has heard on the telephone that Father will hold responsible for his Loss of Identity, but me al*one*, his daughter = the witness of his ruin.

5

ALEXANDER KLUGE

In the Reich Capital

◆

◆

On the same cobblestones and stone slabs that lead from the underground station entrance to the street and, on earlier Mondays, were walked on by the quick steps of the clerks rushing to the ministries, there now lie pieces of debris and a layer of dust and ownerless objects. Soldiers are fighting at close quarters in the city. With an aerial view, one could distinguish the quieter districts of Greater Berlin from the parts marked by strings and lines of fire and clouds where the shooting is happening.

Wilhemstrasse and the Reich Chancellery are under harassing fire hour after hour. This, the core of Berlin, is being defended by (among others) the Charlemagne Division, a French SS unit. It is not until the night of 30 April that the Soviet staff find out with certainty the location of the bunker under the Reich Chancellery in which Adolf Hitler was recently staying. They could have deduced the Führer's whereabouts from the symbolic content of the place, if learning to enter the National Socialist mindset had been part of the Red Army's training.

As late as 1943, there had been a construction planning group (decimated by drafting) responsible for reshaping the Reich capital into the megacity GERMANIA. The destruction of traditional districts in Berlin-Mitte (incomparable to the devastation in April 1945) was considered advantageous for urban planning, as the demolition necessary for the new construction no longer required the consent of the residents. At that point, no one would have thought it possible that two years later in that city, the Red Army would advance towards the Spree from three directions.

Division of the City into Combat Sectors

Attached to the bunker of the battle commander of Berlin is a field printing press that still produces batches of combat maps. All parts of Berlin lying to the east are divided into sectors. Each section is marked on one of these cards with command posts and frontlines. It would be too dangerous, however, to bring these informative papers forward to the different units by messenger. The maps could be intercepted by Russians. At the end, the sole purpose of all paper information was not to fall into enemy hands.

How I Lost My Friend

I am a career soldier. In the fourth generation of my family which consists of military men. To avoid any misunderstandings—my lover and I would not have been punishable according to Section 175 of the criminal code. We did not express our love through outwards actions.

He married my sister because he could not marry me. In five campaigns we fought in the same division, though in different units. The men were not to see from our glances how much we cared for each other. At the end, when he was surrounded in a wooded area, I could not get him out in time with my people. We took the body with us on our retreat, wrapped in a tarpaulin. That is how I lost the war. What do I care about my country? I only care about my friend. No one saw me cry. One cannot tell when an officer is crying. It will be hard for me to comfort my sister. She is a cheerful sort. Even my invisible tears have dried up. They were shot away.

Since his love I no more keep
I have also ceased to weep.

Heinrich Heine, *Book of Songs*

FIGURE 11 (RIGHT). Wartime wedding in late April (unknown photographer).

FIGURE 12 (BELOW). Distribution of cardboard sheets as a substitute for window panes.

As the Last Poet in the Reich Ministry of Propaganda

The empty hallways of the Ministry of Propaganda branch off to offices whose doors are no longer shut. There are no more typists left. The building is sufficiently damaged to be termed a ruin, or perhaps a cave system. For the propaganda employee, who is waiting at his workplace because he knows that his superior in the neighbouring bunker is still working (also, the employee would not be able to explain his existence as soon as he left the office; why is he not in one of the combat units, did he remove himself from his duty on his own authority?), the time is growing long. The working method in the Ministry of Propaganda is that texts for tomorrow are written today. One needs source material for that.

Some possible source material is lying on the propagandist's desk—the file concerning 1 May 1933, Labour Day. The Führer's statement is set in the type of the Führer's typewriter, that is to say in unusually large letters: 'I WILL FEEL NO GREATER PRIDE DURING MY LIFETIME THAN THAT OF BEING ABLE TO SAY, AT THE END OF MY DAYS: I WON THE GERMAN WORKER FOR THE GERMAN REICH.'

One planned surprise for this holiday was the flight of the *Graf Zeppelin* from Lake Constance up the Rhine, over the Ruhr region, Berlin, Saxony, and back to Friedrichshafen. A test flight the day before, a Sunday. On that day, the currently unemployed and accordingly contemplative propaganda employee, still five ranks below his current position, took part in the test flight as a reporter, with the assignment to submit the articles on the following day's events ready for printing the previous evening. For that he had to imagine now, on Sunday, as he glanced at the ground from the gondola, the events that would take place below when the airship appeared on Monday. He had written:

> Rhythm of the day: torchlight processions, streams of flame move through street canyons, gusts of wind fragment marching music.

> The sirens of the Rhine steamers give a salutatory wail. It is a splendid idea to show the German people *Graf Zeppelin* on the day of national labour: 'Behold, no other people has matched that; you can take pride in it, German worker!'

> From Andernach we can see the contours of the Siebengebirge over there, behind the Rolandsbogen ruin, etched sharply into the sky. Directly after that, Haus Dreesen in dear old Godesberg. The crowns of blossoms on the trees looked like snow bonnets.

> Hamburg, the greatest experience of this flight. With irresistible force, broad streams of people flood to the rallying places to receive the word to march into the new Reich.

> The Swabian countryside lies silver-coated in the moonlight.

That, the propaganda employee tells himself in an inner monologue, was like 'getting blood from a stone', even though I took office as a poet, not an author of prose texts—and am certainly not inclined to describe things one cannot actually see. But I was able to imagine (and thus formulate poetically) that *Graf Zeppelin* will be flying over Swabia after dusk falls, and, as a poet, I can say that it shines 'silver-coated' independently of any terrestrial actions (unless hidden by clouds, in which case the zeppelin would have to climb above the clouds to navigate). Even in the gloom of the current April day, the moon, that friend of poets, is undoubtedly perched unseen above the burning city.

There is nothing practical to take care of for tomorrow. This last desk in the ministry has no radio or printing capabilities. I am waiting for an opportunity to surrender to some enemy authority. And so I remain in my position. My chair has an armrest of the kind to which, according to the guidelines, officials from the rank of assistant head of department upwards are entitled. One should be a chronicler, I say, not a propaganda clerk. For, as a poet, one can put ongoing events into words better than merely expected ones.

Skirmishes on the Eve of 30 April at Heerstrasse City Train Station

A Hitler Youth combat group from Subdivision 129 had entrenched itself in a position on the track section from Heerstrasse up to the Olympic Bridge. A Red Army unit attacked with superior firepower from the wooded area behind the city train station Heerstrasse. The advance was intended to reach Westendallee beyond the rail embankment. From there it would have been possible to open fire directly on Reichskanzlerplatz. Under the flexible leadership of SS Deputy Staff Sergeant Fritzsche, who had studied the campaigns of Frederick the Great, the underage combat group, which at that point was barely the size of a platoon, succeeded in keeping the enemy at bay. The boys spent the night in the basements of the Reich Ministry of Youth.

An Unreal Final Connection between 1936 and April 1945

In the early hours of Monday, further groups from Subdivision 129 appeared. An artillery lieutenant-colonel took command. Now there were 1,200 Hitler Youth fighters, all equipped with anti-tank rocket launchers and infantry weapons, standing in a drawn-out line and led by an experienced old man (still with the zealous deputy staff sergeant as his assistant), moved towards the Olympic area. The lieutenant-general, who had been discharged from active service and sent to oversee various offices in Bendlerstrasse, and had come from his pensioner's flat in Wilmersdorf without having breakfast, had begun by addressing the sleepy group in the basements of the ministry and then received the arriving reinforcements bit by bit, all of them young blood. Not much later, the group took over the bell tower in the Olympic area that Red Army soldiers had occupied only the day before.

Two films were going through the old man's head: Carl Raddatz and Ilse Werner first met when they snatched up the last two tickets for the opening ceremony of the 1936 Olympics. Now the two of them, who have been strangers up to this moment, are sitting together simply because the numbers on the tickets dictate it. Before their eyes the bell tower. This building is a monument. The two, who have only just met, know nothing about it; in the basements of the bell tower, a tomb has been planned for the sixth-form students who fell in the First World War near Langenmarck after charging at the enemy's machine guns. The lieutenant-colonel saw both: the two lovers from the film *Request Concert* and the burial place with carved statues of the 'mowed-down youths'. A further film was competing with these images in his mind. A cavalry captain dishonourably discharged from the army of Frederick the Great is defending an East Prussian fortress against the Russians in the Seven Years' War, commanding a troop of underage cadets, and dies a hero's death at the very moment when his country's relief army liberates the border fortress. The retired military officer would have liked a cinematic monument to himself. Not a chance. No camera unit of the Ufa could have reached him, no film plan could have survived the manifestly imminent end of resistance. Later reports state that Red Army units had left the bell tower to the charging National Socialist youths out of bewilderment. According to other statements, no fighting had even taken place there. Rather, the Red Army forces gathering in front of the Olympic area had waited for a long time. They requested orders. They could not decide whether to view these youths as military enemies. They considered the occupation of the militarily insignificant gate a theatre coup (a masquerade). The Hitler Youth troops were unmistakably armed; these make-believe soldiers were dangerous. The Red Army soldiers had no desire to die for the sake of retaking a single point when they only had to wait for the whole of Berlin to fall into their hands. The commanding officer of the entrenched soldiers, advised by his political commissioner, remained indecisive. Much time was spent on the telephone talking to superiors. The difficulty lay in describing the precise situation that was before their eyes, but not easy to translate into the language of usual military action. They were dealing with 'wild boys'—and, at the same time, anti-tank weapons and machine guns.

The imaginative lieutenant-colonel had divided his group of youths (adopting the method of the Battle of Cannae), who were joined by more stragglers from the city, into two wings and a centre (covered by the bell tower). A few fighters, encouraged by the deputy staff sergeant, visited the intact exhibition in the basement that was dedicated to the dead. Had they known about it previously, they would have brought cameras. Pressing the button and choosing motifs would not have been hard. What was more difficult in the dim light was setting up some form of illumination, for example a torch, in such a way that the photographed object was sufficiently well lit. So the basement windows on the east side would have to be covered first, and one would have to light a fire in front of the photographic motif with the wooden crates that were used to transport ammunition. None of this mattered, as there was no camera to hand. It was not their weapons but, rather, the enemy's perplexity that protected the young strike force until they disappeared back to their families in the neighbourhoods after Berlin's surrender. They were encased in imagined ideas and cinematic-theatrical notions. In this respect, they were invisible on the cards of the staff (their own and those of the enemy)—a late echo of 1936, a nebulous reverberation of April 1945, a no man's land between the old man leading them and the undefined future they carried within themselves. However long the Russian commanders on site spoke on the telephone, they could not penetrate the magic hood of illusion donned by the LAST CONTINGENT OF GERMANS.

FIGURES **13A** (ABOVE) and **B** (RIGHT)

Commemoration of Dead Words

The majority of stenographers from the Führer's headquarters were on standby in Berchtesgaden, where they had been evacuated from Berlin. The valuable typists were residing in the garden house on a property adjoining the buildings of the Wehrmacht Supreme Command. They were busy all Monday, stoking a fire in a wooded area by burning the records they had made regularly since Winniza 1942. Secret documents could not fall into the hands of the Allies. This course of action was responsible, but could also be viewed as defeatist. After all, originals that all contained words uttered by the Führer in meetings were being destroyed as if the outcome of the war was absolutely certain. Over 3,000 hours of copying! That was painful for these masters of shorthand.

The retired teacher and Reichstag stenographer Hängst, one of the fastest stenographers in the Reich, walked around the fire, making sure there were no half-burnt remains in the zone where the flames gave way to the wet grass which had been snowed on during the night. When great Vikings died, they were laid out on ships which were then set on fire and sent out to sea in the direction of the sunset.

Reading Time

Waiting all day. I am commanding the task force whose assignment is to take the Führer out of the Reich capital with a seaplane that will land on the Havel, then fly him to Northern Germany. The order came seven days ago. We will take off at the word 'pickup'. The aim would be to continue via Oslo to Greenland, where the Führer could spend the winter in a weather station unknown to the Allies; and, just as Bonaparte returned to Paris from Elba in 1815, he would return to the German Reich as Reich Chancellor

Then we and our four seaplanes seem to have been forgotten. We don't know whether the superiors who gave us the order are even alive any more. We're not going anywhere without new orders.

I am reading a typed manuscript that my colleagues are passing around. The text is entitled *The Blue Chamberlain*. The author, Wolf von Niebelschütz, is a comrade who was serving in France until recently. The novel describes a world of the eighteenth century in which the gods appear on Greek islands like those we are still occupying. A figure from a novel, the blue chamberlain, seems to be Jupiter. But the elegant Venetian envoy at the court of the enchanting princess, who defends the autonomy of her island kingdom, is most likely a divine incarnation too. Everyone is eager to seduce the young woman, whose self-will permits no subjugation. As long as there are books, a person can disappear from the present to another world at any moment. If I am under fire, I open my book and am transported to a Greek island in a different time. But we, the rescuers of the Führer, are currently 'cut off from the war'. Towards evening, a handful of British fighters fly overhead. Our planes are lying camouflaged in a tree-covered cove. The Russians won't get this far. The Canadian division that will reach us sooner or later from the west leaves me with plenty of reading time.

As a Faithful Eyewitness

We had installed ourselves in the basements of Wilhelmstrasse. The leftovers from the military hospital. Gulped down barley soup. Then an order reached us to gather a fuel supply from the units occupying the Ministry of Propaganda, the motor pools, as they are called, and the storm gun crews positioned towards the banks of the Spree, and to bring it to the Führer's bunker at the base of the Reich Chancellery. We had written orders to do so. We took petrol cans and filled up others that were empty. Some of the cans had Romanian labels. Along the paths of rubble. Travelling in haste with our precious cargo, under the artillery's searching fire.

I am a faithful eyewitness. We felt the historic moment; I intended to remember the details accurately. I saw virtually nothing of the main event. I was wrong to think I would later be questioned. Only recently, on the 67th anniversary of 30 April, was I discovered in my room in Bad Godesberg and interviewed. I am 86 years old. My memory is excellent.

We had handed over part of the security force's cans to the Führer's bunker. Another part was deposited in the corridor leading to the bunker's external door. Guarded by us. We felt an urge to cast a glance at the events. But we were pushed away by the sentries, having just gained an inkling that objects wrapped in blankets had been taken outside through the bunker door. This impression came more from whispers and hearsay than from seeing anything first hand, however. The appearance would have been the same if the cloth-wrapped object being carried past had been a beam, a mannequin or (as in the fairy tale) a dead stranger. We only concluded that the Führer had died because of the effort it had cost to acquire the supply of petrol we had brought along. I was in a solemn mood. I would like to have taken away something of lasting value from the environment of this closing act. At the end, four of our cans had still not been emptied; we were told that the cans were no longer needed, and that it was impossible to approach an open fire holding the 'water from Ploieşti' without the can itself bursting into flames. One would have had to pour the petrol on at the start of the fire (which we never laid eyes on, however).

As a medic, I know that when a body is set on fire, it is only the clothes that burn at first. If an incendiary agent (in this case our petrol) is added, the fat under the skin—like the wick of a candle—starts burning immediately, followed by the tissue deeper down. The bones and most of the dead body, on the other hand, are charred rather than burnt up. If the aim were to prevent the enemy from identifying the body, I would also have had the eminent corpse's teeth smashed out and stored away from the two bodies, as teeth (and fillings) do not burn at all, or char, or disintegrate in any way; on the contrary, they enable identification for a very long time afterwards. Such obvious questions did not occur to any of the comrades gathered at the scene of the crime. We, the petrol carriers, without whom the BURIAL OF THE RULER would have been impossible, continue to stand separated in the inside corridor leading to the bunker entrance. So what I can tell you as one of the last eyewitnesses is gossip—assumptions. I can, however, describe precisely the path across the smashed stones from the ministers' gardens to the turning that leads to the cone next to the bunker entrance. There are 12 steps. Then one drops them and waist for a lull in the artillery fire. The cans are supposed to 'stand' rather than 'lie', to prevent any liquid from leaking out and endangering us, the carriers, if it caught fire.

Comforting that there were several of us for the whole time. We carried out our orders, and thus kept our composure. Though we were inside an UNREAL BUBBLE whose consistency I could not even have confirmed any more the following day, when we got as far as Spandau.

The Last and Only Action
by the New Reich Chancellor in Matters of Foreign Policy

A few hours after the bodies of Hitler and his wife had been removed from view through fire and burial under emergency conditions, the last chief of general staff in the high command of the army, General Krebs, was ordered by Joseph Goebbels, now appointed Reich Chancellor by last will, to have himself brought across Russian lines and take up contact with the commanders of the Red Army, whose troops were fighting their way through to Berlin-Mitte. The goal was a ceasefire that would enable the new Reich government to convene and possibly reach an arrangement with the Soviet side at the last moment, the same way they had in 1939. The top cadres of the Reich still overestimated the deviousness that existed between the Allies. The idea General Krebs was supposed to convey did not strike Goebbels as violating Hitler's ban on a surrender of the Reich, but, rather, was intended as a REAWAKENING OF THE POLITICAL. The new Reich Chancellor was still thinking in the same way he had ruled as Minister of Propaganda, namely in poetry: 'Night of destruction, laughing death.' Everything could still change spiritually. Or else everything was ending.

An artillery specialist, commanding the section of the front opposite the vanguards of the Red Army in the bend of the Spree, called for radio contact to be established with the enemy. One of the radio operators turned out to be faster by making contact via telephone, as the German side knew the street and house number of the Russian command post. During the winters at the eastern front, the artillery specialist had made use of the long periods of waiting to learn Russian. He accompanied the chief of general staff on his way across the front at the agreed point, waving a white cloth. General Krebs, who had been the military attaché in Moscow in the Reich's happier times, spoke Russian. He did not reveal this when the negotiations began, and thus heard what the Russians were saying when speaking among themselves and when they spoke to higher-ranking staff on the telephone. Once again, the Reich leadership's misjudgement became clear; they had assumed that the local Soviet commanders could make decisions without clearance from Moscow. Neither the staff of Marshal Konev nor those of his superior, Marshal Chuikov, were authorized to do so. The latter reported the negotiation attempt to Stalin; the answer was negative. General Krebs, who had understood the sequence of events before it was related to him, requested radio contact with the Führer's bunker. Having learnt that this last attempt at a 'negotiated peace' had failed, Goebbels prepared for his suicide.

Last Connection

My assignment was to install a telephone line passing through the fronts between our defenders and the Red Army, connecting the Russian headquarters to the bunker in the Reich Chancellery. The aim was to find artists of my kind. My boss said, 'The connection you're installing here can be the connection to the final victory.' Even as a radio engineer, I know enough about politics to know that this was a roundabout way of describing a surrender of the Reich government to victors who had already occupied the entire surroundings.

My seven men and I did not even have to lay a cable concretely
through the fronts; it was enough to know the intersections where
one could connect the remaining working lines that supplied the subterranean network for Greater Berlin. I had set up the connection by
late afternoon. Then there were two telephone conversations between
the Reich's negotiators, General Krebs and a phone in the bunker
of the Reich Chancellery. What I had assumed from the start, as a
communicator, turned out to be the case—no result. Around 9 p.m.
I received the order to destroy the connection. As if it could have
affected anything without being used.

FIGURE 14. Russian tanks on the way from the Brandenburg Gate to Potsdam Square.

Everything Went Too Quickly to Process the New Realities Inwardly

The furniture, accumulated by three generations in a villa in
Grunewald who had so far been unaffected by any wartime events,

burnt up in just under an hour. A sluggishness spread among the victims—partly because they could not judge whether action (fleeing) or inaction (staying) promised more security. The blows of the last two years had come in too fast a succession. May 1943 was already too closely connected to the feeling of May 1942, a time in which an expansion of the Reich still seemed possible.

The teaching staff and clerks at the institute in Berlin-Mitte, tied to the Humboldt University, whose task was to carry out large-scale research and implement the findings in training courses, were still working on the question of how the German civil service should prepare itself for the world domination that was expected to be achieved by 1952. Or did anyone assume that one could manage India thanks to a law degree, the experience of a Prussian district administrator or that of a governor of the Province of Hanover?

One of the best methodologies for administrating conquered areas could be found in the practice of the Dutch East India Company in the seventeenth century, which followed a personality-based capitalism and was thus closer to the National Socialist idea than was the cold-hearted British style of government. The accumulated stores of such experience were still being worked on, amid bombs and enemy fire, until the last days of April. The training guidelines, some of them already printed, were stored in 17 spacious basements. The head of the institute, mentally agile and still on his toes, was checking how one could procure vehicles despite the hardships in order to transport the material, which was valuable after all, to the alpine fortress (possibly through a gap in the Russian front near Spandau).

In the Basements of the Charité

In one of the evacuated wards of the Charité's maternity hospital, a basement, abortions were carried out in three shifts during the night. The pregnancies in question had come about in March in West Prussia. No doctor could do anything about the current rapes in Berlin. No leaflet had been distributed explaining how a woman should react to the violent strangers. A research group at Humboldt University had set up a data collection that extended back to Assur and gathered information from historical and ancient sources relating to women's behaviour in the face of rape. The staff carrying out the abortions in the basement was assisted by two Russian female physicians who, as prisoners of war, were still attached to the Charité. Later, after the Red Army had penetrated the hospital district, they were interrogated as to why they had let themselves be taken prisoner and placed in the service of the Germans.

Island of Civilization

Six women came together in a partly destroyed block of flats in the south of Berlin. The ground-floor flats still had the cosy, lamp-filled furnishings characteristic of the 1930s. There the women set up a reception area for Soviet officers who then returned and, in the following days, protected this 'German group' (including the girls and women hidden in the attics) from attacks by their soldiers. The enterprise resembled a canteen, certainly not a brothel.

Not that these women, who respected one another and had the same assessment of the situation (German men would never help them in this war any more), were prim. But they considered it a tactical error to offer themselves as sexual objects. That would only lead to new desires, and ultimately to fantasies without end or any possibility of fulfilment. Rather, they acted as hostesses (only granting special attention in exceptional cases); thus lively communicative activity, vitality, visits by interested parties and civility formed the protective space that cordoned off this small part of Berlin from the open violence that filled the city's districts. At the entrance to this establishment, this 'conspiracy of six women', there were occasionally brawls or duels between the 'civilized' and the 'conquerors'.

Normally One Pays for Erotic Services; Here One Pays for Lives to Be Saved

Until the end, the Barn Quarter near the Berlin Police Headquarters was home to criminal gangs and businesses engaged in prostitution. Despite many attempts by the law enforcement authorities to crush or drive away this milieu, it proved impossible to get rid of it. The group viewed itself as remote from the state.

A number of Jews with forged papers survived here, for a fee. 'It's a mystery,' said Police Councillor Schwiers after solving once such case, 'where the wanted men get the money. They most have buried it somewhere—in a place their "rescuers" don't know about. We really don't know everything.'

The 'system' was still working for some of those hidden on 30 April. There was no longer any danger for them from the police headquarters. The status of a Jew persecuted by the Third Reich was difficult to explain to the Red Army soldiers who reached them, however, without any papers to prove it. This was compounded by the language barrier. Once again, the services of pimps and prostitutes, who successfully continued their trade under the new circumstances, saved the day. The erotic trade and flexible, communicative criminal practice, which had much exchange material at their disposal, preserved their paying protégés from attacks by Red Army soldiers. Some of the pimps spoke perfect Russian.

Education Struggle to the Last

Just before Easter, the 'Science Department' of the Reich Ministry of Education had departed in several trucks from Berlin-Gesundbrunnen, where it had moved after the ministry building in Wilhelmstrasse burnt down, to Eisenach. After all intended places of accommodation turned out to have been destroyed already, Head of Department Menzel, who initially stayed behind in Berlin with the minister, instructed by telephone that the files should be stored at Rossleben Monastery and in a hidden barn near Tröbsdorf. That was the current location of the 'education reform'.

In Berlin, Undersecretary von Rottenburg was guarding the 'handling office' that was attempting to make an inventory of the ministry's remains. Some of its employees were still 'clinging' to their workplace. The few conference rooms still intact, with their high windows, had long been impossible to warm up. In the canteen, the wife of the killed canteen operator was keeping a provisional serving counter going.

In Berlin, alternatives to continuing the ministry's work were serving at the front or working in an arms factory. It was only remaining in the office (whether evacuated or improvised in the ministry building) that prevented the OFFICIALS OF THE EDUCATION SYSTEM, passionate educators, from being 'used by others' at the end.

For research projects important for the war, money transfers were still being made to the 'outside' on 30 April as a result of blanket authorizations. The senior civil servant Rabe forced the continuation of work on the third volume of the reader for A-level classes; the aim of this innovation was to give the material, last revised in 1928, its final form by 1952.

He Had Only Got Three of His Students Through to Spandau-West

The educator Dr Friedrich Ruhl, who had led 18 pupils into a military intervention and only got three of them through to Berlin, attempted to report to the Ministry of Education, a ruin, where there was nonetheless work going on in some rooms. He was getting on the nerves of the porter, who was still active in his cubicle reinforced by wooden cladding, because he kept appearing day after day and asking for someone to report to. But there was no official left in the remnants of the building to whom he could have spoken about the loss of pupils in a military intervention.

Thirst in the Wasteland

The animals in one of the enclosures of the Zoological Garden had been forgotten. The birds were screaming horribly. A lieutenant left the zoo bunker with seven men to place a tub of water in there for them. The wires of the large cage were torn. The birds could have escaped to the sides and upwards, the young officer said, but stayed close together, no matter how thirsty they were. The care group returned safely to the bunker entrance; during their expedition, they had been provided with cover by one of the almighty anti-aircraft guns on the plateau of the bunker.

News across the International Date Line

Two radio operators were still sitting in the ruins of the Japanese Embassy on the edge of the Tiergarten park. Russian snipers were nearby. No panes in the windows. They learnt of Hir's death late in the evening by listening in to German radio communications (as they had been trained to do). It was unclear for a while whether the Führer had died through enemy artillery fire, through a coup or by his own hand. They translated the news into Japanese, encrypted it and transmitted the text to Tokyo. The message reached head-quarters in Tokyo at 3 a.m. At that time, an aerial attack on the city with explosive and incendiary bombs was imminent. The news went unnoticed for many hours. The transmission of the message from Berlin and the arrival of the information in Japan were separated by the International Date Line.

6

REINHARD JIRGL

◆

A Proletarian Clytemnestra

In the municipal archives of the township of X. in Lower Saxony lies a report on an incident that occurred in April 1945, during the final days of The War.

The worker Ilse A. (22) had been conscripted into Home-Front-Service & assigned to factory-labour since 1941. The-Works (a munitions-factory under-contract to the German Wehrmacht) not far from X and close to the village of Y on the main rail-line to Hanover, provided logistically=favourable conditions for the transport of-goods and workers to&from work. Moreover, the lines, after Allied-bombing, were always swiftly repaired, shifts were rarely cancelled & production barely faltered; the relentless=bombardments evidently had Other Aims than eliminating arms-production.—In the factory Ilse A. got to know the mechanic Harald P. They were the same age and soon got married. Their marriage had lasted only 2 nights when Harald P. was called-up & transported to The Eastern-Front as an army private; that was 2 years ago. Ilse P., née A., wrote regularly to her husband on-the-Front, sending him food parcels & other useful items, for Ilse was a practical-minded woman. Most of her letters & parcels reached her husband in whatever region The War had taken him to; very little was lost or confiscated. Replying, Harald P. sent home loving-words of gratitude for his wife's gifts; sometimes his sentiments were couched in such purple passages as may blossom in the mind of a *lonely* man absorbed in longing=

thoughts of his=Beloved wife=at-home.—Ilse P. continued to work in the factory. The-Works used slave-labourers who were kept in segregated areas, as well as some foreign-workers, who were housed in quarters that were less strictly=regulated & who had been recruited to work in the German Reich before-The War. Ilse P. fell in love with a Polish foreign-worker called Károl S. Because he had come to-the-Reich=to-work voluntarily, Károl enjoyed a number of significant privileges over the-forced-labourers. He too was obliged to dwell in The-Works' own (guarded) barracks but besides pay & better food he was Free-to-Leave the-premises 3x a week and to-stay out until 10 p.m. So 3x every=week The *Pole* Károl S. visited The *Frau* Ilse P. in her lonely flat in the small town of X. She had no Polish, and his German consisted only of the basics he needed at-work. It was said they fucked mutely & roughly, as hurriedly & rapaciously as-beasts: without ceremony, but with unequivocal attention=to-detail. Hours of panting lust. (The-neighbours, who of course knew=everything, gave nothing away; the days of reporting a woman to-the-authorities for *racial defilement* were over. By early 1945 the time had come to restructure the relations-of-deference, and no-1 has a better instinct in such matters than The People...... They took the necessary= courage from above=from the Incendiary Bombs that rained-down nightly from on-high and the firestorms to which even the small town of X. had now succumbed.) So it came about that people hoarded their=knowledge-of-this=relationship like a banker stock-piling Capital. The moment for realizing their stocks, at New Values dictated by the New Currency of *Resistance*, would surely come, for even the hardest-of-hearing among them had heard the rumour of distant artilleryFire approaching by-day-and-night=from-The-West, the Howling of bomber-squadrons in the skies and the endlessImpact=

of-bombs...... The night reared up in towers=of-flame, the earth shook, quaking with dreadful tremors, and what remained of the winter-ice on rivers & puddles was smashed under successive convulsions of this shudderingMachine—. And when the beams of the flak-searchlights penetrated=the-night-sky they revealed squadron= upon=squadron of bombers passing overhead with the dogged patience of the Death-Machine, like flying crosses bound for a land-of=graves. (During the past one-and-a-half years there had been talk too of an unrelieved retreat of the Wehrmacht & its allies from the-East (some, thinking themselves safe from eavesdroppers, whispered: *They aint straightenin out the Front no more, aint even a retreat if you ask me— the army's bein smashed, it is, slaughtered, any-1 who's smart's doin a bunk, every man for hisself, n the rest is goin to snuff-it, or end up as=Russian-prisoners then snuff-it. The whole=Eastern Front's ka=put.*) Iron&fire—The-Floodtide-of-War that had swept Death into Russia's vastness from-the-West just four years previously was now ebbing with All-Force from the Enormous Expanse of the Soviet Union—.) And yet the Black Uniforms and slim, pipe-like wax-shiny Jackboots were still strutting about the small town of X. with silver ⚡ ⚡-runes on their collar patches—Danger-Signs meaning electric shocks could strike down any=1 any=time.

3 x a=week Ilse P. & Kàrol S. met, kept their peace & fucked. They were wild, animal, driven=by-lust, just as they had been the very 1st time. In-due-course, to prevent him finding out about their=affair when he returned from the-Front, Ilse P. sent her Husband=in-the-Field a parcel, as always containing gifts sent-with-love from=his-Native-Land, among which, baked with ingredients she had saved & squirrelled away, was her husband's favourite : nut cake, with a sponge mixed with ground hazelnuts or: nut-substitute

(?who would notice the taste of bitter almonds......).—Before the parcel arrived Private Harald P. was wounded, discharged from The-Army and, judged Unfit for Active Service, returned=home where he caught his wife in flagrante with the Polish worker. Harald P. killed his-wife's=lover and then beat up his wife. Screaming she ran out into the blacked-out streets. Silver forks of lightning flashed on their collar-patches in the night sky, flak-searchlights penetrating the smoke-filled sky in search of The Enemy...... The air, hot with flames, stank of kerosene, of smoke from burning houses & parched mortar dust. A police-patrol apprehended the raving screaming woman in the burning streets. At the station the woman spoke in confused terms of the assault she had suffered at-the-hands-of her husband following his return from-the-Front (she did not mention her=relationship with the Polish worker). Without further ado the police escorted her back to the air raid shelter in the cellar of her house which the bombing had hitherto left intact.—In the meantime, the parcel containing the poisoned cake had arrived at-the-Front. Because Harald P. was no longer serving in the company, his fellow soldiers had eaten the cake and died a miserable death; their Commander reported the incident to the Authorities=back-home. On 1 of the following mornings, just as the Field Gendarmerie, who had entered the house in X., were about to arrest the unfit Private Harald P., an American Combat Patrol, having made their way up from the cellar of the house, suddenly appeared in the living-room. : The German Field Gendarmerie trained their guns on Private P. &: the Americans; Private P., armed with a pistol he had hidden=in the-house, threatened the American intruders and German Field Gendarmerie; the Americans pointed their weapons at Private P. &: the German Field Gendarmerie. Ilse P., bleeding after her husband had beaten her again that morning, was the only person not being threatened. Once again she succeeded in escaping from the flat into the streets, battling her way through chaotic scenes as far as the north-western suburbs, where she ran into advancing American troops to whom she offered her services as a Red Cross Helper (the bloody-marks on her face, emblems of her credibility, may have expedited her enrolment). In the meantime, the standoff continued between the men confronting 1:another in= the-house. Since 30 April 1945 when this classic set-up was enacted in a flat in the Lower Saxon township of X., it has gone on to estab- lish itself as=a-standard in Hollywood-Westerns, a tradition which extends even to the work of Quentin Tarantino. In movies such= standoffs are always resolved in the same manner: everybody shoots, blood flows in=enormous-quantities, and everybody dies. However, this solution is less conducive to the success of Wars & Other Business Ventures.—Today X. in Lower Saxony is a smart little spa town with a restored=historic-town-centre; the town houses of earlier centuries gleam under freshly applied terracotta-&-sand-coloured surfaces. At the southern edge-of-town stands a memorial-stone, a monument commemorating the slave-&-foreign-workers who worked at the town's munitions-factory serving the German Wehrmacht. The names of those who died here are engraved on the memorial stone. 1 name is missing: Károl S.

7

ALEXANDER KLUGE

In a Small Town

◆

◆

The small town had experienced many different rules during its over 1,000-year existence. The bombing that transformed its centre into a crater landscape, however, struck it harder than any of the destructions and fires in the Middle Ages. But even with such destructions, it matters little who holds power over them.

People are taking back life which had been the property of the ethnic community only a moment earlier. All over the country, zones of happiness and unhappiness split into localities. A dozen of these form a district. A shock forms a stretch of land. Fräulein Hilde walked the whole way from Neuekrug-Hahausen, near Goslar, to Halberstadt only to meet Harald Reck, who assists at a military hospital and whom she first met in March at a dance event organized by the Reich Labour Service. 'My country extends as far as I can walk to my beloved.'

In a Small Town

The telephone connections do not extend far. There are no trains. Thus the town and its population are on their own. But migrants arrive with handcarts and bicycles, and refugees come from the area east of the Elbe.

Before, the town was part of a network—the Reich. The net has been torn apart, so now the town breaks up into pieces. It was not the bombs that caused this division 22 days ago. On the contrary, the destruction re-mobilized the old organizational structures—the city council, the National Socialist People's Welfare, the activity of teachers as organizational directors, and the notion that a quick reconstruction was possible. Now the people in the lower town refuse to be ordered around by the authorities. The refugees are not registered, so they obey no one either. The employees of the post office and the district library on the cathedral square appear for work. But they no longer act together with anyone. The regression to a 'new reality' releases energies from earlier realities that were simply covered up.

Like foxes we roam through the town's basements, the deserted public buildings. One can find plenty of usable material there; but first one has to find out what it can be used for. The third building of the primary school, for example, a solid brick building, was recently a reserve military hospital. One can get blankets and bedclothes there; piles of books and games, collected from donations by private households towards the end of the war for the entertainment of the wounded in their periods of convalescence; test tubes and many types of medical vessels. One can fill 'German sparkling wine', which can be found by the crateful in one of the lower town's cellars (from an air force supply that had been transferred there), into such test tubes and vessels and have a drinking bout with six or seven school pupils.

My father showed a master bricklayer the rubble-filled ruin of our house. The facade, foundation wall and fire wall are still standing up to the first floor. One could rebuild it up to the first floor for 80,000 Reichsmark, the master bricklayer says. Maybe, he says, the fire even made the stonework harder. But the expert can't say more than that. Then a slope will have to be built on the first floor and covered with roofing paper so that the rainwater can drain off. Where will we get the roofing paper? There might still be some at the Junkers factory. The days are cold and damp. Finding fuel is one of the aims of the residents' trips of conquest. Once again in the basements of deserted public buildings—piles of black coal. They can transport it in handcarts and crates.

The churches are standing open and bare. There is strangely little to be had there. Not that the vicars and sextons took anything for themselves; rather, the houses of prayer were emptied of their treasures in the Reformation (and the Counter-Reformation emulated it). One larger looting expedition reached the Rübeland caves, where some people had transferred their effects (furniture, pictures, silver, stamp collections). The caves are deep in the mountain and considered safe from bombs. One possible danger to the valuables comes from the dampness of these dripstone caves, where a lot of brine gathers at the bottom. The explorers from the small town inspect the unguarded stores of possessions. But here in the mountains, they see little possibility of removing them at the moment. One can't cover the distance from the town to the mountains on foot and with a handcart (or even a simple horse-drawn cart) several times a day.

An officer of the occupying power from Minnesota, a teacher by profession, experienced how energetically the residents entered the undestroyed basements of the Büttner department store (there are five, going back to the Middle Ages) at the Fischmarkt only two weeks ago. The throng of people, including children, could not be stopped by guards or military means. In the case of those who poured out of the basements carrying food on the side leading towards Lindenweg, the US guards knocked the loot (boxes of food and other goods) out of their hands. But while the soldiers were doing so, other people carrying spoils went past them, so most of it reached the town. And there was no point in leaving the unroasted coffee beans, tins of sardines and biscuits, and preserved meat lying on the floor around the basement exits. The officer, who was acting as commander and supervisor, was ultimately only concerned with preventing the population from being shot at which resulted in the agitated crows overrunning the few soldiers. The US Infantry was not trained in the administration of a town. The best way of forcing the people to obey was to leave them alone.

Digging for the Dead

A burnt smell emanates from the ruins of the town. At Hoher Weg, a column of German prisoners of war is busy digging up dead bodies unsupervised. Supervision by US personnel is unnecessary, as the work gang is kept together by the bond of food and the prospect of receiving official discharge papers when the work is done. As soon as people suspect that dead bodies will be discovered at the excavation site, all witnesses think that the smell of burning mingles with a 'corpse smell'. It is not clear, however, what kinds of stench or vapours are actually mixing here. The people's noses have no well-founded experience of how to classify individually the perceptions of such odours which are unfamiliar at first but become familiar in these days, and how to distinguish them according to origin.

The US administration has set up stations where it expects finds of corpses and their removal. It assumes that dead bodies spread disease. It is therefore necessary, the Allied town administration states, to extract all bodies from the ruins and either bury or burn them. Most attention is being paid to the air-raid shelters that were buried by rubble. The public health officer, Dr Meyer, is speaking to the non-commissioned officer in charge of the dig. He is a trained medic.

—What kind of disease do you think the corpses will spread?

—Poisonous gases and resulting diseases.

—What diseases are you thinking of?

—Poisoning.

Corpse gases are not poisonous, answers Dr Meyer. He is about to mention experiences with the accumulation of corpses on the German side during the war, but refrains after a moment's thought. Dead bodies are unpalatable, and therefore poisonous, the US sergeant argues. Bodies decompose, they rot. Dr Meyer nods. He is hesitant to bring up experiences showing that even decomposition causes an unbearable smell but does not trigger diseases. Nor is there any question of eating the dead. But taking this argumentation any further strikes the German health officer as a downward slope.

Loot with No Practical Value

Still no school. But a working day nonetheless. We are 'organizing'. It is like a competition to get hold of something that one can show one's friends. The others looking at the booty in amazement is reward enough. How useful the organized goods are is unimportant.

Five of us head for the southern end of the Klus Hills with hedge shears, pliers and hammers. The site of the find was explored the previous week. Unfinished aeroplanes are parked here, a kilometre from the airfield, still hidden in the woods. They were brought here from the endangered production halls at the Junkers factory (evidently because components were no longer being delivered). In their concealed position, they could not be recognized as fighter bombers.

The planes, which were easy to break into, had leather interior fittings. We used the hedge shears to cut out broad pieces of this precious material, making rectangles that could be used as a carpet substitute or other flooring material, or for the seats of chairs. We had occupied the basements that had survived in the ruined family homes. That was the purpose of our booty—it was meant to create a certain 'cosiness' there. Essentially, all our efforts were aimed at restoring conditions from the time before the destruction, or at least hinting at them through signs. We worked until noon, then turned our attention to bartering in the lower town. We exchanged a crate of cigar stubs, taken from airport canteen supplies that had been stored in a bombed-out basement and not collected again (presumably because those now in charge of the airport knew nothing about the hiding place), for two rolls of barbed wire. These were for protecting one of our basements from intruders. Our miscalculation lay in the fact that such a security measure only attracted the attention of other groups of thieves or 'organizers', and that the protective barbed wire is an obstacle that can, with a certain effort, be overcome. A fence does not protect—it announces the presence of unknown treasures. We were energetic, but not experienced.

A long working day came to an end. The red sunset in the west, by Burchardi Green and the Gate Pond, does not look much different from the red sunrise so many hours before in the east.

Domeyer Garden Centre at Burchardi Green

It is easy to draw water for Domeyer Garden Centre from the Holtemme which flows into the Bode. The cucumber patch is soaked. The greenhouses are already being heated again, as there is enough available wood from the ruins of the town. The French migrant workers, in their quarters on the grounds, are still showing no inclination to leave the business and go home. They have settled into their workplace, and feel that they are partners in the garden centre. There is also no information about travel connections to France. French papers would have to be issued authorizing them to return home; there is no suitable agency for that at the moment. So everything stays the same for weeks. Every week, new plants grow on the sprawling grounds of the garden centre, and then have to be harvested and taken to town.

Assigned to Removal Work:
From the Large Space to Simple Cultivation

The senior teacher Schürke, who had taught mathematics, physics and sport, had had a horse at his disposal during his four years as reserve colonel. He had an off-road vehicle with a driver for longer distances. An ambush by partisans had put an abrupt end to the expansion of his ego and his SPACE OF ACTION. Injured by gunfire, he was bedridden for months, confined to an area of 180 x 60 centimetres. Bedsores on his back and posterior. At the end he only lay on his belly. The notion of wide areas in Eurasia and Africa as an image of a German-ruled empire had disappeared. Thanks to petitions he dictated to the nurses at the military hospital, he managed to be transferred to that of his home garrison. Not fit for active service. His joints were weary, his head was lively. Now discharged to his home, only allowed to go out on doctor's orders. There he was tidying things in his study and in the garden. He had buried his insignias and securities (which could perhaps acquire some value later, if the occupying power that had meanwhile arrived left again) in an excavation two metres deep that he had made in his garden. The square metre of removed soil had been carefully levelled and the site disguised with professional expertise.

FIGURE 15. The International Prototype Metre in Paris.

Realistically viewed, a person's right to the piece of property they actually cultivate—be it an area of soil, a natural resource or a tool—diminishes over time. The compost heap the major had set up in the garden already occupied more than a square metre. The human right to a grave of one's own, Schürke thought, also relates to more than a metre of soil, unless one wants to put the dead person in an extreme squatting position or shortens the legs. It was from these concrete standards, which also included the long nocturnal walk on which the senior teacher gathered his thoughts and fought his insomnia (the 'nomadic' right to freedom of movement, as it were), that participation in the OVERSTRETCHED PEOPLE'S COMMUNITY had fallen away. The school had still not been reopened. Along with other men—a colourful mixture, as the occupying power had prescribed this for all adult male residents, whether they had a National Socialist past or not—Schürke had been assigned to removal work in the town's mountains of rubble. Other work gangs were composed of women.

The major was not currently in the frame of mind for larger units like the 'world' or a 'fatherland'. He was content if no one brought up his experiences during the last 12 years. His children tolerated him in the garden, in his study, using the toilet and at meals. Negotiating and smoothing over, his wife kept things bearable at the demarcation lines of the family members' interests; these lines could not be defined in exact spatial or temporal units. That would work out better in the summer. It was not a 'new time' but, rather, the part of the 'old time' that had existed all along during the MENTAL BUBBLE OF GREATER GERMANY without attracting particular attention.

Re-Enacting Conquest

The war died outside. Twenty-two days ago. The excitement is still shaking our idle schoolboys' hearts. I don't know what we were thinking during our games.

We are playing in the Müllers' attic. The house is at the end of Spiegelsbergenweg. Frau Müller is in charge. Her daughter Irmhild is her confidant. Father Müller returned from the war two days ago, released early from captivity with papers. His son Alfred, my best friend. We used to be able to play in his father's study; now we play in the attic. The game is called 'defending and conquering empires'. Alfred Müller's brother Gerhard is playing too. We have marked out our terrain: coastlines and countries are hinted at with threads and matchsticks. All areas together form the world. Generously marked off: colonies, areas of interest and home countries.

We have formed 'battleships' and 'tanks' from metal prongs, roughly 10 centimetres long, that we looted from aircraft fuselages. Lead letters, from an 'organized' typecase taken from a burnt-out print shop, can be placed on the metal prongs or on oblong pieces of tree bark. Then they mean 'artillery'. For the threat and for battle, what counts is to load these 'bodies' with 'superstructures'. Seven beats two. If there is an advantage of four to three, one has to roll the dice.

I occupy the coastline of an area that is part of Alfred's empire. First I 'trick' him by attacking a different zone of interest. But he predicted that, and by shifting all his prongs and lead-loaded pieces of bark onto my 'home areas', he makes my 'empire' shrink while the late afternoon light fades. Alfred and his brother Gerhard are essentially peaceful types. They respond to my aggression with imitative aggression. How remarkable that after sobering days, already under American occupation and after an impressive air strike that destroyed the town, this playful tension, the ambition to gain territory, still persists! It will take a long time for the undercurrent that seized us in an abstract (or dreamlike) manner to ebb away. Ears red with eagerness. We are hungry when Alfred's mother calls us to come downstairs.

Life in the Rhythm of Haircuts

In April 1945, Hartmut Eisert was 13 years old. At that time (his parents had fled with him from the east) his hair was only cut on an irregular basis, whenever a barber shop was open in town and his parents urged him to go. Later, at the age of 20, he went for a haircut every eight weeks, which gave the years and life an imperceptible, quiet yet steady beat. This rhythm varied by a few days, sometimes a week, before major public holidays or holiday trips. Then the frequency of haircuts increased. Sometimes such a cut can bring good fortune; and sometimes it opens an indifferent phase of life. Hartmut was superstitious. It was terrible if his hair was cut badly (by a new, inexperienced employee). He did not like changing hairdressers.

Thus he will experience roughly 560 haircuts until his death in 2014. He always wears 'reliable' clothes when he goes for a haircut, which means clothes that have brought him good luck at some time in the past. An unsuccessful haircut can spoil his life, assuming he knows when his end will come. And so his shock upon seeing in the mirror that the haircut was botched is lessened by the fact that he does not know the hour of his death.

Haircut for the New Times

On the nineteenth day after the Americans invaded, my father had his hair cut in his medical practice by a hairdresser who had come from Silesia as a refugee. With his bald head, there was little cutting or hairdressing to do. His eyebrows at least offered a little trimming work. My father was in a good mood and gave him a present. It is a luxury, he said for such a hairdresser to make a house call, something that normally only doctors do. He wanted to enter the new century, which had begun either with the air raid on Halberstadt or the American invasion, or was perhaps still to come, with a fresh head— after the end of the city, as it were. In those last days of April, one historical epoch replaced another with lightning speed. The barber's house call still belonged to the feudal period (in the Austro-Hungarian style of the former south-east), while the black-market trading and appropriation of unguarded possessions belonged to the bourgeois age (the doctor does not practise that himself, but lets others 'confiscate' things for him—for example, by asking a discharged soldier to organize the espied goods bit by bit and deliver them to his house in exchange for a present). The helpfulness that ignores neighbourhood boundaries and has affected the whole city anticipates a socialist virtue. Even without being sick, a gardener from the lower town brought the doctor some asparagus which could be cut early this year.

Bartering

Twelve pairs of gloves in a cardboard box in exchange for a bucket of sugar from the sugar factory in the lower town. Two such buckets as a loyalty gift to the administrator of the city index that lists all promotions and professional accolades from the last 12 years. Certain career jumps do not need to be publicly accessible. Detective Sergeant Fülpe, who looks after the index, takes the buckets to his family's temporary quarters.

Six handcarts of briquettes for a ball of cloth. A hundredweight of coke for the goodwill of the deputy authority representative in the town business office which issues trade permits. A swap: three of Frau Märker's children for two days for Frau Stolpe (so that she can trek through the Harz to Göttingen and bring back merchandise) in exchange for Frau Märker getting the same number of Frau Stolpe's children for two days, with no compensation for the required food, as the amounts should more or less cancel each other out.

Early Commercial Flowering, Blown away a Moment Later

The stores of the Funger & Co. glove and cap factory are fully stocked. Until early April, following plans and instructions from 1941, they produced military gloves, head protection and later also windbreakers and sleeve guards. The products were manufactured at an increased rate but no longer transported, owing to the collapse of communication lines. With the arrival of the Americans, the 'military supplies' had become 'goods'.

Then the British took over the town's administration from the Americans. Until their arrival, the beginnings of a capitalist natural economy—initially with no new production, simply as a redistribution of the precious inheritance of the Reich's fortune, flourished. The British military administration issued a flood of directives, thus choking the early flowering of the later economic miracle.

It was replaced by the principle of 'fair distribution among the population'. At that point, however, the supplies had already disappeared into thin air. Even Kraux the scrap dealer claimed (at a time when junk was lying visibly everywhere) he could not deliver. That the stores were empty. There was, after all, no iron production that might have required scrap metal. We 'organizers', however, knew that there were caves in the Huy (a mountain ridge north of Halberstadt) where valuable supplies of discarded metal, including zinc and tin, had been stored. We were already eliminated as scouts in early May, however, when all of us, divided according to class and school, were sent to Emersleben Manor to thin turnips.

Gitti and the Captain Wandered along the Shore, Holding Hands ('Several heavens walked beside them')[1]

Captain Sinclair and Gitti wandered along the shore, holding hands ('several heavens walked beside them'). The rapprochement between

---

[1] A quotation from Jean Paul's short story 'Leben des vergnügten Schulmeisterlein Maria Wutz in Auenthal' (from *Die unsichtbare Loge*, 1790).

former enemies had gained momentum after a long afternoon in which her English (drilled into her at school, purely theoretically) had proved fresh and articulate. The mistakes in her school English had made Captain Sinclair laugh. Eagerness had brought them together and had now given way to affection. The working day—hectic.

The cold spell that had gripped the country for the last four days prevented Gitti and the Captain from meeting outdoors. They could not have intimacy at the captain's headquarters either, as it was off-limits for Germans; fraternizing was still forbidden. Having felt for 24 hours that they were closely connected (like siblings, like a lover and his beloved, like conspirators, like people who have worked together for years), they felt an urge for intimate contact. They no longer took their eyes off each other. They could not find any better a location for intimacy than the wooden shack in one of the air-raid shelters of a burnt-out house. They took the door beam of the tiny storeroom out of its bracket and placed it on the bare floor as a kind of wooden bed.

After the town was handed over to the British, which took place in June, the two never saw each other again. The captain had been transferred back to the US to lead a recruiting station. No voice of the heart can do anything against such a command-based CHANGE OF EXTERNAL CIRCUMSTANCES. Unexpectedly, an ocean lay between the two lovers. They wrote each other letters. The memory remained. Calling up details of a bodily contact which, in the moment, they had thought they would not forget, proved more difficult than expected. What stuck in the memory was more the feeling of cold and dust in that basement room.

In certain moments of that afternoon, when an intense exchange at work had turned into a love affair, Gitti had hoped that her sweetheart (she had touched his hand, but did not yet know that they would be in a relationship only hours later) would take her with him to a different country, a victorious country. He, on the other hand, during their farewell crisis, had toyed with the idea of going underground in the former enemy territory and starting a new life with Gitti. The mere explanation of the individual steps in this plan already showed how unfeasible it was. They were both too intelligent for adventures in the groundwater of life. Just as the darkness in the storeroom (there were no lights in the basement) was clearly different from any 'moonlight over the love nest'.

Transatlantic Door

Lisbeth Lehmann from Klein Quenstadt had been drafted in 1943 as part of an initiative to mobilize women for German armament. She was assigned to the canteen at Halberstadt Airbase. The barracks near the Theken Mountains was then taken over by the Americans in April 1945. The service obligation was no longer in force, but Lisbeth kept going to work out of habit; now she was simply serving the enemy. It had been like that for 19 days. From Klein Quenstadt through Halberstadt (with no tram), up Klusstrasse, through the bottleneck between the Klusberg and the Spiegelsberg, and then another 10 minutes to the canteen. That was a stiff walk.

The idea of emigrating formed from this (and the new reality supported such a notion). In the defeated country there was little future, as far as men were concerned. If one of the non-commissioned officers of the Air Force married her—she knew this from books—a new life could begin far off in the west. She had agricultural knowledge.

Only a few days later, two sergeants drove her the long way back to her village in a jeep. Lisbeth's mother served them both bread and jam, pancakes, then ham sandwiches. They were allowed to stay the night. Now Lisbeth had to decide to which of the two she would get closer. If she stuck to both, she would lose both. Her mother's advice was precious.

She chose the older one, who struck her as more mature and decisive. On 30 April they were engaged. Happy days. Lisbeth's mother had cleared out the living room. Four weeks later, the regrouping of the US Air Force also affected Halberstadt Airbase. Lisbeth's fiancé was transferred to an island in the Pacific. They wrote each other 'fiery' letters, memorizing their experiences. But soon Lisbeth no longer believed that anything practical would come of their connection. She tried to find out under what conditions a private engagement (documented, if necessary, by love letters containing larger plans and promises) could result in admission to the US, and there be converted into a marriage. To strengthen their bond, she enclosed intimate photographs with her letters to her fiancé. The connection, promising at first, dissolved. Later she received a letter— still in a tender, reminiscing tone, but also with the news that her fiancé had married in the US and now had children. She sent her warmest congratulations; by this point she had stopped looking westwards and chosen a future in her home town. A sudden visit from her former lover, demanding the fulfilment of the promise made on 30 April 1945, would have been embarrassing. The way to her new job was half as long as to the airbase (now only three kilometres instead of six). Soon she lived there too.

Tufts of Grass

Now, in April, the turf—several tufts—was growing opulently only two metres from the edge of the bomb crater. The crater was a remnant of the attack on 14 February 1945 which had been aimed at the Junkers factory. The group of craters was a few hundred metres away from the target, towards the mountains. Clumps of earth and stony material from the depths had fallen over the tufts of grass. Not enough to cause any damage. The destructive part of what had come out of the crater had gone down at a greater distance from the plants. The substances from the depths, meanwhile swept away by weather conditions, were evidently nutritious—at the end of April, the plants seemed as agile as in the summer.

View of the Brocken

In the dampness of these days, the Brocken could only be seen from the town for one or two hours—between two low-pressure troughs, as it were. I am curious by nature. It would have been logical to visit this mountain peak, an icy rock plateau. The highest mountain of the Harz is subjected all year to the westerly winds coming from the sea and the plains. In my childhood, one could see the distant mountain in good weather. Now, on 30 April, a hike (which would have taken more than a day) was out of the question. How would I have explained to a military police patrol what I was doing on the way there? Would they have checked me for weapons? What would I have done for food if unable to return the same day?

In the 82 years of my life I had never been to the Brocken, despite feeling a strong bond in my imagination. Postcards and photos do not give one an urge to visit; they are different from the image of a rocky ice desert. In my mind's eye, two irreconcilable images of the peak's terrain coexist. That of a plateau which is inhospitable to people on account of the storm winds, and the opposing notion of the drinking room in the Brocken Hotel which I had often heard about. Well heated, cosy. My curiosity never drove me to unite the two images.

A Day with a Surprise

Friday, 1 June 1945, was a cold day. A rain front overhead. We, the pupils of the cathedral school, supervised by our teachers who remained incompetent in agricultural matters and went to the edge of the field just when they would have prevented us from stopping working, were freezing in the turnip fields, our clothes wet. That day was unforgettable for me. We pulled up the weeds that were consuming the soil's nutrients next to the turnips and placed them together in piles. Around noon, because the rain was getting stronger, the estate inspector decided to fill us up with semolina from a cauldron and take us back to town in trucks. As workers, we were useless to him. I rang the doorbell. My mother opened up; she had come to Halberstadt from Berlin, a patchwork journey by train and motor vehicles.

I had not seen my mother for a year. Unmistakably herself in her worn-out, once-elegant clothes with a blouse. I know few 'leaps' from misery (freezing in the fields, under a raining open sky in the morning) to happiness on the same day. For me, that day is unforgettable and more important than 30 April 1945. But it cannot really be connected to anything else in Halberstadt, or the world as a whole. It is also difficult to give a precise account of this 'impetuous emotion', what one calls a 'happy surprise'. It only takes on precision if I describe it in a story about other people. Nor can that upsurge (a door opens and a person I am not expecting embraces me) be documented in the form of a 'photo with music'.

8

REINHARD JIRGL

◆

Uncanny Bridge-Building

The widower Otto Huber, a veteran 1st World War lieutenant and
Bearer of the Iron-Cross 1st Class, lately charged-with commanding
the VOLKSSTURM-Home Guard in the single-street Altmark village of A., spends his so-called leisure hours working in his small
garden in front of his half-timbered house at the southern end of the
village. The house once belonged to his wife, whose family had lived
in the region for-generations, and who, thirty-years-ago, married the
Bavarian-ex-lieutenant & travelling seed-salesman Otto Huber and
brought=him back to her small property in the Altmark-flatlands. His
wife died in 1938, and Otto Huber, not having remarried, has
lived here a*lone* ever since. Today he is tending his spring flowerbeds,
relishing the beguilingly silky fragrance of the blossoming lilac, treas-
uring the white pearls of lily-of-the-valley that Spring's hand has so
lavishly scattered on the velvet-green cushions of his fresh lawn growth;
even the narcissi have begun to unfold their yellow stars. In Otto
Huber's mind his=garden provides a counterweight=to-the horror-of-
the-times, a way of preventing the balance of individual dignity from
tipping into the abyss. Earlier, the local Party-Group-Leader, the
ORTS-GRUPPEN-LEITER, had shown up on the other side of his
garden fence and reminded the retired lieutenant that it was His Duty
to line up the village VOLK-STURM !immediately & to see to it that
they take=up-positions for=battle. Turning on his heels to leave, the
ORTS-GRUPPEN-LEITER had barked a particularly acrimonious

!HEIL !HITLER, whereupon Otto H. had responded with a !GRÜSZ !GOTT—after all, he had kept up this form of greeting, customary in his native Bavaria, throughout his-years-in=North Germany. The ORTS-GRUPPEN-LEITER, as if somebody had doused him with acid, winced at the greeting; he said nothing, but seemed to shuffle-off with his shoulders slumped.—To an old-soldier like Otto H. it is clear that any=sort-of FOLX-STURM-ing is going to be pointless: less incitement of the people than their=incineration. So he stays put and cultivates his=garden at the edge of the road. : On the other side of the low fence, a few arms' lengths from where he is standing, army vehicles come dashing past with engines howling & soldiers, perched on an open-backed truck, shouting to him, gesticulating wildly & pointing to the other end of the village; Otto H. can't make out their words, their calls are mangled-by=the engines: suddenly the column has vanished—clouds of exhaust-fumes, dust (it hasn't rained for some-time) & gravel-powder swirl through the air to sink slowly & heavily on the road opposite Otto Huber's garden fence and blossoming freshly-turned flowerbeds. The scene reminds the retired lieutenant of the kind of images that crop up in dreams, also of scenes he saw in the volcanic regions of Europe during WWI : deep-red glowing rivers of all=scorching lava, channelled by exuberantly green banks of lush untouched Mediterranean forest. Not even the pestilential breath of the searing lava had succeeded in spoiling !that green. *Thus every raging torrent touches at its edge the redeeming=terra firma. No river is without banks,* our FOLX-STORM-leader muses, & as a consequence of this intimation, which he takes to be A Sign, decides to refrain from executing on that day the-command to assemble= his-troop of pensioners juveniles & women (at the other end of the village's 2-km-long single street some FOLK-STORMERS, who have taken-up= position of-their-own=accord, are now banging away...... at something they take to be The Enemy).—Otto H. is weeding an especially recalcitrant root in a flowerbed when suddenly he becomes aware of a Profound Silence. The thunder-of military-vehicles rattling past has ceased, the artillery and other cannon are holding-their-fire, not a strafing plane or exploding shell is to be heard—All Quiet (not a bird singing in the sky) o how very quiet in the spring-blue afternoon light is the shimmer of dust on the street. No escaped POWs either, no prisoners from The Camps...... strays plundering, sometimes even murdering—just recently 3 Russians, escaped from a-transfer...... had turned up in the village, threatening the place with-fire, rolling their eyes, screaming & brandishing scythes, & could only be mollified by giving them bacon eggs & schnapps. They eventually moved on. (For in=the-depths of Otto Huber's cellar are copious crates of wine cognac and schnapps, shelves full of preserves & other food-stuffs—stocks belonging to a businessman friend from Hamburg who wanted to safeguard himself & his goods from the recurrent firestorms that were transforming his home town into a gigantic furnace. That merchant is now somewhere in Hamburg, baked in boiling asphalt—but his goods are stored here: !*Dangerous treasures in my cellar—an endangered strong-room which, like all strong-rooms, rather than offering protection against thieves actually attracts them.* The important thing now is !not to let !all-of This Vast Treasure slip into=the-hands& down-the-throats of the Victorious Occupying Forces; his own experience in WWI has taught him: all Conquerors, at their=Victory Banquets, first want Firewater, then Women, and finally Flames&the- Scalps of-the-vanquished......)

Deep yellow sunlight streams from the flat skyline across the vast expanse of unresisting fields & earth, striking the brickwork of the western gable of his small half-timbered house. The wall glows an orange-red, as if the old bricks were being refired, albeit in invisible flames.—Otto H., standing in the middle of his garden, straining his ears into=the-silence like an animal trying to sense the direction of approaching Danger...... discerns again the grinding-clatter & rattling-chains of tanks rapidly approaching from the end of the village to which the men on the truck had been pointing, and there is something different about the roaring engines as they noisily advance along the road—: Then Otto H. sees the smoke-blackened tank veering this way and that, waving its gun-barrel about in the air like a drunken Cyclops as it zigzags up the street, on-course for his garden fence : fence-posts bushes flowers & fruit trees snap like matchsticks & the all-crushing Steel-tracks churn-up Otto H.'s= freshly-turned beds. The American tank, part of an advance-party, partially disabled by the anti-tank rockets of the last village VOLXSTORMERS, finally crashes into the front wall of Otto Huber's house—as if hit by an earthquake the small building shudders at the impact & the tank comes to a standstill half-way through the wall, its gun-barrel protruding into the living-room like a battering ram: Bridge-Building with an iron fist. The powerful tube of steel in=Otto H.'s living-room is now pointing=directly-at a small porcelain sugar bowl, a family heirloom left intact on the dresser & just a little dusty after wall GlassBeams&Rubble heaped=themselves on-the carpet chairs table and other pieces of furniture (a suffocating column of clay Cement& Dust replacing the air in=the-room). Otto Huber, glued-to-the-spot, views the mishap from his garden. The engines of the tank have stalled, nothing else seems to be happening, just this unfamiliar steel vehicle embedded=in-the wall of his house, resting now like some triumphantly intrusive animal after a rough bout of copulation. Otto H. finds it odd that not-1 of the tank-crew has climbed out of the vehicle (he has mustered all the English he can remember with the intention of proclaiming: *I am unarmed I surrender*). It is only=now that Otto H. notices the open hatch on the gun-turret and wisps of acrid smoke rising from-within : 1-of-those VOLK-STORMING-heroes must have climbed up & lobbed a grenade down the hatch; the crew are dead. Again, that Silence—an uncanny silence in the Great Numbness of the hour——

In=Otto H.'s mind: indecision & terror—people are bound to think !he threw the-grenade into the tank, that !he was responsible for the death of these American soldiers. Yesterday's acts=of-heroism will be today's call=for the-bullet...... Cautiously, Otto H. steals away from his devastated garden and goes inside. Once there he peeks back outside through the smashed living-room wall: still all-quiet—not a military vehicle in sight, no American shock-troops following the tank—still deep-sky-blue, a star-shaped chunk of daylight the gun-barrel has knocked through the wall & hurled down with steely=force spills into the front-room. The silence is total. In the dying light the big white five-pointed star gleams for a while on the gun-turret of the smoke-begrimed Cyclops, in=whose entrails of twisted steel the dead Americans lie. Otto Huber uses this opportunity to remove the sugar-bowl from what is likely to remain a precarious position on the dresser of his living-room. *The gun may end-up firing, and then what—.*—— He doesn't know what to do with the dainty little sugar bowl, his wife's heirloom & acme of the riches amassed= in-his-cellar, so for the time being he will just hold on to it. Otto H. stands there & listens for a sign of anything about-to happen. An expert on dreams, he knows it is vital to wait until you wake-up. But first, evening comes, and then, descending dreamlessly over-the land: The 1st Night of Peace——

Early Shift. Scene for an Imaginary Front Theatre.

Winter. Bare open fields. A straight icy road, powdered with snow. Colourless Sky. No wind.

A group of soldiers, attired in various uniforms, marching abreast without haste. They are kicking an empty shell-case in front of them. Whoever kicks the case forward says his lines. And stops speaking as soon as he loses the case to a neighbour. The soldiers are marching in=step, without joy, without anger, as resigned-as factory workers on their wonted way=to-the-conveyor-belt. Not 1 of them attempts to take the case from his neighbour or to hold=on to it for unreasonably long. Nor do they deliberately pass the case to each: other; whoever gets the case is a matter-of-chance. What the soldiers say to each: other as they pass=on-their-way is neither-here-nor-there; it isn't the content that is important, but the rhythms & intervals, structure.

From-time-to-time, out of the Colourless Sky, a transparent film falls in front of the scene like a curtain, but without hindrance to the proceedings on the road.

An old lady, her hair November-grey, enters the scene & smiling amicably unfurls a large American flag made of several sheets she has presumably sewn together. A voice comes over the loudspeaker: 'It's how she earns=her-living. Nobody has ordered the flag & nobody needs it.' Whereupon the old woman, smiling amicably, rolls up the flag-cloth and removes herself, the film hung in front of the scene disappearing too.

Then repeat as a loop, a routine.

9

ALEXANDER KLUGE

On the Globe

◆

◆

Independently of all war-related events, Planet Earth moves around the central star on its elliptical orbit, reaching the point of springtime. The waters trickling down the drain of a sink or a well in the southern hemisphere turn in the opposite direction to those in the north. What is happening inside people, far more slowly than a water buffalo moves, flows towards horizons of hope that were still invisible only recently, even without any news in the papers or on the radio.

Civil war in Greece since Christmas. Labour leaders of organizations who have not met since the failure of the Second International in August 1914 travel to a global meeting on the West Coast of the USA. Will there be emancipation (for whom and by what) after the upheavals of this war? In San Francisco, removed from events in Europe by nine hours, the United Nations is founded.

Immense Redistribution of Military Forces Halfway around the Globe

Two mighty lever arms have been organized, one on the French Atlantic coast and the other in Malta. They shovel materials and soldiers from Europe to the Asian war zone on ships and by airlift. Allied secret services claim to have heard from Moscow about overtures by the Japanese ambassador towards the neutral Soviet government—a ceasefire is to be negotiated. On the other side, the planning staff in Washington fear the murderous details that would result from the conquest of the Japanese homeland in the case of a final battle. The massive transfer of armed forces and equipment to the Pacific also has the function of countering the troops' tendency to view the war as over. Surveys show that the majority of US soldiers in East Asia would no longer give their lives now that the end of the war is in sight.

A Stock-Market Leap

At 4 p.m., shares at the New York Stock Exchange leapt upwards after word had spread that income tax would be lowered not after Japan's defeat but immediately, owing to the collapse of the Axis in Europe. South American shares were the front runners.

The System of Certificates

Many Greek ships had escaped the German attack in 1941. The majority of those were now in the service of the British. Ten ships belonging to a ship owner who worked for England received certificates stating that he could use them for 'free seafaring'. They had the status of neutral ships.

FIGURE 16. Globe with Australia.

Circumnavigation of the Earth by Ship

A ship that dares to cross the belt of Japanese patrols (usually fishing boats) moves from the Pacific into the Indian Ocean, where further boats of the Japanese and British navy also keep watch. Now, in April 1945, passage from Cape Town across the Atlantic is unproblematic, meaning that because of the certificates, which display sections like land allotment maps, one can circumnavigate the earth twice through the Panama Canal.

Disappointing Arrival in East Asia

Germany could have done with those Type XXI submarines in 1941. Twelve of those would have been capable of controlling the Indian Ocean. Now, on 30 April, one such vessel, loaded with rare metals, patent drawings and relief supplies, entered a Japanese naval base in Java. The goods were unloaded and handed over to the Japanese authorities. They already no longer saw themselves as allies of the German Reich. Frosty negotiations about the transfer of fuel. The diesel here was viscous, unsuitable for the submarine's engines. Was there any other fuel? It had been a mistake to deliver the boat's cargo to the Japanese so quickly. It would have been better to leave the base on the first night, drop to the ocean bed in the sound and conduct negotiations with the authorities from there. But then one could only have trusted promises until the boat had reached the pier again and been unloaded; after that, promises would no longer have been kept. The frosty negotiations ground on. During the long journey through the Indian Ocean, the German seamen had prepared themselves for steam baths and Japanese massages upon arrival. They were emotionally starved. They were taken to a camp and guarded by the Japanese military police. They did not even have the rights of prisoners of war, as they were not in the custody of enemies but, rather, held captive by disappointed allies.

The empty boat was taken over by Japanese engineers. They came to the camp at night and tried to get some information about how it worked. Together, they could have searched for a large US aircraft carrier and sunk it with a few torpedoes that had been brought along. But such cooperation was no longer conceivable in the depressed atmosphere.

Robinsonad in the Ice

In April 1945, two high-ranking SS and police leaders, entangled in murderous actions and united by friendship, were in the service of the German Embassy in Tokyo. The friends certainly had no intention of being taken prisoner by the Allies (for the dissolution of the German Embassy was inevitable within a certain time frame). They chartered a Japanese whaling ship that brought them to the Kerguelen Islands, to an ice-covered, almost empty French island in the outermost South Pacific.

By 30 April—they had been keeping a calendar like Robinson— they had already lived in isolation for a few weeks in their tent. The whaler would have reached the Japanese mother island again by now. There was so little chance of ever leaving this island, a terrain of gravel and ice, and hence of being in the company of other people (even if these would arrest and punish them for their deeds), that they had decided to shoot each other. And so each shot the other. But there was a fraction of a second between the shots, which meant that one of them was fatally struck but the other was not. The one who had been spared still held out heavily wounded for a few more days, under the protection of the tent, as a 'survival'. Then he felt sufficiently recovered and shot himself (he had feared nothing more than an inaccurate shot). No one can survive without the company of others.

Neutral Ship

In all those years, the Portuguese mail steamer *Albuquerque* had sailed from Portuguese India (bypassing the embattled Dutch-Indian archipelago to the south) across the Pacific and the Panama Canal to Brazil, and from there, after transferring some of its cargo, sailed onwards to Porto. The ship barely transported mail any more. But the goods were of immense value for the neutral trade routes, and partly also for war parties. The steamer was marked as neutral and sailed illuminated at night. Spotlights were directed at the large Portuguese flag which flapped in the wind like a sail.

Fortunate Landing

One of the last steamers to leave the port of Warna before the Russians confiscated all seaworthy material brought a number of Jewish families, whose deportation to Poland was now obsolete, from one of the

Transylvanian camps to Palestine. The ship unloaded its human cargo on the beach a few kilometres from Tel Aviv. Boats had been sent to intercept the steamer beyond the surf zone by the organization that had made the transportation possible. The British frigate patrolling this stretch of coast came rushing along too late, and could only inspect the empty steamer. The passengers had long since disappeared in the city, where the repressive colonial power could no longer distinguish them from the residents.

Coup in Argentina

A participant in war crimes from the Third Reich, rightly feeling that he was in danger, had fled as far as Tierra del Fuego. Shortly before that, he had been a military attaché in a neutral country (responsible for investigations by the secret service). He had left that office and crossed the Atlantic, and had now been settled on a hacienda for six weeks. Technically, as far as his home country was concerned, he was a deserter.

Even here, in the south of Argentina, he found himself in danger on 30 April. An association of military officers forced into retirement, disappointed fascists and groups of left-wing extremists had conspired to bring about a coup. Once the fall of Berlin became known, the group, which was in contact with exiled Argentine politicians in Montevideo, planned to kill members of government and commanders loyal to the government, then seize power. The coup plan was uncovered, and the wave of arrests extended into the province of Tierra del Fuego. The German fugitive, who was living under a new name, saw a neighbour being taken away by a police car. The convoy drove heedlessly past his hacienda.

In the Seven-Hill City of San Francisco

In no way, states the *Neue Zürcher Zeitung* on 29 April 1945, can the seven-hill city of San Francisco be compared to the seven-hill city of Rome, where an empire was born, or with Versailles, where the League of Nations was founded. The delegations from 51 nations initially forming the UN convened in two large halls that constitute the conference centre. In fact, however, such assemblies rarely take place. Diplomatic relations are maintained between the four major powers and the heads of the other states' delegations.

An Indian delegation led by Pandit Nehru has taken up residence at a hotel. This unaccredited group is being closely and conspicuously observed by British secret agents. The intention is to disrupt their communication with the other three major power and the delegations of other influential states. The British agents are in turn being followed by US agents, which prevents them from using illegal methods on American soil to drive away the 'Indian guests'. Officials from the bureaus of the former League of Nations (whose statute, however, is officially in force until the final establishment of the United Nations), as well as previous secretaries-general, are present. Together with the idealist Richard Nikolaus Coudenhove-Kalergi, they form a personnel that deviates from the modern, pragmatic, war-marked type of politician. The congress is presided over by businessmen who act in a sober fashion and focus on specific goals, like Paul-Henri Spaak, Georges Bidault and Eelco van Kleffens. They are not innovators.

The Genesis of the Veto

With their strong voting bloc, the South American nations demanded the admission of Argentina to the United Nations. The Soviet Union objected, citing Argentina's close connections to the Axis powers. A further concern was the balance between the four major powers (were the sessions of the United Nations to be led by a single chairman chosen by a majority, or four chairmen provided by the four major powers?). In the end a compromise was reached—Argentina was admitted, but, in addition to the Soviet Union, the Ukraine and Belarus received member status and the right to vote. Also, the veto power of the four major powers in the Security Council (USA, Great Britain, France and China) was agreed upon, meaning that in future no voting bloc of smaller nations would be able to push meaningful decisions against the objections of any major powers. This is what occupied the diplomats on 30 April 1945, which is why news from the European war zone faded into the background.

FIGURE 17. Assembly Hall of the United Nations.

The Patriot of Lviv

The man from Lviv came from Alexandria, where he had lived since the thirties and directed a society whose aim was to restore the old Austro-Hungarian province of Galicia as a sovereign state and LVIV as a free city. In conjunction with US citizens whose ancestors came from Lviv, this society maintained a not-inconsiderable lobby. Before Roosevelt's death, they had succeeded in igniting the president's imagination with the idea of SAVING LVIV; because of this, nothing occupied the president more during the Yalta Conference and afterwards than this historical pledge of freedom that, taking significant immigrants into account, he possibly wanted to declare part of the USA. This town should remain an autonomous territory (as an island in the Ukrainian-Polish environs). But it should at least not belong to the Soviet Union, nor be subject to the puppet regime installed in Lublin by the Russians. Like Tangier or Gdansk, the city should be guaranteed the status of an independent community by the incipient United Nations. Then he, the president, would visit and be welcomed. For the short time Roosevelt still had to live, the Soviet Union could have received an inordinately handsome reward from the US government for such a solution.

The documents of the man from Lviv showed that since September 1914, Lviv (the Paris of the east) had never again become the city it had been during the empire—a relay station for generations thirsty for life and advancement between the villages and small towns on the one hand, and between Vienna and the USA on the other hand. Then the Russian army occupied the city. And it was no longer the same when the Austrian army administration took up residence there again. After the massacres of the German special units against the Jewish population, it lay desolate and decimated while the hostile rural population surrounding it had greatly multiplied.

FIGURE 18. Horticultural decoration in San Francisco on 30 April 1945.

That morning in San Francisco, the influence of the Lviv lobby was still strong. The South American nations and the USA were seeking a 'mediation' with Russia. Foreign Minister Molotov remained in the minority in all plenary meetings, in other questions too, and threatened twice daily with the Soviet delegation's departure. Had the delegation left (and it would have had to return weeks later), Lviv would presumably have received a guarantee from the United Nations. But as soon as the four major powers had agreed to introduce the veto in the Security Council, such a 'beneficial coup' was no longer possible. Russia would have prevented Lviv's secession through its veto. And so in this one point too, a finer, richer world fell victim to the pragmatic advance of the new world order. The Lvivian from Alexandria had spent the entire funds of his society.

COLOSSAL CRISES, RECURRING IN CYCLES, SIMILAR TO HUGE / & BLINDLY GROPING HANDS THAT GRIP & THROTTLE COMMERCE, / CONVULSE IN SPEECHLESS RAGE COMPANIES, MARKETS & HOMES. / [. . .] IF THE PRODUCT HOWEVER IS ONLY USED, BUT NOT ALSO BOUGHT / SINCE THE PRODUCER'S PAY IS TOO SMALL— WERE THE SALARY RAISED / IT WOULDN'T PAY TO PRO- DUCE THE COMMODITY—WHY THEN / HIRE THE HANDS? [. . .] YET WHAT THEN WITH THE COMMODI- TIES? IN GOOD LOGIC THEREFORE:

WOOLLENS & GRAIN, COFFEE & FRUITS & FISH & PORK / ALL ARE CONSUMED BY FIRE, TO WARM THE GOD OF PROFIT! / [. . .] YET THEIR GOD OF PROFIT IS SMITTEN WITH BLINDNESS. HE NEVER SEES / THE VICTIMS. HE'S IGNORANT. WHILE HE COUNSELS BELIEVERS HE MUMBLES / FORMULAS NOBODY GRASPS. THE LAWS OF ECONOMICS / ARE REVEALED AS THE LAW OF GRAVITY AT THE TIME THE HOUSE COLLAPSES / CRASHING ON OUR HEADS. (Bertolt Brecht, 'The Manifesto')[1]

'What to do?'

On 30 April, Bert Brecht noted: 'What is the European working class doing?' He expected some of the revolutionary upheaval of 1917 or 1918 to repeat itself after Hitler's downfall. As a playwright, he imag- ined scenes of uproar and social reconstruction.

1 Translated by Darko Suvin, *Socialism and Democracy Online* 16(1). Available at sd online.org/31/the-manifesto-2/ (last accessed 11 March 2015). [Capitalization by Alexander Kluge. Trans.]

FIGURE 19. Bertolt Brecht. At the time, he was working on a version of the COMMUNIST MANIFESTO in Homeric hexameter.

'All wheels stand still if your strong arm wills it'[2]

Oakland. City and port. Not far from San Francisco. The labour organization of the Henry Kaiser Shipyards has sent an invitation. Here the constitutive INTERNATIONAL CONGRESS OF LABOUR ORGANIZATIONS takes place. It is meant to act as a counterweight to the founding of the United Nations in neighbouring San Francisco.

There has been no gathering of all labour organizations since 1914. The disappointment over the fact that the Second International and the working classes of all countries could not prevent the World War from breaking out had broken up the labour movement into factions. Some of them were in fierce conflict.

---

2 A quotation from the 'Bundeslied', a song on a text by Georg Herwegh used by the General German Workers' Association (*Allgemeiner Deutsche Arbeiterverein*) as a hymn to the revolutionary proletariat. [Trans.]

The Congress of Labour Organizations has a strong element of British associations and US trade unions. One Swiss and one Swedish delegation are also represented. Many not-yet-accredited delegations and lone fighters are waiting for admission. The Red Chinese delegation, provocatively, is composed of farming envoys. No national Chinese figures have appeared. From the colonial regions of Africa: no representatives.

Accreditations are decided by a committee of three. Many organizations that historically emerged from labour struggles are no longer active and have no members, but are represented by functionaries awaiting political rebirth at this HEARTH OF UNITY. Looking at the hall chaotically filled with racks, Fritz Schuster, a newly minted US citizen from Chicago who has been arrested for agitation on several occasions, states: This will be the seat of the TOTAL WORKER. There will be no TOTAL CAPITALIST, he knows. The basic element of capital is competition; solidarity, by contrast, permits cooperation. That sums up the theoretical foundation.

It must be possible, Schuster says, if one considers the immense production activities set in motion by the war, to clothe the cooperation of all workers (joined by the scientists at Berkeley, and musicians are, incidentally, also workers) in a CONSTITUTION. Only this, and not the founding of a world association of nations in the spirit of democracy like the UN, would constitute the WORLD REGIME. This will still require much research and organization, Schuster says. The day is beginning.

On Folding Beds

The rooms for the delegations are set up in a giant, abandoned factory hall. The assembly room was designed by the shipyard workers like something for an equestrian circus, but also similar to an anatomy theatre in which the spectators are placed in slanted rows of seats. Verbal duels are supposed to take place here. A chairman's table is being prepared.

There are only a few hotels with vacancies in the city. The majority of participants are sleeping in folding beds set up in local trade union offices. Others are staying with families of workers. Representatives of the Barcelona anarchists who fought there in 1937 have also come. Their admission and status are controversial. These comrades get into fistfights with the Russians at dockside bars.

With Embers that Burn for Over 40 Years

As I sit here in Oakland and watch, I see no familiar faces. *My* comrades are dead. I myself am viewed with suspicion by the Soviet delegates. I struggled through to get here; my last stop was Mexico. I was an assistant, a typist for my sharp-tongued boss Karl Radek, and on New Year's Eve 1918 I listened to Rosa Luxemburg's speech 'Proletarians in Uniform' with him, 16 days before her death.

My boss at the time was beaten to death. I don't think any of the participants of the gathering in Kiental are still alive. As a 16-year-old I served coffee there and listened. That was where the Spartacus oath came about: Follow the majority, even when it's in the wrong. When the majority of socialists voted for the war credits, our minority kept its oath in for the sake of the proletarian revolution and its victory.

We were not naive. The proletarians had to be armed. An autonomous new society strong enough to prevent wars and world wars can't be defended without weapons. But it can be defended without repression of the kind Lenin later used. I carry our ideal in my heart. My facial expressions don't show it.

Nothing can be achieved immediately here in Oakland. On the long journey here, I made notes for a speech before the assembly. I wanted to stir things up. So far I haven't been given any speaking time by the congressional committee.

So many factions! Many stranded organizations. They all want to report. We have a historian too. He comes from Stockholm and collects statements for an archive of the labour movement funded by a foundation there. If one could bring together all the experiences of our dead comrades and the living ones present here, that is, the experiences of all workers' struggles—would that be the NEW ENCYCLOPEDIA? Or the raw material for a MANUAL OF EMANCIPATION?

The coffee here is excellent. But even without it, I am wide awake.

In the Eye of the Secret Service

The Office of Strategic Services (OSS) had to build up the organs of its secret service within a short time. For émigré groups supporting the fight against Hitler, this secret service was an attractor. Conversely, the service was concerned in this war with mobilizing all forces against the 'devious enemy' who kept proving his inventiveness. An unorthodox Marxist study group formed a cell in the OSS. The OSS leadership checked several times that the members of this group were not passing on information to the Soviet Union. Trotskyites, as the head of department knows, do not generally do so.

But some former labour leaders not organized in any party have also been recruited for the cell. The concern, it is said, is 'to deprive Hitler of the workers who temporarily placed their trust in him'. Next to this, but unrelated—the anti-fascism studies of the Institution of

Social Research. The OSS was in contact with the jurist and social researcher Franz Neumann who wrote the book BEHEMOTH. An analysis of 'fascist economy' (drive economy and industrial practice) that is useful for the long-term fight against National Socialism. If only such a theory had been available before 1932!

A Labour Leader at the Hotel Palace

'I saw Harry Bridges, the head of the West Coast dockworkers' union, and notorious in East Coast circles, over here from Oakland, at a cocktail party at the Hotel Palace,' reports the journalist William L. Shirer from San Francisco. 'He spoke to the business leader Roy Howard in a friendly and casual tone, but not like an "elegant devil". He didn't strike me as elegant at all, though smartly dressed. I suspect that he speaks differently when he is somewhere else and with other people. He has been charged with communism and sentenced to deportation. His lawyers, however, have appealed to the Supreme Court. The cocktails and snacks at the press meeting were paid for by the union. If one can't bring this man down over an accounting matter, one will never be able to bring him down from the outside, as it were.'

A Senior Comrade

An exiled labour leader who had made it to Oakland across six Customs borders had developed something of a belly. Not because he had eaten too much in recent years, but because he had had too little exercise. He had waited abroad for many years. Compared to his body, his sense of self had a different form—that of the 20-year-old from the revolutionary year of 1905, which he had not forgotten. It resembled the slim figure of a passionate man devoted to the revolution.

He sealed that up in his heart, warned by the experience that the comrades in the labour movement preferred conservative ways. So he had travelled to the congress and, for the first time, he was having breakfast and conversations with companions again. The younger delegates had little interest in him; they did not want to hear stories about the old battles, and he had no new battles to tell of. Whenever he joined a group, it gradually dispersed. But he was expecting these days in Oakland to renew the elan that had still moved him in Spain in 1936.

Finally he opened up to a comrade, but this one was a Soviet secret agent and betrayed him to the American authorities. In the days following 30 April, they expelled him from the country as a conspirator. They did not understand that his intentions had nothing to do with conspiracy, but rather a GLOBAL PUBLIC defined by workers.

Pilloried by the New Generation

It happened during the exciting days of the 1968 student protest movement. It was an unfortunate idea of mine to tell my son, who was with his comrades and belonged to a rival group to the SDS that called itself the 'Frankfurt Leather Jackets', how we were smuggled into Germany by the American secret service at the end of the war. We were not recruited by the secret service; a group of émigrés had formed a department at the Office of Strategic Services and co-opted us, as it were.

The comrades already misunderstood my account after a few words. They called me a US agent. But for a Marxist emigrant in the war years, it was impossible to doubt that our socialist struggle was only possible at all in the shadow of a powerful secret service. The situation could not be clarified now, 23 years later—at least, not in a cider pub in Frankfurt's Nordend district, where the gathering, which soon became an interrogation, took place.

The fact that we, as a Trotskyite group, would not have fit into a conspiratorial network controlled by the Soviet Union was of no interest to the boys. What a fool I had been to tell them anything! What we fought for and won in 1945 had nothing to do with the Vietnam of 1968.

But now I was despised by my son, a traitor to the workers, a spy for the White House. My head could take it, but my body could not. At the factory gate, the group handed out leaflets with accusations against me. The porter and the security officials, who did not want to get on bad terms with me, kept the distributors at a distance. After all, I was a member of the works council and a union steward. The workers who had the papers with the 'disclosure' pressed into their hands at five in the morning did not read them; they did not read anything so early in the morning. And they would not have been swayed to distrust me by a pamphlet from a radical group unknown to them. So the danger to me did not come from the company but from my body cells and nerves. The arteries, already hardened, became narrower because of the anger I felt. It demonstrated an impulse to strike out when deeds and words that were valid in April 1945 were twisted into suspicion and ostracism in the comfortable world of 1968, just so that one group could make an ACCUSATION PROFIT.

My son as a pimp for these interrogation specialists. But I also sensed the shame he felt in front of his comrades for having a father who was a 'US agent'.

That year one could feel the public impact of the Auschwitz trials for the first time. Such changes in the public sphere take place slowly.

The student protests had led to the formation of a group in IG Metall (led by Brenner), which was favourable for the labour conflict and had a mobilizing effect on the working class. The comrades I worked with saw open horizons. While I was still telling myself to stay calm, my body blared against the injustice of the accusation. Billions of tiny advocates blocked the flow through my vessels. I had first a mild stroke, then a heavy one with hearing loss. The workers found me in my flat, where I withdraw to when I don't want to see anyone, and in which I also store confidential documents (the place is the remainder of my private property, so to speak). According to the company doctor, I was lying there as if lifeless. They cooled my face with wet cloths, massaged the extremities. They revived me with a large dose of *ouabain*. I mustn't give up, the doctor said repeatedly. But she also said some other things, leading me to I assume that I will not physically experience the triumph of the working class (even if it were only a modest goal, like success in a series of labour conflicts).

> *Bitter it is not to see the long-desired light,*
> *To go to one's grave in its dawning.*

Nikolaus Lenau, *The Albigensians*

WITH *USURA*

by EZRA POUND

WITH USURA HATH NO MAN A HOUSE OF GOOD STONE
EACH BLOCK CUT SMOOTH AND WELL FITTING
THAT DESIGN MIGHT COVER THEIR FACE
[. . .]
USURA SLAYETH THE CHILD IN THE WOMB

IT STAYETH THE YOUNG MAN'S COURTING

IT HATH BROUGHT PALSEY TO BED, LYETH

BETWEEN THE YOUNG BRIDE AND HER BRIDEGROOM

CONTRA NATURAM

THEY HAVE BROUGHT WHORES FOR ELEUSIS

CORPSES ARE SET NO BANQUET

AT BEHEST OF USURA.[3]

An Attempt at Contact

Ezra Pound felt an overwhelming urge to descend from his abode in the hills to the village, establish contact with one of the American patrols and say his piece. Partisans and armed civilians were driving along the coastal road with commandeered vehicles. The poet was clutching a leather bag containing manuscripts and a Chinese dictionary. He was working on a translation of texts by Confucius. He walked down the steep path, holding the bag as if it were a talisman.

In the village, he went up to a sergeant and told him that he, Ezra Pound, was expected in the State Department. The American soldiers did not know him. A neutral outsider, unaware of the accumulation of saturated experience and fresh impressions that controlled Pound, might have taken him for a crazy old man. None of the GIs, who were being patient partly because they were surprised to be addressed by someone in English here, wanted to question or arrest him. The American unit, a kind of reconnaissance patrol that was supposed to supply superior positions with an overview of what territory had been conquered, left for the next village in their jeeps. The poet, unarrested, gazed after them for some time.

3 Capitalization by Alexander Kluge. [Trans.]

10

REINHARD JIRGL

◆

(From the papers of Alfred Krugk)

After Midnight

Under the cover of dimly shimmering night a row of figures flits resolutely & silently along the main street of the Saxon village of S.
towards a local manor house. Each of these silent beings is carrying
a bundle or package, several hold longer objects wrapped in sack-
cloth, probably rifles. Entering the manor yard (the-owner has upped
and left=for-the-West the previous day) they head equally quietly &
deliberately for the grand cesspit. 1-by-1, as if attending a funeral,
they step forward to the edge of the pit. Without-further-ado these
band=wagoners throw their swastika-flags medals official documents
pictures-of-the-Führer & weapons into the sewage along with their
brown & black uniforms—the sinking fabrics practically invisible in
the shit, their colours having matched it all-along. Each waits till
his=burden has sunk into the stinking sludge. This cesspit is their
first step to Deliverance, the slurry their Holy Water, their=cleansing
in innocence, and everything now at the bottom of the pit can
from=this-day-forward be chalked up against the fugitive Lord of
the Manor.

These people now disperse to the darkness of their own hovels.
I keep well out of their...... way, for: !beware: hominids switching=
gods...... : from Adolf to Joseph.—From-now=on the-old-talk is=

!taboo. New Speak: unknown. At the deaf=mute heart-of- language: silence. This is reflected in the way New Man dresses: washed-out darned-to-death flannels. Ever=since that episode after midnight the cloak-of-oblivion...... purblind, shtum, has spread itself over their shadowy faces.

The Oldest Peace

About 600 million years ago an enormous celestial body is said to have crashed into the Earth. Life=on=the=planet prior to thatImpact had consisted of primitive forms—unicellular organisms mosses lichens stromatolites. Genetic codes reveal that these=forms eradicated themselves after relatively short periods of development, only to return in the same form & reach the same stage-of-development.— *Short cycles, millions-of-years=long. As if the span of all life had been limited from the very beginning to a single season*—as the geneticist Dr Eugen Rasch of the Second-Reich-Research-Council put it. With theImpact of the celestial-body the entire planet Earth was subjected to a complete= and=sudden metamorphosis. Existing life was burnt-to-smithereens in the flames & heat. All that Once Was had dissolved along with the sundered continental shelves and evaporating seas—. Then, after an Ice Age lasting many million years more, life of an entirely !different nature took possession of planet Earth : this life was characterized by diversity of species, explosive growth, absolute perseverance & exclusive assertiveness of each-against-each among all life forms, according to the sole principle of self=preservation & development.

　　—!*What an effect this had on the human race*—declared the geneticist Eugen Rasch, generally somewhat given to emphasis.—!*How people strive to get* !*out=there,* !*how they* !*burn-for=untrod ground.* !*How they* !*lust to take-possession of their own=lebensraum, to have their-own=will with it & inhabit it in accordance with their-own=rules, without interference by neighbours.* !*Only untrammelled by rules & conventions can the-Ego truly blossom.* !*That is=*!*precisely what the human-race is looking for, whatever=the-price, even—as we can observe today—at the price of 1's-own=life.* This gave our scientist pause, and he proceeded to his peroration in a more sober vein while assembling the last of his documents for transport (for the-Institute was to be evacuated in the coming hours, bound for the West:=the-Americans).—*A heavenly body battered=all-life-on-Earth to=perversion. It bludgeoned into the world what it had brought with it from the hell-fires of the distant universe, letting it unfold its power on=this-planet. The Earth is a terrible place. Some make=money here. Some survive.*—Dr Rasch opined, adding: *With the end of this-war comes the* !*unique opportunity to cauterize, to finally blast=out-the-perversion that has entered Earth's=genetic-codes, and to help earthly-life regain its originally modest cyclical format. Only=then would the-peace-Earth=enjoyed some 600 million years ago return. However,*—he said, standing at the door with his coat tails flying about him—*we do* !*not have time for peace.*

(*From the papers of Alfred Krugk*)

Shadow Figures 1. *We all fall down.*

Berlin East in the last days of April 1945, near the bomb-gutted Schlesischer Bahnhof. In its enormity grimly=determined in War& Subjugation the-massed=Red-Army with its engines-of-war devours its way forward through devastated stonework, disintegrating human-firing-machines with spidery-souls & enormous monkey- jaws, people bound by delusional=fears to-a-dwindling hourglass. House-*stalag*mites: where once stood a town is now a collapsed cave with smoke for sky. Stink of all that can burn. Lightning strikes of the monstrousStorm smash war-fists into what remains of the city (?can any-1 in the cellars and bunkers possibly now be ?eating ?sleeping ?loving ?shitting: ?living every=day-?life.)

3 Wehrmacht soldiers, the scattered remnant of some infantry company, straggle between ruined walls down torn-up streets⸺?quo vadis. They no longer speak, communicating only by signs. Their !Forwards !Freezes & !Get-downs are dictated by the shells whistling= this-way-and-that overhead. An especially badly bomb-ravaged facade sports a shop sign: "Trimmings for Fine La" (the rest is missing). Soldier 1 has just stopped to stare at the sign, shred of a schoolboy's fantasy⸺when out of the solidSmokeSky a whining diabolical= crescendo hurtling towards them can only mean 1 thing: detonation-Wall-of-fireBlast-wave brick&rubble-storm⸺: the 3 soldiers are hoisted upward and hurled like flesh&rag missiles through a blizzard= of-fieryDebris, earth-and:-sky tumble, switching places they have occupied since-the-dawn=of-time: the earth is smoke, the sky full-of=stony ruins, the bizarre-looking wrecks of houses hang like stalagtites from the roof of a giant cave. Whatever flung the 3 soldiers into=the-air now sends them soaring into a deep bomb-crater=in-the-heavens. Dashed into the bomb-debris they hang=there like cursed angels-of-war: unconscious, bleeding, deaf. Beneath them: nothing, death's=home, to which not-1 of these 3 soldiers wants to belong yet. Suddenly noises rumble up from the centre of the crater (the 3 soldiers hear nothing)⸺a column of water, clear and glassy, shoots straight up through the layers of rubble⸺a burst, still active pipeline. It rains on the 3 soldiers, who immediately recover con-

sciousness. They start to crawl, trying to get to their feet. Soldier 1 can't move, can't get up, stays doubled over on his side, moaning. Screaming. !*Screaming*. Soldier 2 covers Soldier 1's mouth with his scabby dirt&mortar-caked hand—'!Enemy !is !listening'—he takes a look at his mate : a bombSplinter, not unlike a carving-knife, is sticking out under Soldier 1's=lowest-vertebra. Soldier 2 turns to 3, in their deafness he mouths the words: I'll-get-help.—He crawls up the slope of the crater, after a couple of failed attempts he disappears from sight, gone to further-flung regions of the heavenly ruins. Soldier 2 will not return from the sky.

Darkness, the stoneSlab of-night, the never-ending howl of Steel-Hammers as Bombs&Shell-Fire hack glaring chunks off houses, a hail of bricks from the rubble-choked sky, for whosoever hath much, to him more shall be given. Anything still standing reels as showers of explosions come through in-waves, as if the sky were a pond of miasmic sludge. The fountain hisses relentlessly and the water sprays down on Soldier 1 & Soldier 2, gradually stripping them of the last shreds of their uniforms & bandages until their almost naked bodies gleam in the darkness like freshly defleshed bones. Soldier 3, without a word, his leg injured, creeps arduously up the slope of the crater, then vanishes. He, too, swallowed by the maw-of-war, or by cowardice. Soldier 1 is now a*lone*.

Night and morning and day and evening seeping into the pit of toppled heavens. Lying there, still alive, curled up on 1 side with the shrapnel splinter in=his-back, is Soldier 1. Night again: the beast, deep black, wounded, its hide scorched by fire, heaves itself bellowing onto its other side to face the morning of Flames&Blood. And in the light of the new morning the old figure of yesterday's chillingTerror rises again—All that was is still here & here it comes again—paralysing the beating heart's courage to countenance life that is this.

Forlorn...... Beside Soldier 1 crouches the-God=of-Pain, dark & mute. He is in no hurry.

With the fountainSpoutingIncessantly and the bomb-crater gradually filling with cold muddy water, Soldier 1's legs (he is lying on his side in=the-rubble, incapable of moving) are knee-deep-in=mire. And the filthy water goes on rising. The bomb-crater in the sky seems to exist outside the world, nobody shows up, neither-friend-nor-foe, while all around it the rubble of a whole city is pounded to rubble again and again.—

Yet another shiting day pours its sodding light-dregs down the evening's plughole—murky vomit-brew dripping from the puss-stain of sun in=the-debris-sky, then the long-night of painAndMorePain that stabs spiky stars in the darkness of my being nailed=to=here. No loss of consciousness. No end. And after the feverflickering wreck of sleep the dulling bone-chill of a new morning, with old misery in full abundance lying-in wait for any-1 forced to go on living...... The shortest route from Zero to Infinity & back : God=of-misery, ?who else is ?here-with=me, God=over life-and-death : deadly-wounded and yet: despite All-His-Power still unable to die. How tragic——

The dark God=of-pain gives a snort of disdain but stays where He is, for He still needs this deadly-wounded soldier.

The day after Hitler shot himself. The stream of water peters out at the bottom of the crater, the war-sky with its clouds of ash dust & smoke is empty of rain, the weather changes. A Russian soldier appears, standing at the edge of the bomb hole above, surely he has been wafted here, an angel sent by some other crew. He looks into the crater. Discovers the bone-white body of Soldier 1 doubled over on his side. He is clutching his rifle as if it were the railing at the edge of a precipice. He doesn't let go. Doesn't cast his weapon aside. It is his last anchor as he climbs ever upwards into a ruined sky, desperately clinging=to-the-debris. But nothing can hold the climbing body now, a figure incapable of withstanding the storm of images swirling backwards through his mind, images unknown to any-1, even this Red-Army soldier, the only testimony to which are his tangled, scurf-incrusted hair & the feverish numbness of a gaze too delirious to go on seeing.

—*Gittler kaa*!*put*, yells the Red-Army soldier, turning his submachine-gun on Soldier 1. Because the latter refuses to react to his-commands—!*Ruki* !*vverkh* & !*It'di* !*sjudà*—:—to throw his weapon aside & come up=the-side of the bomb-crater—even his loudest shouting achieves nothing, after all Soldier 1 is stone deaf - !*Now*: *the moment has come*: *the end of all despair*—the Red-Army soldier raises his submachine-gun & opens fire on Soldier-1, who is evidently resisting-capture in-his-bomb-crater.—This is Peace—stammers Soldier 1 in his deafness. At that moment The-God-of=Pain gets up from his side & leaves; He has=much-to-do & long-will-it-take, His patience with this mercenary is at=an-end. He may die at last. Every=human-being is very alone. And sky and: earth tip back over into their old positions, 1-above-the-other as required by the order-of-things.

Strains of an accordion—the last victors for the moment in the last war for the moment, singing drunken=songs of joy, dance around the rim of a crater in which a man lies dead=in-the-mud.

11

ALEXANDER KLUGE

Heidegger at Wildenstein Castle

◆

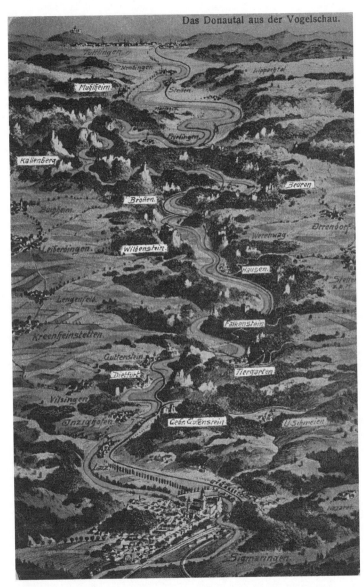

Das Donautal aus der Vogelschau.

FIGURE 20. Map of the Upper Danube Valley with Wildenstein Castle, on the left.

♦

Grey geese swept across the land. Above them, fighter bombers on their morning patrol, too high to hear. The valley lay silent between the mountains on one side and those on the opposite side. The river that divided the terrain was unrecognizable beneath the whitish cover of the early morning mist. The gods once lived here, Hölderlin says. The moon, still visible from the night, hung as a crescent in the western sky.

Students shuffled half-asleep into the morning. None of this, not even the stores in the castle's larders, paid suitable tribute to the hardship and gravity of these days. Wildenstein Castle hosted 10 teachers and 30 students. These were joined by others, whether they had come along, escaped or been invited, who felt kinship with the circle. Martin Heidegger, who had not belonged to the faculty since being drafted into the Volkssturm (though the house of his grandparents lay directly beneath the castle), had installed himself as a teacher and was welcomed gratefully by all present.

An Enclave of German Spirit

It was strange, Hannah Arendt opined much later on, when she learnt of this scene, that this INTELLECTUAL CONSPIRACY OF THE REICH'S FINAL HOUR was not noticed by any Allied secret service or any of the front units that occupied the country and had already passed very close by days ago, heading for Sigmaringen—an enclave of German spirit that, at this moment, could not be precisely assigned to any present, any past or any future.

From the Attendance List

A senior forester had joined the teaching and learning staff at this ISLAND OF KNOWLEDGE. An engineer (a subscriber to the world ice theory) had struggled over from Hungary and joined one of the seminars. Two theologians who had been unable to find accommodation in Beuron (as a reserve military hospital, it was overcrowded, and closed to academic arrivals) were visiting as emissaries of the Freiburg theology department. The tenured professor of Old High German specialized in the language of the early Holy Roman Emperors in Germany, and taught that today's Swiss dialect originated from imperial German before 1050. He carried out exercises for advanced students using the relevant texts.

In Leibertingen, the village where most of the students and faculty lived, a merchant from southern Italy had also been put up. His wares were collected in a barn: half pigs, icons of Byzantine origin, various stamp collections and two sacks of unroasted coffee beans. At night, carts and motor vehicles drove up to this exchange centre.

Still driven by the momentum of his last four years of research, the methodologist Schirdewan, who, being unable to walk and dependent on a wheelchair, had escaped military service and more recently drafting to the Volkssturm (though he could have been used there as a wireless operator) despite his young age, was working on his thoroughgoing polemic ANTI-POPPER: Against the Icy Veneer of Logic! According to a plan made in 1943, the text was to be translated into Italian and read out at an Immanuel Kant congress in Rome in 1950, which would now never take place.

Wildenstein Castle Was No Ship

Sailing away from contemporary events, that which is merely existent in the world, and landing on German shores 10 years later—that would be a project worth committing oneself to. There was a box deposited in Wildenstein Castle's wine cellar containing 'messages to posterity'. But there were no means to bring the product of Wildenstein Castle into the world. After the air raids, it would already have been impossible to send telegrams into the world from Freiburg. And what was 'world' supposed to mean, considering the closure of the German Reich? How could one have connected a message to the invisible network of the worldwide scholars' republic?

One could just about have sent a message in a bottle from Wildenstein Castle down the Danube in a closed container, like a one-man boat! But whom would one reach across the Black Sea, given that the coasts of Abkhazia no longer harbour any Mingrelians or Medea?

Transients

Towards evening, refugees came from Sigmaringen. They had certain files with them. They had been the last to escape the troops of their own country, 'Free France', who had occupied the seat of the Pétain government in Sigmaringen Castle (an enclave of French territory).

French authorities at certain locations in the world still obeyed the legitimate government of France which had fled from Vichy to Hohenzollern Castle. Radio devices were standing ready in the attic for the transmission of directives and the reception of reports, but were no longer used.

One of the visitors (they ate with the scholars at the castle tavern, slept in the garrets and stayed up late packing for their onward journeys) was planning to slog through to a neutral country. He thought he could start by reaching Genoa, where he would find passage on a ship. He considered the authority installed in Paris by the Allies, which had been infiltrated by communism as well, wholly illegitimate. He had a written authorization to conclude all affairs in the name of the absent marshal. He had a wide range of passports. He belonged to the secret service.

Now, in the time of greatest need, he explained, it was necessary to revert to the time before the Treaty of Verdun, the disastrous division of the empire, and—counterfactually but insistently, with the millennial gaze of the right-pointing leaf of the lily, which meant under the authority of Paris University—restore the Merovingian-Thuringian connection. This would herald Germany–France reunification in parallel, albeit in the opposite direction, with Churchill's suggestion in 1940 to merge French and British citizenship. One could start by giving German citizenship to all French prisoners of war still working on the German Reich's soil, with a stepwise expansion of such integration. He vehemently objected to the statement made in the round that 'militarily, the die is cast'. There are no dice for historical processes but, rather, a predestination extending across aeons. Part of this, as a kind of last resort, is the unification of Germany and France, which he had espoused since 1940. There was old wine from one of the volcanic rocks of the Rhine Valley, matured not only by the sun's warmth but also through the earth itself.

Unoccupiable Territory

A group of students with experience at the front, consisting of the heavily wounded who could no longer be used in the war and had been discharged to study, had set up a kind of stand at the junction where one path leads from the valley road to the castle, and were taking turns to keep watch. The visitor from the imaginary France had reported how ex-territoriality was represented by a similar guard at Sigmaringen Castle. Even the German ambassador to the Pétain government had to lay down his weapons and show his passport before he was admitted to the area of 'sacred France'. Similarly, the students imagined, members of the future occupying power should only be allowed to enter the enclave of the scholars' island at Wildenstein Castle as a 'world of its own', not as conquerors.

Crossing to Switzerland

For two days and two nights, people were busy tying things up and packing. An exodus of the 'castle troops' had been decided on (only two of the students and one of the professors hesitated). The march was supposed to lead into Switzerland through the Hegau, keeping to the hills for the whole distance, away from the roads. The whole group included two fellow students and a lecturer with Swiss citizenship. The Swiss said that they could give security if the column were discovered by Swiss border officials. At Thayngen, where Pétain had already driven across the border, albeit accompanied by the German ambassador and with passports, crossing over to a neutral country seemed the most promising option. Heidegger's standing could be seen as transnational. The plan was to stay together as an academy in secure Switzerland, for only a genuine dialogue could hope to soften the hardened fronts of the war.

—Why was there no march into the more highly situated neighbouring country? Was it the usual sluggishness that prevented it?

—None of us were sluggish.

—So why was there no attempt?

—Some of the students had experience of marches from the eastern front. They considered it impossible to manage a march like that (while avoiding the Allied-controlled roads) if one only had experience of hiking in the Black Forest.

Heidegger had referred mockingly to the night march of the Freiburg Volkssturm in November the previous year. Everyone checked their maps. That march, which had ruined the marchers' feet, was noticeably shorter than the planned one through the Hegau; for that reason alone, it had to be considered a warning example, as it had followed the road rather than leading through the wilderness.

The Night March to Neu-Breisach

We marched quickly, Heidegger said. Through the night, the Volkssturm battalion keeps moving towards Neu-Breisach with bags and weapons. The first four units of the column consist of academics. Two cases of cancer, three prostate infections, one foot injury from the First World War. The doctor, a party member and slightly mad, did not issue anyone a certificate exempting them from drafting to the Volkssturm.

Heidegger walked in the first row of troops. (Those in the first few rows can set their own rhythm. The last in the column have to run to keep pace.) One could hear enemy night-fighters, but they did not find the road. It was because of those aeroplanes, which were hunting everywhere, that the march took place at night, as no larger group could show itself on the Reichsstrasse by day any more. It was cold and foggy. The fog gave the marchers cover in addition to the night.

The weapons of the men in this Volkssturm were unsuitable to fend off the expected attempt by a French tank army to cross the Rhine. Some of them carried anti-tank rocket launchers on their shoulders, and they all had guns. They would only have had a chance if they had been incorporated into a professionally trained army unit. No such intention was known.

Letters had been sent to save the philosopher. Friends asked the Reich University Teachers' Leader, who was also a Gauleiter, to issue a letter of discharge for Heidegger. Heidegger had not agreed to that, for a task must be taken as it is set. His friends had written nonetheless. The reply was noncommittal, and called for a new attempt. The Reich University Teachers' Leader was known as an opponent of Heidegger.

By five in the morning we had marched any 'what for?' out of our systems, Heidegger reported. Only a 'wherever the way leads' was driving us forward. Then we lay down in barns near Neu-Breisach.

The column lay there, mowed down and tired. The bodies of the eight academics rested in dreams alongside one another. Dream is close to death. The following morning, the news came that the French advance from the Vosges mountains to the Rhine had turned north towards Strasbourg. These were the troops of General Leclerc.

The order to march back to Freiburg that night came around noon.
There was pea stew. Pushed around like tin figures. No contact with
myself. None with the enemy. None with the land we were defending.
Like lemurs.

Mineness of Concern

In a state of emergency, the definition of concern (as already-being-
ahead-of-oneself-in- . . . - as-Being-with) is confronted with the question of whether a deployment is even possible. Thus thought is no
help in the face of an oncoming tank. An individual with a gun could
fire at such a vehicle, but it would be in vain. The individual could
make use of his anti-tank rocket launcher, but a single shot is pointless
against an attacking unit. Pointless battle cuts us off from the world,
even more than any border.

This being-ahead-of-oneself, or indeed lagging-behind (being
where one was still an intact self a moment earlier), is the hallmark
of concern. It must be connectable to a me, a single or multiple you,
or a we, and an outsider should be able to refer to the Volkssturm
column with a personal pronoun—that is, an allocation in reality.

The fact that the longer the night proceeded, the more the
march to Neu-Breisach consumed hope, also destroyed the primary
human quality of being characterized by concern. But this did not
make any of those marching unconcerned.

Cura: concern; 'fearful effort', 'caution, 'devotion'.

Being-ahead-of-oneself-in-Dasein.

The disintegrating flight of Dasein.

No one can say 'I' to any of this.

Those were not my people any more, said Heidegger, who was commanding five ranks of this troop—one could just as easily have called them wandering sticks. It was impossible to adopt the image of war.

The Three Leaves of the Lily

The tenured professor of medieval history could precisely reproduce the stages that had led the teaching and learning group here, to the high castle, at the end (that is, within 750 years). From the University of Paris, an exodus of the discontent leads to the founding of the University of Prague. An exodus of the discontent from Prague leads to the founding of the University of Freiburg. This is followed by a chain of inner emigrations and mental reservations. And so, the historian concludes his exposition, this current emergency march from Freiburg into the temporary quarters is a gathering of forces, a new foundation, similar to an exodus.

'I shall dip my soul / In the chalice of the lily', Heidegger interjected into the debate. With its right-pointing leaf, the lily of which the visitor from Sigmaringen had spoken stood for the University of Paris. With its left-pointing leaf, it stood for the armed nobility, *La Chevalerie*. The leaf of the lily pointing upwards was the empire (including the *sacerdotium*). But this no longer existed, nor was it resurrected in 1933 (despite certain initial signs). So the concern was to envisage a new empire in the absence of practically all three leaves of the lily—the spirit, the sword and the emperor—almost like the soil dwellers of the forest, the ants and the mites. And to write? interjected an impertinent student. Heidegger passed over her remark.

Curiosity and the Lust of the Eyes

That morning, after a long march in the forest that extended around the castle, Heidegger convened a reading circle he had announced shortly beforehand. The topic—consciously remote from daily events. 'Reading' meant that he interpreted a text by Saint Augustine about 'seeing'. *Ad oculos enim videre proprie pertinet*: 'For seeing belongs properly to the eyes'. *Utimur autem hoc verbo etiam in ceteris sensibus cum eos ad cognoscendum intendimus*: 'Yet we apply this word to the other senses also, when we exercise them in the search after knowledge. [. . .]And yet we say not only, "See how it shines", which the eyes alone can perceive; but also, "See how it sounds", "see how it smells", "see how it tastes", "see how hard it is."' *Ideoque generalis experientia sensuum concupiscentia sicut dictum est oculorum vocatur* [. . .]: 'And thus the general experience of the senses, as was said before, is termed "the lust of the eyes", because the function of seeing, [. . .] the other senses by way of similitude take possession of [. . .].'[1]

Is It Possible, as Hölderlin says, to 'Fall' Upwards?

A Spanish-German couple from Salamanca (he was still politically burdened by events in the Spanish Civil War, and later because of participation in war crimes in the east) had already studied for three semesters at the humanities department of the University of Freiburg and was intending to complete a PhD on a scholastic legal theory by 1949. They were looking forward to the 1945 summer semester. Contrary to all information that such a semester would presumably never take place. Over the course of the day, they had attended a colloquium on the world ice theory, an exercise on Heidegger's lecture 'Leibniz:

---

1 St Augustine, *Confessions*, Book 10, Chapter 35.

The Twenty-Four Theses', an astronomy seminar and a theological dispute. They felt animated and confused. At night, having climbed up to a cave in the witch's tower, they saw the cloud cover tear apart and the firmament form its calm circle, perceptible through the movement behind the treetops at the edges of their field of view. That was the direction in which they wanted to let themselves fall. One only had to 'forget' the gravity that keeps us here. And so they would shoot up into the cosmos and escape the reality that threatened them, for they did not want to separate, yet one of the two bore a burden of guilt.

'The Aroundness of the Environment'

While thinking, Heidegger had his strong legs as companions. The NODAL LINES OF THE INNER GAZE, the origin of thoughts and literature, come from the body's movement in the landscape. In that sense, thought happens of its own accord. The philosopher's work consists of retaining that which has produced itself in the memory for long enough to put it in writing at one's desk.

'When I speak of "thinking while walking" and of my legs,' Heidegger added, 'I do not mean that the thoughts come from the muscles (as opposed to the head). The movement of the body is to a particular degree a part of the equipment.[2] This movement "is" not, it acts "in order to", it consists in its movement. In this respect there is no concrete place, either in the landscape or the body, or merely its history, where the connecting of ideas and the "compaction of thought" would be carried out. A favourable place such as this one,

---

2 'To the Being of any equipment there always belongs a totality of equipment, in which it can be this equipment that it is. Equipment is essentially "something-in-order-to . . .". A totality of equipment is constituted by various ways of the "in-order-to", such as serviceability, conduciveness, usability, manipulability.' (Martin Heidegger, *Being and Time* [John Macquarrie & Edward Robinson trans] [Oxford, 1978], p. 97.)

full of calm in the midst of the turmoil of war, is the precondition
for calm thought; yet even the latter is not a reflection of this outside
but an in-between, just as blind mirrors cast their light on one
another.' This, according to Heidegger, was why Heraclitus was
called SKOTEINOS, the Obscure.

Heidegger was infused with passion when he spoke. The sentences had a propulsive force, he stated. The less one thinks about
them while speaking, the more vigorously they rush ahead.

Heidegger then brought up Wilhelm von Humboldt and his
1829 text 'On the Connections Between Adverbs of Place and Pronouns in Some Languages'. In it, Humboldt referred to languages
that expressed 'I' with 'here', 'you' with 'there' and 'he' with 'yon-
der'—that is, which reproduced personal pronouns via adverbs of
place. This specifies the coexistence of the others in both intraworldly
and local terms. 'We encounter person-things "at work",' Heidegger
continued. 'Just as the mother occupied with her work enters the
room in which the children are playing—previously she had only
supervised events from the next room, using her ears. Now the
playing groups itself around the maternal person who dominates the
room. The children begin to imitate the mother's work. They invent
new games, "they work".'

The conversation group had meanwhile arrived at the castle tavern, where a breakfast measured out according to food voucher
rations was waiting: 300 grams of bread had to suffice for the day;
jam equivalent to 15 grams of sugar (which yielded as much as 40
grams of red-coloured mass) had to be spread out over the day.

'Wars are not capable of deciding destinies historically [. . .].
Even world wars cannot do so.' How were we to understand this
statement made by Heidegger the previous day? Heidegger was not
in the mood to explain the apodictic statement, even if he was well-

disposed to the questioner. He certainly did not want it to be taken as 'the day's words of consolation'. The military situation was decided, he said, even if one did not feel it in the silence of this castle. We were in a bad way. But the underlying mood of sorrow and unrest which accompanied it had always been there during the last 10 years. He would address that at the right time. Was the right time before envoys of the occupying power arrived? Or before teaching was shut down? Heidegger, still carried by the momentum of the earlier hike, replied: 'There is no rush.'

'MAN WAS ORIGINALLY SIMILAR TO OTHER CREATURES, NAMELY, FISH'

ANAXIMANDER OF MILET ASSUMED THAT WHEN THE WATER AND THE EARTH GRADUALLY BECAME WARMER, THEY GAVE RISE TO FISH OR, AT LEAST, CREATURES RESEMBLING FISH. HUMANS GREW INSIDE THESE CREATURES LIKE EMBRYOS, KEPT THERE UNTIL

FIGURE 21. People settling on the 'Great Fish'.

THEY REACHED MATURITY, AND ONLY THEN DID
THOSE CREATURES BURST OPEN AND HUMANS, BOTH
WOMEN AND MEN, COME FORTH INTO THE WORLD.

Announcement on Swiss Radio

Monday, 30 April 1945

Bern. As was revealed in Bern, the German imperial regalia, namely
the imperial crown, scepter and orb, have been found by the Americans in a copper mine near Siegen. The imperial regalia had been
handed over to Hitler on 7 September 1938, at the Party Congress
for Greater Germany, by the Mayor of Vienna with the following
words 'With this symbolic act, I present the imperial insignias to the
restorer of German greatness, the Führer Adolf Hitler, after the
return of the Eastern March to the Reich.

Sankt Margarethen. The party refugees will resort to any trick to get
across the border. Ferdinand Schramm, the Reich Master of Crafts
and SA Obergruppenführer, attempted in vain to slip past the Swiss
border officials in the uniform of a German Red Cross medic.
Schramm was at the wheel of a truck done up like those from the
International Red Cross that had lately brought food for the prisoners
of war in the Reich. Near Rheineck, the German proxy minister in
Croatia, SA Obergruppenführer Siegfried Kasche, appeared at the
Swiss border equipped with Croatian papers and a car with an oval
sign and the red letters of the Diplomatic Corps, 'CD'—but that was
no use either. No less than four major party figures, whose identities
are still being kept secret, decided not to bother with the embarrassing
interrogation at the border at all and took a Luftwaffe plane to
Lucerne. But they had to repeat the journey in reverse only a few
days later, like the former German envoy in Vichy, Krug von Nidda.
Krug von Nidda entered Switzerland a few days ago on the pretext

of intending to negotiate with the International Red Cross in Geneva. His application for an indefinite extension of his residency permit was turned down, however. Now a Swiss patrol has taken him to the Reich border. The wife of Gauleiter Wagner, likewise seeking in vain to enter Switzerland, has now been arrested by the French in Constance. Gauleiter Wagner, Baden-Alsace, who abandoned his wife, has vanished without a trace.

News on Radio Beromünster at 9.40 a.m.

The voice of the Radio Beromünster presenter had an intonation that had been acquired through training but in which an attentive listener could still hear that, at the same time as speaking this language, the newsreader was always thinking those words in his native dialect. In the past seven weeks, the presenter said, the port city of Antwerp had still been reached by single V2 missiles. A total of 4,000 flying bombs had been fired at the city. The fire was heaviest between November and late March. During that time, the Allied arsenals had needed up to a million flak grenades per day to fend off the V missiles. The newsreader's script contained terms that had not existed in that form before 1944 and had no equivalents in Swiss German, and which could therefore only be imagined in dialect using analogies. The presenter read each of these terms with the hint of a parenthesis or a tonal equivalent of quotation marks.

Heidegger on Actuality

Martin Heidegger best liked to let the day's news sink in at breakfast time, a custom familiar to him from Hegel. The only newspapers available at the castle were weeks-old issues in the toilet. But the group enclosed in the castle had a radio device, an Italian model made of plastic, quite small, with an illuminated dial. Heidegger's

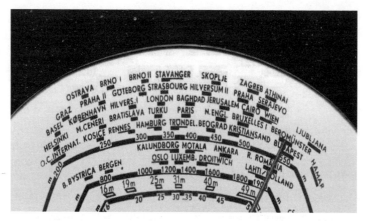

FIGURE 22. Radio Beromünster

favourite was the Swiss station Beromünster. The current as some-thing ephemeral, he said, as something derived from the degenerated form of idle talk, was not simply distracting or superficial.

He stated that through the intonation of the news, with the real voices sprinkled in, even a propaganda broadcast contained much that was unsaid, a broad stream of impressions that were certainly capable of establishing a connection with the outside.

One should not speak at all disparagingly of what is referred to as 'idle talk', he said. 'Idle talk is the possibility of understanding everything without any previous appropriation of the matter.' 'The fact that something has been said groundlessly, and then gets passed along in further retelling, amounts to perverting the act of disclosing into an act of closing off.' 'Thus, by its very nature, idle talk is a closing off since it *omits* going back to the foundation of what was being talked about.'[3] This applied to the radio as much as to printed news.

3 Heidegger, *Being and Time*, p. 213.

But why, Heidegger asked further, did Hegel entrust himself so willingly to this 'byway of the thoughts'?

That morning, Heidegger wanted to connect his judgement on the quality of the news, especially if they came to us from abroad, meaning from a distance, to the daily events that had changed so greatly. The historical (and violent) events of the present could not be transformed in the vessel of a landscape, that is to say, through walking and thinking, not even through the probing of the spirit (sensing), into a substance that the soul would have to inhale in order to be present itself. Such an approximate materialization would be more possible in a superficial mode of apprehension that used secondary things for orientation, he reasoned. The advantage of the self-evidence and self-assurance of average interpretedness was that under its protection, 'the uncanniness of the suspension in which Dasein can drift towards an increasing groundlessness remains concealed to actual Dasein itself.'[4] The curiosity for which nothing remains closed was not a good guarantor in that context. Even with the 'hardness of the concept', a situation like ours could not be 'grasped alive'.

Abyss gapes beneath my feet—
Take me now, O ancient night!
Heinrich Heine, *Book of Songs*

'Primordial Will as Spirit'

Twenty-one-year-old Fritze Billung, who went by her middle name Bertha (rather than Friederieke) during her time at the Reich Labour Service, but was always addressed as 'Kiki', found the term 'primal

4 Ibid., p. 214.

will' (Nietzsche) confirmed by something she observed in a forest. The head forester's vehicle had driven over a column of ants. Now parked in the courtyard (how was the petrol acquired, evidently illegally?), the dead creatures were still stuck to its tyres. But a few hours later in the pine plantation, the column had long since been completed again. These primordially willing things came from a very distant time. Short of a grenade impact at least eight metres wide near them, nothing could kill them as a collective. A SUBSTANCE: the over 500,000 years in which their kind had set itself in motion, before pine forests even existed. A SUBJECT: their community. This life form consisting of such numerous individuals could only exist together with the SUBSTANCE, namely the time of its genesis.

Possessed by the same primordial will, her child had grumbled in Kiki Billung's body since a lieutenant seduced her (or vice versa). He pushed his feet against her abdominal wall. Again: each was a SUBJECT (until birth). The SUBSTANCE, namely, the vessel of their life, was the uncertain time, the tireless unrest inside this child.

> The essence of spirit is the primordial will that wills itself, which is thought sometimes as substance, sometimes as subject, and sometimes as the unity of both.

The Entertainment[5] Character of Thought

Sitting with others around a table, Heidegger did not speak the way he wrote. Only the listeners had the tendency to silently chant along with what they heard in the terminology of his writings. It is conversationally enjoyable: it is *entertaining* when the facts of life are sung together with certain attributes of eternity (like the fashion of 1630

---

5 There is a play on words here and a few lines below, as *Unterhaltung* can mean both 'entertainment' and 'conversation'. [Trans.]

in which protracted melodies were added to a *basso ostinato*, as far apart and different as possible).

The Brothers Grimm and the 'Small Border Traffic of Fairy Tales'

Dr habil. Gilberte Hahnwald was seen as an eternal outside lecturer. The professor who had supervised her habilitation was driven out of Germany along with the comparative branch of knowledge he had developed. Dr Hahnwald was not offered a position by any other university, which would have been a prerequisite for permanent employment at her own. Not because it was the dominant trend, but because she was genuinely interested in medieval texts only kept on the outskirts of Europe, in Iceland and Norway, she immersed herself in Nordic myths and fairy tales. Before her research could bear fruit here (she was hoping for a second or third university in the Reich alongside Strasbourg that needed fresh staff for research and teaching), she found herself surrounded by the troops of a foreign country. Now it acted in her favour that, out of sheer thoroughness, she had kept up her comparative 'excavations' which had long been academically uncompetitive. She had examined the tales of the Brothers Grimm and their sources. And it had been hitherto unknown in research circles that Frau Hassenpflug, one of those who had passed the tales on to the Brothers Grimm, was of Huguenot descent. The same applied to the background of Frau Viehmann, the woman who had contributed the majority of the fairy tales. She also came from France. This pointed to a tunnel that had been used to exchange intellectual contrabands under the Rhine (despite the wall of hatred between France and Germany)—through oral transmission from great-grandmothers down to the children. The Brothers Grimm, as Dr Hahnwald formulated it, positioned themselves by this river-bed or tunnel. Once the university was reopened by the occupying power, she, Dr Hahnwald, would admittedly be tainted by her Indo-Germanic research, which was open to misinterpretation (and was documented in a publication from 1944); on the other hand, she would stand out from the crowd of applicants for teaching posts with the find that numerous fairy tales previously considered German had French origins. Dr Hahnwald had never intended to 'fit in'. She had always wanted to teach.

'Fallen Into the Well'

On 30 April, Heidegger noted down some keywords for a planned lecture on Hölderlin's motto 'For us, everything is focused on the spiritual; we have become poor to become rich':

> What does 'poor' mean? [. . .] Poverty is a not-having, a lack of the necessary. Wealth is a non-lack of the necessary, namely having more than what is necessary. [. . .] Beyng truly poor means: beyng such that we lack nothing, except for the unnecessary.
>
> But what is the unnecessary? [. . .] What does 'necessary' mean? [. . .] The essence of need, in the fundamental meaning of the word, is compulsion. [. . .] The unnecessary is that which does not come from need, i.e. not from compulsion but from the free.

The free—he continued the train of thought without writing it down—is, in our oldest language, the unharmed, the spared, that which is not used for a purpose. It is by no means limited to the negative quality of the non-touching or the useless. The free is that which is preserved from the compulsion of need, that which is left in its essence. He wrote down: 'Thus, when we think the essence of free-

dom and necessity, then necessity is by no means the opposite of freedom, as the whole of metaphysics believes; only freedom is in itself
a turning towards need.'

Need that has become turning. Quiet unrest, the sorrowful joy
of never being poor enough. The palaeontologist and one of the
female students had meanwhile joined the group. That did not interrupt Heidegger's train of thought; far from it. And instead of speaking
to himself and the things he had written, he now spoke once more to
these guests. Lean years lie ahead. Heidegger sought to convey the
decline of prospects. The danger of famine, he said without waiting
for questions, viewed in terms of the whole and authentic part of occi-
dental destiny, does not lie in the fact that many people might die, but
in the fact that those who survive will be living only to live. Isn't that
enough? asked a female student. The palaeontologist supported her.
There were chains of life extending over more than 40,000 years that
deserved respect. In these times, one joined such chains. In one of the
radio commentaries that morning, Heidegger had heard the statement
that Central Europe was now falling victim to Bolshevism. That, he
said, could only apply if we did not ward off the destiny awaiting the
historical world, that thing bearing the inappropriate name 'communism', through poverty. He noted: 'Communism is not avoided and
circumvented in beyng poor; it is overtaken in its essence.' For a
moment the palaeontologist, who was reading along with what had
already been taken down, saw the political dimension of that day:
COMMUNISM CAN ONLY HELP AGAINST BOLSHEVISM
ONCE IT ATTAINS CONCEPTUALIZATION.

The Temporality of Hope

The palaeontologist belonged to the humanities department. He had
carried out excavations in the Swabian Alps during the previous years.

Always following the path the Ister (the Danube) had bitten through the limestone mountains. It was not to be taken for granted that the river, as thin as it was here, would have the force to reach the Black Sea. Had it been impossible to channel the waters through the Swabian Alps, they would have moved west towards the Rhine. The palaeontologist had not been able to publish the most valuable insights from his excavations which primarily concerned the caves and subterranean lakes near Blaubeuren. For nothing Indo-Germanic, let alone Germanic, ever appeared in his findings. For that, they would have had to reflect periods no earlier than 3,000 years ago.

The researcher had dug up objects, artefacts, that appeared to be musical instruments. Also tools, with functions that were far from primitive. These were signs of life left by ancestors who had migrated up the Danube from the south-east 40,000 years ago. Each generation had journeyed some 15 kilometres with the objects and family members around them—that is, with their 'seats'. Work on that preliminary stage, compared to which later conqueror peoples, including the Nordic ones, probably seemed like barbarians, was now open to worldwide publications. In the face of the authentic ancestors from such a long time ago, racial contrasts between Semites and Indo-Germans were certainly inconsequential. The excavator conferred—often whispering on account of a sore throat—with Martin Heidegger, whose authority he hoped to win for a foreword. Plans like never before in the palaeontologist's mind. Heidegger, he requested, should paraphrase his statement: 'The entity that we ourselves respectively are is ontologically the most distant.' One could not think more than 40,000 years back in time through excavation.

12

REINHARD JIRGL

◆

Shadow Figures 2. *Into the Light*

(*In memory of G. Kl.*)

A. In the Beginning

Somewhere in Poland. Late winter 1945. Sixteen-year-old Wolfgang H., the sole survivor of an ethnic German East Prussian family, is on the run. Following the Red-Army's invasion on 21 October 1944 & subsequent occupation=of-East-Prussia by Soviet troops the rest of his family was lynched by an-angry-mob. He has set his hopes on falling in with 1 of the many refugee treks which, vulnerable=to-threats from all=quarters & doing what they can to avoid attack by armed forces & the local population, are slowly looping & zigzagging their-way=west to the Oder. Folk laden like beasts of burden, dragging pushing their barrows wagons handcarts & prams, lugging suit-cases sacks mattresses crates full of belongings, their clothes torn by winter weather, stinking of sweat hunger disease & fear-for=their-lives: he clings to=these-figures as closely as their own shadows. But even among these hordes of outcasts the boy, a stranger without par-ents, is never accepted for-long—*welcome strangers & invite dangers!*—; the boy with the bright blond hair must fend for=himself. Where pos-sible he avoids the open fields, the common=pastureland & woods (the haunts of highwaymen...... no less so today than in the Middle Ages). Now-and-then he follows a band-of-fugitives making its way across-country, but keeps-his-distance, dodging their attempts to drive him away like some mangy dog. Joining others to steal=provisions or for other small thefts is easy enough. Occasionally he takes a beating or is robbed of his plunder. More beating if he refuses to give up his=grub to one of the Stronger Men. Blows & blood. Better lose blood than grub, blood grows back.

In some of the Polish towns & villages he passes through, women lean out of windows, whistling to the lad with the shock of bright blond hair & shouting:—!*Hodsh tiy gori* !*padovitch* (Come up for a fuck), & making various unambiguous gestures. The boy, at=an-age when !*padovitch* is the most important thing in-the-world, peers up at them: he sees ghastly smiles on the women's mouths, faces daubed as luridly as a seedy bar sign—: he slinks away, has no desire to pay, with his young-boy's flesh, the bill=of-some-old-guy who was there before him. And on. Along-roads. On the verges & in muddy ditches, or on the roads themselves, lie the squashed cadavers of animals, of people, also their wrecked carts, the gaping throats of suitcases, torn eiderdowns raining feathers over corpses—refugees crushed by Russian tanks advancing=to-the-front. When from time-to-time yet another military vehicle runs over them, some of the flattened bodies=in-the-dirt lift smashed skulls or torsos, and the-carnage turns into a twitching par-ody-of-life...... Flies, their malevolent metallic buzzing, the air thick with the stench of corpses: the sticky-sweet fug of Enormous Suffer-ing. And onwards, the road the boy follows leading him past countless dead—.—The further west he walks, and the closer to the Oder he gets, the more chaotic and crowded becomes the throng=of= refugees—densely packed flotsam adrift on the dammed-up torrents-of-war.—One morning in April 1945, just before dawn, he arrives in the vicinity of Küstrin, his intention being to cross the Oder unob-served by the prowling army-patrols & Polish-militia, & to press on to Soviet-occupied Berlin. He knows his parents have relatives there, in Treptow.—

Berlin, belching craters spitting shell-fire death, stink of scorched air, howling & cracking sounds from cellar-doors and havocked houses exploding into the massy reek-of-war—the Spree is a carrion-choked river of tarry grime. According to former neighbours whom the boy discovers rummaging in the rubble, his Treptow relations were bombed out—their house a ruin—& have fled=west. So he is still= al*one*, in Berlin, Death's greatest metropolis.—The boy takes shelter in a cellar, curls up for the night. He holds out. He doesn't want to die. Nor does he want to follow his relations to=the-west. He barely knows them. The next morning he squirms out of the cellar, heaving away the fallen rubble that has blocked the entrance overnight, and sets off to roam through the districts already under Russian-command. The war's-embers are still glowing here, the gutted cadaver of the city glimmering in=fleshy-reds&greys, while at=the-centre of Berlin the Reich Chancellery & Führer's Headquarters are being pounded by=the-fists of=gigantic-shells. It is now the end of April, and with the pall of thick smoke over the city beginning to thin, a radiant spring sky shines through in soothing blues above the stone desert. Wolfgang H., trying to join up with other stragglers, is picked up on several occasions by military patrols, various parties might have made short work of him...... if luck hadn't been on his side.

B. Interlude: With the State

Caught up in post-war-events, Wolfgang H. is well-aware he will need a new pair of gloves for=the-peacetime-boxing-ring : the new German authorities, appointed by the Soviet High Command, are recruiting personnel for equally new police battalions, no easy task after a war that has wiped out all the suitable men. The boy, 16 years old, is made of=just-the-right-material: he 'volunteers' for the Garrisoned Alert Police, who would later become the GeePeePo, the Garrisoned People's Police. He is given a clean blue uniform to wear, and, for the first time

in ?how many months, he finds himself sleeping washed & with his
blond hair closely cropped in a bed of=his-own in the police barracks,
albeit in=a-bunk & a dormitory housing 11 other men. His fellow-
recruits (now called 'comrades'), all much older than him, ignore this
pimpf (as they still call him using Hitler-Youth-jargon), but let him join
in=their-drinking-sessions because, attempting to impress his older
peers, he gets=more-rounds-in than any-1 else. Thus not a day passes
without the lad collapsing, completely plastered, on his sagging mattress
& prickly woollen blanket. Booze & duty, then duty & booze. Their
superiors turn=a-blind-eye : Everyman, even a drunken Everyman, is
needed. On 1 occasion, however, they are unable to turn=a-blind-eye
any longer : Wolfgang H., as full as a tick in his full-police-kit, boards
a train on the by now revamped S-Bahn Circle Line, falls asleep
&, ?who knows for how long, Circles around town until he is picked
up in 1 of the Western Zones, arrested, & turned over to the Eastern
Authorities. Dismissal from police service, youth custody: corrective
labour camp—sentenced to clear ruins&rubble. His old haunts when
he was out stealing, caches for goods & himself, are now being eliminated by the work of his own hands.—This 16-hour-a-day=drudgery
under=the-thumb of screaming overseers at last brings the boy to his-
senses. Barehandedly-heaving away chunks of walls&rubble, he has a
vision of=himself; sees himself as an automaton carrying out movements which have no significant impact (collapsed houses seeming to
consist of manyMoreStones than standing houses), remembers time-
&-again his escape from East Prussia through Poland across the Oder,
how it had seemed at the time that his skin was being ripped from his
body time after time, and yet each time his skin grew back & allowed
him to go on & do what he did: !*I've got to get* !*out of this skin.* He has just
arrived=at-this-conclusion when a lump of cement drops on his feet—
he teeters, falls over and blacks out. Then spends weeks in the infirmary
of a coop=for-young-offenders.

The atrociousThings he has been forced to look at have not blighted his eyes. Tiny, pale-grey eyes gaze like listless marbles from his round face. It is not his sight the abominations of the dead & living have sapped, but his will, tearing with rapacious beaks at the-inward-man he could have become, arresting his=physiognomic-development at a permanently=boyish-stage: 16, for-life.

C. A Friend, a Good Friend

After his release from the-youth-detention-centre Wolfgang H. decamps to the American occupation zone in West-Berlin. Here, in a bar in the Potsdamer Strasse, he gets to know Helmut D., publican, owner of the (to judge by the rest of the building) aptly named bar Nook in the Ruins, & dealer in 'redistributed goods'. Helmut D. is also a (clandestine) pimp; he has, as the saying goes, a few 'in the stable'. In his early 20s, Helmut D. is powerfully built, not to say stout, standing some 1.85 metres tall, and has lost his parents and both brothers to the war. He is a-man=who-knows-how-to-fend-for-himself, who takes-things=into-his-own-hands & gets what he wants;—in-fact, Wolfgang H.'s opposite in-every=way. Ever since their first encounter in that smoky-blue tap-room, their lives have been entwined by that rarest of shrubs: a flourishing firmly rooted friendship. What this means in reality is that Helmut, the older of the two, provides the protection & leadership of a Big Brother (kid-brother Wolfgang, at under 1.70, is somewhat smaller in stature). Burly Helmut D. has thus succeeded in replacing two of his dead with a living brother. This friendship between men of such different character, planted in a miserable little corner bar in a semi-ruin, will thrive for the rest=of-their-lives.

When the-situation in the Potsdamer Strasse gets too hot for Helmut D. (he has 'overdone' things on the smuggling side), he seizes=the-moment & does a bunk to the-Russian-zone before the *fuzz* arrive;—behind him he leaves half-filled beer glasses on the counter, cigarettes in the ashtray, Skat-cards scattered on a table-top & the radio blaring out post-war German song-hits. Helmut D., & riding his coat-tails Wolfgang H., make it through the cellars into=the-Eastern-Sector, friends=for-all-seasons.

In East Berlin, by-command of the Soviet Cultural Authority, the bomb-gutted, burnt-out Volksbühne in the former Scheunenvier-tel has been rebuilt and re=activated as a theatre—its grey walls had resembled hollow teeth, and the entire domed roof had come crashing down into the auditorium. Now they are on the look-out for somebody to run the catering side and it is Helmut D.'s luck to be in=the-right-place-at-the-right-time. He can simply carry=on where he had left off in the Potsdamer, although he does have to jettison his 'stable'. Helmut D. is one of those men who are constantly, even in the company of the real boss, taken for The Big Boss. This enables him to set up his friend Wolfgang H. (who has no professional qual-ifications) with an income & contract as a bit-part actor at the theatre. Through the good-offices of the theatre manager Wolfgang H. is also allocated a back-yard flat (2nd floor, 1 room, WC & running water in the cellar) in the Stargarder Strasse. In the evenings, after the per-formance, Wolfgang H. takes a seat in the lounge or canteen supping beer or schnapps, and after closing time, the publican Helmut H. comes to his table & they sit, smoke, drink & chat for a while about this&that. Thus the-years go by—.

The Soviet-Occupied-Zone has become a state called the German Democratic Republic (Gee-Dee-aaR)—in June 1953, after an unin-terrupted four-year chess tournament with the Western Powers, the Gee-Dee-aaR is in-check; Russian tanks occupy the-board, crushing any piece that refuses to lie down & deploying the 'Russian gambit' to rescue the=Gee-Dee-aaR from mate.—8 years later A Wall and Forests of Barbed-Wire divide Berlin, a city rising-out-of-ruins—in

the SED Politburo they harp on about crushing allOpponents=
against: the=concrete-Wall—shots rip through the air at The-Border,
the 1st death a fugitive on his way from Berlin to Berlin—Russian
and: American tanks face:1:another across the demarcation line at
the Kochstrasse, threatening:1:another with gestures befitting of cold-
warriors & lambasting 1:another with fiery slogans;—however, The-
Wall remains & people learn to live with it, on both sides. Wolfgang
H. and Helmut D. remain friends, inseparable. Only their bodies
have changed over the years, Wolfgang H. is small & chubby, his
formerly bright blond hair grown thin; physiognomically, he is still
the-boy-of-16 he always has been, while Helmut D., still=a publican
& in-recent-years a stage manager to-boot, sports a sizable beer belly,
a shield of fat&flesh between him &: the brutal rest-of-the-world. On
the street, walking to the pubs & back, they have developed their own
marching formation: the avant-garde, with only his beer-gut going-
on-before, is Helmut D., while Wolfgang H. trots along behind. They
do not say very much, but go boozing=together and communicate
by means of gestures glances & silence.

D. A Heavenly Power in Hell=on-Earth

The border between Poland and: the Gee-Dee-aaR is open, nobody
needs a visa or pass to get back&forth—large numbers of Poles come
to Berlin, and trade of all kinds sprouts up from the barren, beggarly
East-Berlin soil. Helmut D. (now 47) falls in love with a young Polish
woman (almost 20 years his younger), but Helmut can't understand Polish. For the first time in his life Wolfgang H. (by virtue of his provenance
in East Prussia) is able to come to the aid of his friend, acting as an
intermediary whenever and wherever words are required. By-and-by,
Helmut D. and Vera, the young Pole, get married. —In the meantime
Helmut D. has succeeded in extending his=sphere-of- influence into
senior theatre management; he is secretly in=charge of The Bank

belonging to the illegal poker games that take place every evening in the cellar=canteen after performances (some of the Theatre Headmen could lose their heads over the heavy=debts they run-up night-after-night with The Bank (alias Helmut D.)......). Thus is he empowered to help his young wife Vera find a job in the theatre canteen. The marriage does not encroach on Wolfgang and Helmut's relationship—the only difference being that they now drink as-a-threesome.

Vera is permitted to retain her Polish citizenship & consequently her=passport, which in turn means that, within-certain-bounds, she can travel to=the-West as often as she likes. She often goes to West Berlin in the evening & doesn't return till the next morning. A former stagehand, now retired and permitted to travel to=West-Berlin & back himself, has seen the Polish-woman—Vera—working-the-Potsdamer-Strasse—. He has had to promise her on-pain-of-death not to tell any-1; consequently, by the following day, the-whole=theatre knows about it. The news hits Helmut D. like a Hammer, his whole world caves in; Heaven crushes him with its Omnipotence and thrusts him deep into his=own-Hell. Wailing & remonstrating as never before he becomes his-own-best-customer at the bar; Wolfgang H. rarely leaves his=best-friend's-side; now&then, instead of saying something, he puffs out his cheeks & expresses the contained air slowly & noisily. That's about as much as he can say about love: that Heavenly Power.—The moment Vera returns to Helmut's flat : strife, screams & beatings. They break a lot of china. And 1 evening, when Vera—in an advanced state=of-inebriation and shortly before the beginning of a performance—runs howling & stark naked through a crowd of theatre-goers assembling in the foyer in their evening attire, her separation from Helmut is complete. On the following morning she is dismissed without notice by the Cadre Officer, but Vera is no longer there, she has absconded to West Berlin, where Helmut D., with all his=insinuations&beatings, cannot follow. Helmut, this man of considerable stature, now begins to ail & dwindle, with an apoplectic look on his face and strands of hair plastered=across his sweaty brow. And next to him sits Wolfgang H., puffing out his cheeks, not out of derision, but because he doesn't know what to say, and therefore says nothing.

E. If It Keeps Too Long It Won't Last

The instant they open The Wall——in fact it wasn't really opened as much as eroded by Floods=of-people from the East & the Scythian-tactics=of-functionaries who, in desperateStraits, sent their=slaves swarming out to induce chaos among the-enemy while the functionaries themselves (crumbling like mummies who are exposed, after sheltering for a thousand-years in-their=pyramid-shrines, to the ruth- lesslySearingLight and tempestWinds of Real Time) were blown away like so-much geriatric dust——as soon as the Wall opens, on the very evening of 9 November 1989, Helmut D. (now 64) sets out to find Polish-Vera in West-Berlin, and indeed does find her in-his=old-stomping-ground, the Potsdamer Strasse. He wants=her-back;—but his entreaties over-the-years have been in-vain.

6 years later Helmut D. suddenly falls down a staircase in the Underground: sudden cardiac arrest. 1995: for the 1st time in almost 50 years Wolfgang H. is al*one* again.

As in=the-old-days he spends his evenings quietly boozing in the theatre canteen. He doesn't drink any more than he used to. He often sits al*one*; he has no inclination to speak to any-1, and: no 1 wants to talk to him. The new personnel manager has been trying to sack him for alcohol addiction. Without the support of hisOldFriend, Wolfgang H. is defenceless; all his life—allThoseYears spent in=the-protective-Shadow of his=partner—he has trotted along on a path he supposed to be The-Right-Path for=him. Whenever he met obstacles he stopped—and waited. For time is like hydrochloric acid; it gnaws through everything, including an obstacle. But pitted against iron-fisted Human Meanness Wolfgang H.'s hands are like those of a child.

A famous actress (who also directs plays at the theatre) manages to get Wolfgang H. what she calls a !Leading-Bit-Part as a 'A Drinker' in an Irish farce she is directing; in it, he repeatedly declaims a single line: 'God bless this house!', after which he has to chalk up a dash on the landlord's debt slate. Wolfgang H.'s costume in-this-play—coarse felt & heavy shoes—is astonishingly similar to the clothes he wore during his=flight from East Prussia.—The personnel manager, who knows a good deal about admin but nothing about theatre, lets the famous actress have her way: Wolfgang H. is allowed to remain what he is, 'A Drinker' & bit player at=the-theatre.

F. For Finale

At the lighting rehearsal for a new production some of the bit-parts are asked to pose on stage as the proper actors. The director says to Wolfgang H.: !Could you take 1 step up to the lights; !this scene plays in daylight.—Wolfgang H., compliant=as=ever, takes 1 step into the light at the front of the stage, and keels=over. Everybody assumes he must be drunk again. But Wolfgang H. is not drunk, or not more so than usual; he lies right at the edge of the stage, quite motionless. Whatever life meant to him, it is all over now.

He never had a wife or learnt a profession. But he had always had enough to drink and had had a good friend for all of 50 years; many-people have less.—The production, in one of whose rehearsals a minor actor had died, did not make it as far as a premiere. Due to *disputes of an artistic nature* between director and: actors the play was dropped from the rehearsal schedule.

13

ALEXANDER KLUGE

I, the Last National Socialist in Kabul

◆

◆

She was a woman of 30. A reporter who was considered talented. She really wanted to concentrate on Syria this year. The fact that her British friend, also a woman reporter, had been killed by targeted artillery fire had stirred her. We can't accept the intimidation of people who make facts public. She had made contacts in the border region between Syria and Lebanon that made filming possible. But then her superior at the station had assigned her to the major documentary on the seventieth anniversary of the end of the war. All television networks were competing in the lead-up to that day, planning features two years in advance. Why is something current now, the filmmaker asked, simply because it happened 70 years ago? The boss insisted on his decision. Crisis with her daughter. Separation from her partner. Suspicion of cancer at a routine check-up. What did she care about the end of the Third Reich?

The suspicion of cancer was later eliminated. Relieved, she decided to obey. No one would have paid for her to travel to the war zone in the Middle East (and insurance policies had meanwhile become unaffordable). Once again, she said to herself: I am tied for 40 weeks of my finite life to a task I don't consider central.

Her superior tempted her with the idea of inserting a portrait of violent right-wing extremists. I don't agree, she answered. She doubted that those offenders had a real (and not simply an imaginary) connection to the last days of National Socialism. The idea is premised on a false notion of currentness. People should have occupied themselves with the end of the war sooner, not only after 70 years. We documentarists have to shift the anniversaries into the future, she said. A retrospective from 2040: What prevented energy from the desert flowing to Europe in 2014? What does the present of 2014 look like to an adolescent in 2034? Her boss remained obstinate.

I, the Last National Socialist in Kabul

People call me the last National Socialist here. That means in the area of the Swiss Embassy here in Kabul, which is harbouring us, the legation councillors and staff of the former German Embassy (and representing the concerns of our country, as formulated by us, to the Afghan Foreign Ministry). I am not only the last remaining party member, I also continue to direct the political training courses we have been carrying out in recent weeks. Now the participants are almost all Afghan citizens. The students often come from afar. My own staff in the service of the Reich avoid me. The conservative skeleton of German diplomacy is coming to the fore. It is becoming clear that many who previously behaved like National Socialists were not National Socialists.

I too find it difficult to live up to the faith placed in me by comrades who sent me to this part of the world (almost all of them fallen by now). I make an effort to summon the radical and partisan stance of the National Socialist as I teach in my courses. But what does that mean, a National Socialist? It is not that I have doubts about my stance. Or that I see no way out now, in the Reich's and the party's hour of need. I have already thought to myself—if all that is left is to escape to the Pamir Mountains, then three or four people like me could head north-east from Kabul with winter equipment and weapons, and make preparations for a FOURTH REICH in one of the monasteries in the Wakhan Mountains. To be effective, an idea does not need to be being espoused by many comrades from the start.

In the course of these thoughts or, rather, this inner examination, I feel that a National Socialist cannot be a National Socialist without the MOVEMENT, that is to say, without the NATIONAL

SOCIALISM OF THE OTHERS surrounding (and flowing through) him. One's own will is not enough; I must be wanted as a National Socialist by others. To lead means to be wanted. In that sense, the National Socialist comes about in a space of activity that is not identical to SIMPLE REALITY or FIRST NATURE. This must be augmented by industry and inalienable assignments from the ancestors—that is, a form of PROVIDENCE—so that alongside each pair of nerves, alongside each muscle in the body, a second, parallel line is laid to determine the National Socialist direction of movement. Like the threads of a jumping jack? No! Rather, in the sense of BREEDING. In that sense, National Socialism was perhaps misplaced in Germany, and would instead belong in a spaceship orbiting an unknown planet—that is, in an ARTIFICIAL WORLD, just as the opera *Rienzi* cannot be staged in a glade or in the mountains but requires the sets of a theatre and the collective willingness of an audience to embrace the action and the music.

I see the wretchedness of the small theatre group at our embassy. British agents stand outside the windows of the rehearsal room, observing our activities. They watch every step, every action of our Swiss hosts and our staff. They probably cannot make much sense of the rehearsals. We are performing the play *Schlageter*, but now, in 1945, it no longer arouses that defiance in me towards the impertinent French rule of the Ruhr region in 1923 that gripped me when I first saw the play in 1934. Not here in Kabul. But we do not wish to cancel the performance in the auditorium of the GERMAN SCHOOL scheduled for May. We are still experiencing surprising successes in our daily work. Despite the severest of threats made by the British envoy, the Foreign Ministry in Kabul accepted in the name of Afghanistan our demand, conveyed by the Swiss ambassador, to rename the GERMAN REICH the GREATER GERMAN REICH.

A National Socialist is a 'man of joint action'. If the action (the 'movement') is broken off, then he, on his own, can no longer be a National Socialist. Thus Othello can no longer strangle Desdemona as soon as, having been disturbed in his delirium by the knocking of Desdemona's confidant, he returns to reality. He has lost contact with his urge for action and lapses back into mere despair, sorrow, because he thinks he has lost Desdemona. This turns a murderer into a weak man. At this point in my monologue (or while quarrelling in my head) I must add that Othello, after all, is no National Socialist and, as a Berber warrior, certainly not a Nordic type. Nor does a mass of jealous characters constitute National Socialism. The mobilization of extraordinary energies needs a vessel, however—a space of action, as my teacher Heidegger formulates it. Whether MOVEMENT is an illusion or reality, it does not exist as ice (solid) or air (gaseous), but by FLOWING. That is why I no longer feel like eating at mealtimes. The provisions and weapons for the escape to the mountains are already packed in weatherproof material. All that is missing now is the will. Just as a fish tossed on land can no longer make its way back to the water! And where, after all, will there still be water if the Reich falls?

A Building Block for the Fourth Reich

I, Knut Fritsche, have long been using a Spanish name. I am a lawyer in the service of a wealthy Spanish family. In these days of the German Reich's defeat, I consider myself one of the few Germans who are still keeping track of things. That demands immersion in history, knowledge of files and agility in conducting negotiations. Marrying into the aforementioned family, who live in Caracas, acted in my favour. Only 'yesterday' (in 1895), the USA and England narrowly avoided a military conflict in the struggle to control mining in the Cordillera de Mérida (at the foot of Pico Bolívar). Germany could then have been the adjudicator in such a war. The Reich likewise had claims to those mines. An alliance between Germany, the USA and England would have brought about lasting peace in the world.

Trials from those days have not yet been concluded, and we hope that we can decide them with a favourable outcome for the German Reich, even if time is short. My firm is fully occupied with objections to the confiscation of German assets. We are concealing the values until other times come. Hence the defence of Greater Germany is continuing here, on the almost opposite axis of the world, even if the weapons in Europe will evidently soon fall silent. This glorious country was once pledged in perpetuity to a German company for a loan to Emperor Charles V. Certain remnants of this claim are still legally pending in court, meaning that the emerald mines near Cabimas in the north-west, for example—passed on through a series of inheritances—are still in German hands, an asset which neither the British nor the Americans know about. If a Fourth Reich were ever founded, the profits from these mines would be a fundamental building block.

The Tunnel to Leuthen

I am interested in the life of my maternal grandfather whom I never met. In 1945, he was the head of a pioneer unit at Fortress Breslau. It is reported that he discovered a tunnel system under the town hall of the besieged city and worked on clearing and restoring this escape route with his people. The tunnel was meant to extend to the battle-field at Leuthen, and had been constructed by Frederick the Great in case Breslau should be besieged in the Seven Years' War. The sub-terranean passage was supposedly so wide that horse-drawn carts could drive through it. Behind a mountainous area, once the rubble had been cleared away and the tunnel had been concealed, there would then have been a route for the besieged to reach the Army Group Centre. My grandfather, a young officer, did not survive this period of his life. But all witnesses speak of him as a figure of hope, an imaginative man who was never nervous and, above all, techni-cally adept. I wonder whether the 'Tunnel to Leuthen' was a fever dream of the besieged or a fact.

A Warlike Bunch

At Fortress Breslau, I, Dr Guido Weiser, battalion doctor, am caring for three regiments—though they do not have any more fighters or wounded than a battalion used to. With the supplies of dressing and medicine (as well as 126 complete sets of surgical instruments) that I brought to my forward deployed military hospital from the garrison stores, I could hold out until the spring of 1946. Despite these supplies, treating my patients in the field is difficult. How do I bandage a boil in the rectum? There is nothing in the body's curves for the bandage to grip. A neck injury! I have everything except for plaster casts. A grazing shot to the head. Hard to bandage in such a way that air can reach the wound. My battalion fought its way through the broken-through walls in the cellars and advanced to meet the Russians from behind; thus they managed to occupy and control the first floor of the rearward houses in Goethestrasse, the area of the backyards. We dominated this part of the main line of battle until the surrender. The unit had grown out of Cavalry Regiment 8 (Oels garrison), was then called Combat Group Hanf, was briefly assigned to the 269th Division, and temporarily belonged to Regiment Reinkober of the 609th Division under the name of Batallion Schmidt. Each renaming was a new beginning. While the injured limbs of my patients are only growing together very slowly, stormy turbulence at the higher command levels of command. Thus the names of the units change, even though the people remain the same.[1]

Economy of Leftovers

On 30 April, the 3rd Tank Army and 21st Army were located on the line Demmin-Lake Kummerow-Waren/Müritz-Rheinsberg-Neuruppin. Together the armies formed the Army Group Weichsel. The tank army still bore its name but no longer had any tanks. The army group took its name from a front that had not existed since January. Its commander-in-chief, Gotthard Heinrici, had been removed from his position. But he stayed close to his staff and his successor, General von Tippelskirch, questioned him about the few measures that were still being ordered from the command post. At this point, however, Colonel-General Student, who had been in charge of the Cretan landing and was considered a 'stayer' in these last weeks of the war too, was chosen to command this fragment that called itself an army group. He had taken over three different chief commands in recent weeks. He never had time to get a grip on the

---

1 As Cavalry Regiment 8 they were the elite, as part of the 609th Division they were rabble, as Combat Group Hanf they were the 'sworn community of a wearer of the Knight's Cross', and as the 269th Division they were not supplied, not even noticed. As already stated—always the same people, defending their section despite all orders.

group under his command through telephone calls, visits, addresses or other leadership actions. When he arrived at the command post of the Army Group Weichsel, all he could do was join in with the mass flight that was taking place with 18 vehicles. Of the three cars with which he had arrived, two were lost over the course of the day due to attacks by fighter bombers.

Radio Work in the Final Hour

The three, a radio technician and two editors, had fled with their equipment from the broadcasting centre in Masurenallee to the Zoo flak tower. It was not easy to penetrate the concrete with the radio signals but it was still possible at certain frequencies. The shots from the heavy flak guns on the roof platform, which kept the Russian tanks at a distance from the bunker entrances, gave the hit songs with which they were meant to supply the combat units a real-time character.

The two editors set up boards from the equipment they had rapidly thrown together and brought with them. The speakers' microphones were poorly suited to music recordings. But, for all the obstacles to this RADIO WORK IN THE FINAL HOUR (not including the presumably absurd reception in the inner city combat positions, assuming the soldiers had a sense of melody—and there were no radios for music there; the military radio devices were set to receive the 'station'), the intention was simply to create MARKERS FOR THE MEMORY in a brief moment—whoever knew the hit songs could put them together by combining what they heard with their memory. That was not music. Much contemplation while playing the records. 'The Next Spring Like This Will Be in a Hundred Years': the popular song reminded the radio staff of 'happy days we had experienced in 1938, in which we imagined a couple in a hundred years, when we're not around any more.' But right now, in the besieged Zoo tower (facing forward), we imagined that in a hundred years, counting from this 30 April (that would make it spring too), there would either be another war or a picture of an unknown period of freedom and reconstruction would come into view.

Group Photo with Capitulators

No one would have used the word 'surrender'. I am visible as the sixth liaison officer from the left on the group photo of the German Supreme Authority, which governed Denmark to the end (in indirect rule, a unique case among the Reich's administrative structures in the occupied territories). I am marking my position with a cross. At the time this photo was taken, we were informed via confidential channels and a letter from our superior that we should accept the entry of 5,000 Danish policemen trained in Sweden into the kingdom and accompany their induction. We emphatically refused to hand over our power to the Danish resistance which did not present itself to us in any official position or with any identification or official authentication, not even as a guarantor power. We would rather take up negotiations with British agencies or wait for the final surrender of the whole Reich, and then slip into this final battle position or handover at the last moment, as an intact power centre, without having to use the word 'surrender' ourselves.

Our remaining power is sufficient to have a say in the conditions, namely, the time and the partner who will receive the handover. Part of our power also lies in pointing to the chaos of uncontrollable hostilities. In that sense, our potential to threaten lies not in the power we actually have but in the obvious gaps in this power which our partners should fear more than ourselves. We desire a 'soft transition' and have no cause to spell the word 'unconditional' as that is found in the declarations of the Allies. While we are getting in position for the group picture, the representatives of the king and the Danish cabinet leave the building without having achieved anything. The Swedes have been waiting for some time in a nearby restaurant.

As far as steadfastness of character and persistence are concerned, we are still men of 1940. As far as the situation of the fatherland and the real circumstances now confronting us are concerned, we are equally resolutely creatures of late April 1945. Hence the 'amphibian gaze'—that is what the photographer assigned by the propaganda company (the only one here in the north), who, for all his exhortations, did not manage to make our faces look uniformly 'serious' or 'cheerful'. In fact, our faces looked 'doubting' and 'cautious'—which I liked, as it corresponded to the actual situation. By late afternoon we had already made progress with the Swedes. There was much talk of us in the newspapers of the neutral countries. Transports with prisoners (including ones we had asked be sent over from the Reich) went to Sweden to reinforce our good will.

A Failed Surrender

Six former shooting instructors from the Paderborn Tank School, filtered out from the prison camps of the Ruhr Pocket and tried by a US military court, were acquitted on the evening of 30 April 1945 of the charge of having 'executed' the American General Maurice Rose for racial reasons (they belonged to the Waffen-SS and the general was a New York Jew). Simply because they were so good at it, the shooting instructors had organized a last resistance outside Paderborn. They owed their acquittal to their American defence lawyer, a captain in the American secret service with a law degree from Harvard. General Rose, nicknamed Big Six, had been warned about the front visit. The US unit that headed for Paderborn was under attack. An air raid on a group of Tiger tanks had failed, as the tanks proved immune to napalm bombs. At that point, Rose was still eight kilometres away from the first frontline.

Meanwhile, half a dozen other German tanks had appeared from the south-east. US General Rose recognized the danger of the situation. His grouping of two jeeps, one motorcycle and a car headed in the direction where he could not hear any shooting. After a short drive through a forested area, his vehicles came under fire from hand weapons. They turned around. From the direction they had come, a heavy tank was now approaching. They took it for one of their own—until they saw from the two exhaust pipes that it was a Tiger tank. The turret hatch opened and the commander of the German tank pointed a machine pistol at the US general. One of Rose's accompanying vehicles left the road and escaped across the fields. Rose's driver and his adjutant undid their gun belts to surrender. Rose, who, unlike his companions, was wearing his gun on his hip rather than in a shoulder holster, reached down to drop it and submit. The German misread his movement and shot him on the spot. The US press wrote about the popular general's death for over a week. The Ruhr Pocket in which two German armies had been surrounded was renamed the 'Rose Pocket'. All this counteracted the efforts to cast light on the facts by the defence counsel of the accused soldiers (only one of them came into consideration as the direct perpetrator but the prosecution spoke of a conspiracy). Nonetheless, he achieved their acquittal.

Episode near Eitting: Taken Prisoner along with Their Prisoners

The air reconnaissance had reported that all bridges over the Isar Canal were destroyed. The US divisions pushing ahead to Munich and the Alpine fortress were accumulating in front of the obstacle. A patrol under Lieutenant Warren Parkins discovered an intact underpass leading under the hydraulic structure to the other bank. At the other end of the tunnel—an anti-tank barrier. Parkins severed the ignition cables installed for a detonation of the underpass. Success made the US troops boisterous, and they ran out into the open. They were directly followed by a company from the 342nd US Infantry Regiment. This hasty troop was surprised by a major German counterattack and captured just as Captain Richardson and his radio operator O'Neil were about to report their success. For a while, the Germans wandered around with their prisoners near the town of Eitting, at a large distance from the bank of the canal. They were seeking a chance to surrender to the enemy along with their prisoners. But it had to look as if they were only doing so under duress. They could hardly surrender to a group of three captive GIs. So they asked the GIs they had captured to mediate for them. A larger US troop was radioed to come with their vehicles to the tunnel, where the Germans and the captive GIs received them.

Surrender at Unusual Times[2]

In the First World War, on 4 April 1915, Easter Sunday, the Russians attacked an Austro-Hungarian infantry regiment at the Carpathian

---

[2] Based on Holger Afflerbach's *Die Kunst der Niederlage. Eine Geschichte der Kapitulation* (Munich, 2013). The following stories likewise draw on this study.

front that was composed of officers and men from the vicinity of Prague. The soldiers had no reason to defend themselves. A few minutes after the attack began, the regiment surrendered without firing a shot and marched into captivity in an orderly fashion, led by its own commissioned and non-commissioned officers. The lack of any spirit to resist was a harbinger of the later collapse of the Habsburg monarchy. In the historiography already presented by the Viennese authorities during the war, the actions of the regiment became legendary—cowardice and high treason. The traditional regiment, whose standing extended back to the Thirty Years' War, was disbanded. The families of the soldiers and officers were subject to disadvantages at home.

The capture of the last Japanese soldier from the Second World War is an opposite case. The Japanese second lieutenant Onoda Hirō surrendered on the Philippine island of Lubang in March 1974, 29 years after the end of the war. He had indeed heard the loudspeaker vans calling for him to give himself up (with his combat unit, he was terrorizing the island from the jungle), even the voice of his brother, who had urged him to stop. But, he related, he had come to the island in 1944 in a situation where it seemed impossible to him that Japan could surrender unless all Japanese were killed. He had therefore taken the loudspeaker announcements for enemy propaganda, a means of deception.

Bite Inhibition in Wolves

In the history of evolution, only those wolves have survived who were reliably capable of bite inhibition within the pack. A wolf defeated in battle will extend its throat to the noticeably larger specimen which plays the victor and need only bite to destroy the inferior animal. It will not do that, said the breeder who had been an Austrian again for a few days, and was showing the Soviet officer the enclosure because he needed an allowance of meat for the animals that had to be approved by the new occupying power. And there are no exceptions? asked the officer. There is no such thing as a mad wolf, answered the breeder.

Failed Surrender by the Last Followers of Antony and Cleopatra

Antony and Cleopatra, still riding the wave of triumph they saw as their future until the Battle of Actium, had sent a troop of gladiators ahead towards Rome, who were supposed to appear at the games that would follow the victory over Octavian. Then this column of combat specialists, who were famous among the people but of low social standing, learnt of their rulers' defeat in the decisive battle. Antony and Cleopatra had retreated to Alexandria. One by one, the legions from Africa and the Orient fell away from the two, quickly reckoning who were likely to be the new masters. Only the gladiators remained loyal, fighting their way to the tower to which the ruling couple had withdrawn. Only after the queen's death did these fighters surrender to the victorious Octavian, who accepted what was called the DEDITIO (unconditional submission in the firm expectation of pardon). In a base act of deception, he gave the gladiators fields. On those same fields he then had each of the capitulators—one could also call them the last followers of Antony and Cleopatra—massacred individually on their property.

Certain Captivity, an Uncertain Status

Aristocratic warriors in the late Middle Ages, as Johan Huizinga notes, had a low opinion of common people. But they were terrified (which meant they were also attentive and respectful) of falling into the hands of such foot soldiers in battle or afterwards. Faced with someone of equal standing, they could have surrendered and been released for a ransom. A foot soldier of humble origins could not be assured that the noble captive's family would genuinely pay the ransom once he was delivered to them. They were more likely to chase the prisoner's escort away. So it was better to kill him directly in combat, and take his armour which could be sold for a good price.

In one battle, an ancestor of the Seneschal von Waldburg attempted to escape this fate. To that end, he had to convince within a very short time the peasants who had captured him that—contrary to past experience—a ransom would definitely be paid for him. But there was neither a formulation nor a gesture that would have achieved this in so short a time. He was butchered and stripped of his armour.

In the Battle of Crécy, 4,000 French lords were gathered as prisoners behind the front of the English crossbowmen. Then it appeared that the main French force would attack again. The English king, either to deter the attackers with an example of his determination or because he expected the prisoners to be freed, ordered the slaughter of the entire mass of prisoners. With each crossbowman having to kill four nobles (which was only possible through the gaps in the armour), this task took the full contingent of bowmen some two hours two perform.

'Whether the governor of a besieged fortress should go out and parley'

In his first book of ESSAYS, Michel de Montaigne writes in Chapter 5 about WHETHER THE GOVERNOR OF A BESIEGED FORTRESS SHOULD GO OUT AND PARLEY. At no time, he quotes other authors as saying, must a commander be more on his guard than during negotiations. He continues: 'That explains why it is a precept on the lips of all fighting-men of our time that no governor of a besieged fortress should ever go out personally to parley.'[3] But then Montaigne adduces an example of a besieged commander saving himself by trusting the besieger's word of honour. The scene took place in the Hundred Years' War. The English commander who laid siege to a castle had had the building undermined. He only had to ignite the gunpowder piled up in the drill hole to blow the fortress to pieces. But he then summoned the lord of the castle, a certain Henry de Vaux, to come out and negotiate his surrender. The latter decided to show faith. Once the besieger had explained to him that his downfall was certain because everything was set up for detonation, he felt the utmost gratitude to his enemy and surrendered unconditionally with his troop. Then 'the fuse of the mine was lighted, the wooden props began to give way and the castle was blown up from roof to basement.'[4]

In this respect, surrender is not the defeated party's act of submission but, rather, the generosity with which the victor takes up his opponent, who has already lost his reality in itself into the new reality, namely, that of his side. Peace follows not from laying down one's

3 Michel de Montaigne, *The Complete Essays* (M. A. Screech ed. and trans.) (London, 2003), p. 23.
4 Ibid., p. 24.

arms (which does not rule out the possibility of later retribution) but, rather, from this 'joint forgetting'. It is a matter of exchanging realities, the chance of a second life—acquired, justly or unjustly, thanks to the enemy.

'I will lay my head on screws until all bridges are blown to pieces'

A popular actress known for her authentic expressivity (she never lied when she acted) had always kept her private life and her profession strictly separated. As her marriage aged, she noticed that her husband had a mistress. A marital war ensued. Both of them suffered, as did their two children. The actress spoke a great deal to her confidant, who worked as a dramaturg. This friend gave her some advice: You must end all fighting, for the sake of the children. They alone are important. He is a traitor, the actress countered. Believe me, her confidant replied, you will not kill your children. You will not even use them as a security. I never 'use' my children at all, the outraged actress responded. Exactly, her confidant insisted. You will not fight to the end. You are no Medea. So you must surrender.

—What's that supposed to mean?

—No court proceedings. No arguments. Submission. Accept the young mistress. Wait and see what happens.

—I can't do that.

—I believe you. But you can act it.

—What role do you mean?

—Perhaps the Marschallin. But I don't mean a known role, I mean 'your' submission. 'I gave myself up with heart and hand.'

—I'm not a masochist.

—But an actress.

—Who will write the role for me?

—You. You will yield in every matter. Not a word about that. You must want it with all your heart, with no ifs or buts. I belong to you, I surrender. He won't be able to bear it.

—Because he feels guilty?

—The guilty conscience has to be eliminated too. You are his prey.

—Unconditionally.

—For better or for worse.

She should call to mind his character and her own very thoroughly, collect everything that accumulated between them (their shared 'ground'), and then build a bridge. With the violence of the hate-filled Medea and the patience of a wise slave (the actress was of Slavic descent), but most of all with the experience of so many plays in which she had already acted both sides: that of generosity and that of revenge—like a Russian grandmother, then, in which lots of playwrights are sitting and telling her what traits to employ in developing her 'campaign', or, rather, her bridge-building. This is about your life, said her confidant.

Before her conversation with this confidant, the actress had enquired about a Swiss address where one could find a gentle death; but she put this idea aside for the children's sake. The energy of this 'mental attempt' entered her peace machine. Surrender, not peace, the confidant corrected her friend. There is no 'peace' in this matter; there is only the chance that your husband will stay in the marriage.

The husband, open to seduction in many directions (this had originally drawn her to him), entered the path cobbled together out of dramaturgical elements (though its details were masterfully evoked in his imagination by the actress). He did not even realize that the route he proceeded along in the next weeks, step by step, was a bridge. It all looked human, not mechanical at all.

All of that fashioned out of determination. None of it simply for a purpose or goal (this was out of question for the actress). NOTHING MERELY A GOAL (it was EXPRESSION).

—Should I hint that I am having an affair?

—Definitely not.

—It would increase my value in his eyes.

—Please, nothing artificial!

—It's better to forget that I'm supposed to be acting all of this?

—That's how you'll transport it in the most authentic possible way. You can't act it if you don't feel it. It's art.

—Outside the theatre?

—It's the opposite of theatre. This is about your life.

The actress summoned a unified will. This encompassed her children and this man (with all his flaws—a no-good to others, but a jewel to her). Added to that, she herself and her happiness (which she wanted to regain as she knew it). All this surrounded her like a magic spell. First her husband (initially relieved) had exploited her yieldingness and hastened his trot, his movement away from her. She evidently complied (which also confused him). A path with no borders lay ahead of him. He had reached the depths of his baseness.

Then one thing and another emphatically drew him to her. If something as precious as this generous, obviously passionate person *entirely* belonged to him, he should not leave her lying there. His sense of property was mightily stirred. She seemed more desirable to him than when he had first courted her.

Within a year, the two were reconciled. He never discovered that dramatic experience from over three centuries (including the French classics) had reunited them, not mere human nature. The marriage remained problematic. But the children were growing up. None of the bridges broke, if only because they had not been built by engineers or from material components. An outsider would not even have seen them.

Handover of a City

Dr Hans Mayer was director of a munitions factory. He learnt from the mayor that the commander of the British division in front of the city had told him to surrender the city by 7 p.m., otherwise it would be destroyed. The mayor felt unable to make such a decision which required him to assure that nothing would happen to the British troops as they marched in (he could not account for any coincidences or guarantee the absence of lunacy). He consulted with the local police chief and Ortsgruppenleiter. The local military commander too could not bring himself to make a decision that would taint his military career just before it was all over. He had a telephone connection from his factory's air-raid-protection cell to the central air defence for Hamburg. He used this connection to seek contact with the Reich Governor of Hamburg.

Dr Hans Mayer, surrounded by engineers at a factory still producing at full steam, wearing a uniform of the Reich Labour Front in which he had often been lucky, and thus full of energy, concentrated on establishing the cable connection. Around 10 p.m. there was still no artillery fire at the city, although the ultimatum had expired. By that time Dr Mayer already had Reich Governor Kaufmann on the line. In our munitions factory, Mayer told him, there is a store with 1,000 cubic metres of aircraft fuel (highly flammable hydrogen peroxide) and 7,000 tonnes of gunpowder. If these reserves were to come under artillery fire, the entire area up to Bergedorf would be chemically burnt. We can do without that, replied the Reich Governor. Maintaining secrecy, he planned Hamburg's surrender. He sent a peace envoy to Geesthacht. Thus the factory director, the mayor and this negotiator crossed the lines to the enemy quarters and arranged the handover of the city.

A Surrender That Was Unprofessional in Form but Successful in Content

The Foreign Office had left 50 people behind in Berlin to keep an eye on its buildings. By chance, staff from the protocol department had been assigned to this purpose. They would much rather have left for Thuringia or Southern Germany with the others. Meanwhile the Foreign Office's Secretary of State, Adolf Steengracht von Moyland, had already been summoned back to the north, and was cunningly struggling through the Allied-occupied areas towards Schleswig-Holstein. He had not arrived there yet. As a result, there was a complete absence of expert advice from the protocol department of the Foreign Office for the northern surrender negotiations. In that sense, an expert from the diplomatic service later commented, the surrender negotiations of General Admiral von Friedeburg with the commander-in-chief of the British armed forces, Montgomery, was not carried out properly in formal terms. As far as the substance was concerned, it was a stroke of luck and a last success.

The first thing one sees on the photos of the negotiations is the following scene: THE SUPERIORITY OF THE VICTOR (not the done thing, but the German side had no influence on the other side's style). Then: WAITING FOR THE CAMERAS TO ARRIVE. The process humiliates the vanquished. This, said Steengracht, was what came of the fact that there had been no training for military head negotiators by diplomats on the German or the English side since 1918. The German delegation made a mistake, the assessor continues, if it pointed out the limits of its authorization. It meant to express that it would be difficult (without the help of the Allies, who had better radio equipment) to inform units fighting on the periphery quickly enough what time the surrender would occur.

As the surrendering party is assuming a guarantor position for the effectiveness of the surrender, that does not have to be brought up in this form. One particular success fell into the general admiral's lap, as it were—the vanity of the British commander-in-chief, who wanted to see as many soldiers as possible kneeling before the victor, caused him to argue that the western surrender should involve not only the Army Group North but, in fact, all German forces in Holland, Denmark and Norway. He did not realize that it was in the German government's interests to have as many troops as possible surrendering to the western Allies while—conversely—delaying surrender on the eastern fronts.

The spoils consisted of an 88-hour reprieve. That was the time between the partial surrender in the north (ships could still take troops and civilians across the Baltic Sea to Denmark or Kiel) and the final overall surrender in Reims. For the units of the First Tank Army in Bohemia, it meant leaving for the west. For the submarines, the reprieve meant a return to the ports. One last time, the telecommunications units rehearsed their techniques, constantly improved during the war, for reaching distant parts of the troops, masterfully outplaying their comrades' coincidence, accident and technical failure. In those 88 hours, the army's telecommunications system, whose reform had been initiated by Guderian in 1916, was given its finishing touches.

Life-Saving Message to the Enemy

The hierarchy, now without the force of sanctions but still alive, so to speak, through inertia and custom, led to bizarre situations here between the wire fences of the prison camp in the Rhine flood plains. Hierarchy of mindset, hierarchy of ranks. Thus Major Salb, a field officer who had led a combat unit in the Lüneburg Heath only two weeks earlier, was invited to a 'conversation' by a military judge and high-ranking fellow officers concerning information he had carelessly provided. It took place in a location near the barbed wire fence, far away from the guards.

Before Salb's troop was captured, that is to say, while he was still a soldier, he had passed on a sketch of the wooded area north-east of Münster to the British enemy through a messenger, Captain von Reitzenstein, who crossed the fronts. He had spread this around. The treasonous map sketch showed the location of containers filled with

4,000 tonnes of combat agent, primarily war gases. Through artillery fire, said Major Salb, these containers would explode. The expansive contamination would endanger the enemy, their own troop and the civilian population in equal measure. And the word 'endangerment' was a euphemism—these combat agents, which were never used in the war but kept as reserves, were directly lethal. In this 'conversation among officers', which the military judge in attendance interpreted as 'a form of military trial', Salb could have talked his way out of the matter by claiming that the message to the enemy had been a strategy to prevent artillery fire. But he insisted that in war, one had to counteract 'unwanted damage' to both sides through communication with the enemy. One was in constant communication with the enemy in various ways, not only through fire. This response gave the conversation among comrades, with its implicit threat of a secret court, a certain edge. What saved the major was the information from one comrade that the Army Group Blumentritt had also informed the British 8th Corps facing it of the combat agent storage facility. Yes, Major Salb expanded his argument, he would soon give courses in the prison camp in correct behaviour during future wars, using his case as an example of communication beyond the frontline. His comrades advised against this, as one should not speak of 'future wars' at all here. Thus the debate, which had begun in a hostile and anxious manner, ended with a conciliatory mood all round.

Emergency Supplying of Shaft Mines Knows No Fronts

In the glory days of the German arms industry, there was a workforce of 20,000 men operating in the shafts and factories of the Eschweiler Mining Association. Now 1,600 people were still active to save the mines in day and night shifts. They waited for the Americans at a

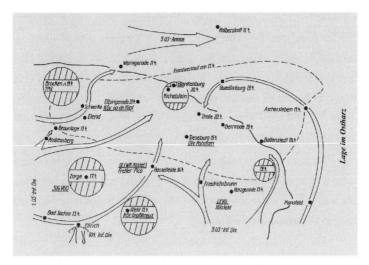

FIGURE 23. The conquest of 'Fortress Harz' in April 1945. On the last day of April, there were still isolated hideouts for fighters.

depth of several hundred metres. Through linguistically complicated contact, they persuaded Allied mining officers near Aachen to carry out preparatory work. There is no 'zero hour' for complex, historically grown facilities like the mine systems of the Mining Association. The facilities self-destruct and fill with water unless there is continuous work inside them. US officers were horrified but then, for technical reasons, tolerated the use of connecting tunnels from the side already occupied by the Allies to the mines beyond the frontline.

Exhausted as We Were

There are three of us left. Our superiors have gone missing. The enemy has also lost sight of us. We are lying on the ridge opposite the Büchenberg. On wet ground, underneath pine trees. Days ago we watched a group of German officers being taken away down the Büchenberg, on the other side. We still have six tins of chasseur sausage. Tins like that can be opened with a bayonet. Eating pure meat (without bread) upsets the bowels. To discharge the thin soup that trickles out of our bottoms, each of us crawls to a pit 12 metres away. We still have that much decency left, enough respect for one another, that we observe proprieties.

The last order from a non-commissioned officer who led us here was to hide and not move an inch. We should not defend anything. He wanted to ensure that we would be safe. He never returned from his reconnaissance expedition.

Now, around noon, our limbs are gradually warming up. It's drizzling. Or there's fog. The pines are keeping away the moisture coming from above. We haven't seen the sun in several days now. So we can't tell the points of the compass. We lack the imagination to know where (with no mission) we should march to. So we stay in waiting in our undergrowth, greedy for every iota of warmth but can only produce it ourselves with the little stoves of our bodies. At night we move close together.

The main difficulty is that we don't know how we can contact the enemy to give ourselves up. We've discussed that we will put our hands up if we encounter an enemy patrol. Is that enough for a surrender, for a guarantee that we'll live? We hope so. But we can't bring ourselves to leave the safe forest yet. We're also exhausted, with no mind for decisions.

At Rest

The last entry in the army journal I keep close to my body (as I saw a standard-bearer doing in a film about Frederick the Great, hiding the regiment's flag on his body and thus saving it from the defeat at Kunersdorf; but we had long stopped carrying flags with us) concerns events that took place four days ago. Lieutenant-General Flörke, completely cornered, radios from the vicinity of Elbingerode. Infantry General Mattenklott entrenched west of Heimburg on the Nackenberg. Artillery General Fretter-Pico at Todtenrode Forester's Lodge, his last command post. No trace of the commander-in-chief.

Our proud 11th Army! Victor of Sevastopol in 1942. After that, it was never again the same as the army that went out and set itself up in front of that legendary fortress. It did not survive von Manstein's recalling to higher tasks in good shape. What is an army? The topic of the journal I am keeping. And also a FRAME STRUCTURE, worth as much and as little as the concrete structures that are connected to this frame, just as a pine tree with candles and decorations becomes a Christmas tree can look rather shredded by early January.

The remnants of the 11th Army recently bore the title 'Fortress Harz'. The mishmash of groups squashed into barely more than 16 square kilometres. The German Reich consists of a few such 'enclaves on enemy territory'. The remaining combat groups allowed themselves to be driven to the mountain peaks. Those are dangerous places to be locked in. Never, we learnt at army college, should one allow oneself to be driven to hopeless heights. That was already a fixed rule for a Roman legion. The fact that an army's leaders no longer have the choice to follow simple rules of war demonstrates the decline.

I have meanwhile gone into hiding at Michaelstein Monastery. Henry the Lion, I am told, once lay in one of these cells with a femoral neck fracture. He remained unable to prostrate himself before the emperor and receive mercy, for he slipped on the frozen path on horseback and did not get beyond Michaelstein Monastery. I slept for three days. I never fought exhaustion so comprehensively in the entire war. Now I will set out from this monastery cell and look for an enemy to take me prisoner.

Devastated Youth:

Hitler Youth Area Leader Friedrich Grupe Reports

[30 April] The last 20 of my Hitler Youth boys left on hidden routes. Only Bannführer Kicki Fischer left with me. No Langemarck, that's the main thing. At least I've kept to that.

Only four days ago I dismissed a hundred boys. They went back to their home towns across the American front.

[23 April] There are granite blocks lying scattered in the woods. The Wurmbach is running into the valley named after it. The Americans have already been through here. I march with the rest of my people to the resting area on the Georgshöhe, near Thale. Here there's a forester's lodge in an oak wood. Let them search for us in vain here, in big Germany. Three days ago (in scruffy old clothes, which is dangerous if I am discovered) I saw my family. The heavy iron gate at the courtyard entrance clangs when there are distant explosions. In the village of Rieder I come upon a command post set up in a school classroom. The Quedlinburg district leader, an oldish air force colonel. Visibly drunk. This is what one calls a 'collected combat group'; they plan to take up position on the Hexentanzplatz plateau.

All-round defence and dignified downfall. I don't supply them with any of my boys.

[**12 April**] We march through Quedlinburg, the city of Emperor Heinrich, singing. Supposedly we are meant to join the army group 'Harz'. We receive guns of a type unfamiliar to me. Two hundred of them. We are joined by a group of 90 students from the Napola and their teachers. Our quarters is only five kilometres away from the property of my parents-in-law, where my wife is staying with our daughter. That's a quick trip by bicycle. I surprise the family at coffee time. In the daytime my boys train on wooded terrain, spread far apart. I meet the 'Hitler Youth Representative for the Army Command in the West', a Hauptbannführer. He is wearing a lieutenant's uniform. We youth leaders are assigned non-commissioned officers and present ourselves like soldiers, even though we are teachers. At the Hitler Youth Area Leader school in Thale that evening. Some of the staff are still there, waiting for instructions. They tell us of a giant sulphur-yellow cloud that passed over Halberstadt three days ago. A blood-red sun illuminated its form. The trainee area leaders appeared distraught.

[**8 April**] That Sunday I was supposed to take over command of the youth training camp in Halberstadt. The troop is meant to be trained as an anti-tank unit and deployed against the tank vanguards of the Americans, which are thought to be in Vienenburg. On that same Sunday, duty began at 5 a.m. for the squad under my command. The Hitler Youth boys are taught by non-commissioned officers with experience at the front. Today's schedule features a march out to the Huy, a ridge above Halberstadt with a monastery complex. Three hundred Hitler Youth boys have fallen in now in front of me, in the courtyard of an expansive, deserted school where they are being put up. Procession with fanfares. One can see that the spectators who have gathered at the gates disapprove of the boys being deployed. I have to say something about the raising of the flag. My words come out haltingly. The procession of 300 marches through town. I am wearing field grey too, like the commissioned and non-commissioned officers accompanying me. We reach the edge of the forest at the Huy. Air-raid alarm. I am standing on the road with my bicycle which I was using to circle the column like a shepherd, and looking back at the town. I see the squadrons of planes. Fire engines are driving towards town on the avenue we came from. The smoke clouds are drifting south-west towards the Harz. I break off the exercise. What use is a compass exercise supposed to be to the boys? The march back to the quarters on the town's lacerated roads leads to a destroyed school. My column leaves the burning town. We search for the way to the towns near the Harz. People on Sunday outings cross our path.

Fair Copy Based on the Latin

It is well known that in Thomas Mann's novel *Doctor Faustus*, the chronicler Serenus Zeitblom ends his written account in April 1945 with the words, 'A lonely man folds his hands and speaks: God have mercy on your poor souls, my friend, my fatherland.' After completing his Herculean task, the humanist experienced such a sudden sense of relief that, in the subsequent days, he began a series of postscripts and was overwhelmed by a dynamic activism.

It is often overlooked here that the character invented by Thomas Mann, who named him Zeitblom, was in fact based on a real person—the headmaster Dr Knut Knorre. And did not experience the end of the war in a southern Bavarian town, as described by Thomas Mann but, rather, in the Harz. He had recently, as an 'educator of educators', been a supervisor at the Napola Ballenstedt and reported to the Magdeburg Senior School Authority. Now, having fled first to Braunlage and then to Torfhaus, he operated within the vicinity of a hut in the hills above the town which was already occupied by American troops. GREEDY FOR ACTION after such intense months and years of writing down events, he attached notes to trees, posts and house facades in Torfhaus, and the following day also in Braunlage, announcing courses for young people that he would give in his hut, as he called it, his 'residence' or 'retreat'. He was contacted by a group of Hitler Youth boys who had buried the weapons entrusted to them, obtained plain clothes and were now trickling into the town. They had read the notes. They saw it as an opportunity to make their stay here in the Harz look plausible by taking part in an educational course. At night they bivouacked in the open, in a meadow next to Knorre's hut, and then the teaching began at seven in the morning. Children and pupils whose school had shut joined them. A US sergeant leading a reconnaissance patrol entered the classroom, checked that they were studying and refrained from further examination. Nor had the occupying authority objected to the notes which Dr Knorre had posted in order to announce the course he was offering.

But this educator saw it as a decisive beginning to start from scratch, namely with Latin, which had been lacking in Central European parts since Varus lost his battle (possibly in the Harz). The chronicler and action-hungry practitioner had everything at his disposal that vibrated in his head, starting with Melanchthon—via the anti-music of education, as it were, rhetoric, logic and the modest

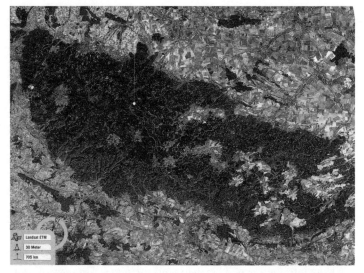

FIGURE 24. The Harz Mountains. Dr Knut Knorre's hut is located around 100 metres from the point marked.

interpretation of faith, that is to say, the anti-diabolical, and he had a copy of a Latin vocabulary book. In addition, Dr Knorre had a German translation of a chapter from the *Annals* of Tacitus, which had been made for the military postal service and was therefore in small print. He had to translate it back from German into Latin from memory in order to teach from it.

A friendly day outside. It seemed to him that the Harz Mountains were located above the cloud cover. Or what looked like a cloud cover over the plains in the north was actually fog. In the unheated room of the hut, the 'pupils' were mouthing the Latin words in alphabetical order.

In this way, thought Dr Knorre, the German youth could learn a new beginning in a language as distant from German as the moon from the earth—that is, on new linguistic ground. For the words pull the souls along with them. And if there are many words (and if they fill up with memory, camaraderie, contact, character and whatever the chronicler pours into them with all his heart and knowledge), they gain wings.

Actually these boys, as one of their leaders coughed up after revealing himself to the teacher in confidence, had been prepared for a Werwolf mission. Explosives were hidden in the grave for their weapons in the upper mountainous area above the hut. Pioneers had trained the youngsters in the work of destruction. They could have dug up their supplies at night and attacked one of the villages and the local garrison. For a moment the chronicler was shocked by the information. Then he became proud of the fact that his authority, that of an old man, was enough to keep this young troop from prejudice, senseless acts, the demon. HE FELT LIKE THE HEAD OF A MONASTERY COMPLEX THAT WAS ALWAYS A PLACE OF EDUCATION, AND WHERE, IN THE YEAR 1000, BECAUSE THE END OF THE WORLD WAS OBVIOUSLY CLOSE AT HAND, YOUNG PEOPLE GATHERED AROUND THE OLD TEXTS AS IF THEY WERE A FIREPLACE. Only in late May did those entrusted to him disperse, 'everyone to his own town'.[5]

Network of Loyalty

Several thousand people wanted by the Gestapo were hidden in the Greater Berlin area. As Harald Welzer told me, it was always networks

---

5 Luke 2:3. [Trans.]

that offered this protection. No one can attempt to hide a person from the henchmen in a block of flats on their own. The caretaker would notice and report it (so he has to be in on the plan and keep quiet). The rushing sound of a flushed toilet at night is suspicious. Even if the individual shares food rations from his coupons with a hidden Jew, everything else needed for survival will be missing. In one case, a married couple much admired in Berlin society, who had too long felt immune to persecution owing to their renown and the friendships they cultivated and missed the right moment to escape, were kept safe by their household staff, the servants, for the duration of the war. No traitor among so many people. After the dissolution of her employers' household, one cook (she was together with the family's chauffeur, who still kept quiet after they separated) rose to become the head of the canteen at an air force base. It was she who put up the aforementioned couple. Meanwhile, 24 people knew about the rescue plot, and they all stuck together. The achievement, Welzer commented, lies in this unifying bond of silence.

—Taking both her employers under her wing—one can say that was how she was brought up.

—Did she have cause to be so loyal?

—Nothing unusual. She was asked and she helped.

—She had already been dismissed by that time?

—The household had been dissolved. The endangered couple sat in station restaurants in disguise, waiting for their arrest.

—Then the persecuted couple ascended to more favourable areas of security with each promotion of their protector?

—And to new dangers. It depended on the cook's prudence (by now she was the head of a canteen) in suitably limiting the number of people in the know. They formed a 'state within the state'. Only a network like that can offer protection.

—You're saying that morality lies *between* individuals, not just *inside* them?

—Some people in this group stuck together for immoral reasons too.

—And the cook's parents were a silent part of the network as well?

—Everyone who played a formative part in her life.

—Would you call that resistance?

—No.

—Would you call it 'uninfluenceable by the powers that be'?

—Yes.

The Loyalty Machine

Magda Bügelsack, née Stolzheise, from Halberstadt, later married in Quedlinburg, had a strong ability to discern: Something is trustworthy if it proves reliable. She felt a yearning for loyalty. Where did it come from? Inherited from all her ancestors, learnt from her parents and from her surroundings, to the extent that all her female friends in the German Reich felt the same need—mirrored in the hit songs and their friendships, in the people they wanted to meet and to whom they would become engaged. When it comes to something as valuable as one's life, the arbitrariness of exchange must be eliminated.

That was not simply longing; it was an empirical judgement. Transforming this sluggish society of troths and dreamers into a rapidly functioning modernity is A MATTER OF ORGANIZATION. Organization, in turn, rests on a currency, according to Niklas Luhmann (still an anti-aircraft assistant at the time). Organization gives the leader of a multiplicity the right to move comrades back and forth with short commands that do not lay out the entire context of justifications, putting them in a state of activity and accelerating them in a way that cannot be explained within the traditions from which the loyalty relationships come. The leader needs recognition which can only come from those followers who owe him loyalty because they expect loyalty from him. Where this system collapsed, for example, on the retreats, its end was accompanied by that of ORGANIZATION, the most important and novel machine that joined the machines of the industrial period in the 1930s.

Nocturnal Confession

One evening in May 1978, on the day when the kidnapped former Italian prime minister was found dead in the trunk of a car in Rome (we experienced police officers were still in a state of shock after the German Autumn), my colleague Reimers from the State Office of Criminal Investigations in Rhineland-Palatinate asked me about politically motivated violent criminals on the FAR RIGHT over some beers. That was part of my domain at the Federal Criminal Police Office. He said that corresponding to the basic level of active violence that could be observed on the so-called left in 1977, there was a considerable parallel tendency among the 'young rightists'. He referred to the generation shift that we both agreed was evident on the far right. Then, because we had been in the same year in the accelerated training as assistant detectives during the last two years of the war, we got on to the question of whether, based on our inner stances, we were better equipped to pursue criminals from the left-wing terror network or those on the right of our field of observation. My colleague Reimers emphasized that for him there were only criminals. Their programmatic inclinations 'towards rightist or leftist slogans' (by which he meant the written material and quotations that accompanied the crimes) were interchangeable. By four in the morning we had openly spoken our minds. I had the feeling that something in me had been working up to a heart-to-heart like that for a long time.

I don't know if I should call myself a National Socialist, as I took up my profession enthusiastically at 23, full of impressions from the spirit of the movement. Before that a Jungbannführer. I was deferred from military service, first to complete my training as a criminal investigator and then because of my obviously successful police work. The curvature of my spine also made me unfit to serve at the front. And so the war ended. I kept my convictions to myself back then. The Allies assigned me to the police service which had to be rebuilt. I signed a declaration that I would carry out this service loyally and reliably. No one asked me what I thought, and in my heart I remained what I had been before, the things I had sworn along with the others in my year during training. Had I interrogated myself, I would have concluded that I was still a National Socialist.

At the same time, my professional behaviour is impeccable. No one can tell what I feel politically, and I proceed on the assumption that one cannot be a National Socialist if National socialism no longer exists as an organic reality, as a movement and as a grouping.

I often think that National Socialists in particular are effectively immunized against the Third Reich. We direct our gaze sharply at what was lost, and are immune to any positive or negative slogan used about National Socialism. There are, after all, no witnesses (except, on that evening over beers, for my colleague Reimers, who will not give me away) to the fact that my feelings are those of a National Socialist—in the literal sense, namely, 'nationalistic' and 'socialist' (the combination now exists only as a world interior or grief work, and even before 1945 it probably only truly existed in fragments or for a few moments; it is, as we said at the time, an IDEA).

When I feel like that, I have interior monologues, I feed a mentality, and no one can see any stirring in my official's face that corresponds to these reflections. The way one guards a secret treasure as a dragon of the soul. I can't even speak about it to my wife—at most with my colleague and superior Dr Friedrich, whom I know to be an anti-fascist (and almost as openly to him as to Reimers). I pause in my account because I am thinking of the pistol (wrapped in oilskins), two hand grenades, a mine with a detonator, all buried near Kiel in a box—that was the last impulse for activity, namely, becoming a Werwolf *at the appropriate time*, not then, so close to surrender. The stuff is still there. Presumably without rusting in its grave, I packaged it that well. My personal file does not contain any shadow that could fall on me. Twenty-three years ago, as a young criminal investigator, I had no opportunity to be criminally active for the state. My successes as a police officer involved fraudsters and forgers. That was my department; robberies were a separate matter.

Today I'm the right hand of the head of the Federal Criminal Police Office, Dr Horst Herold, a passionately skilled man. He seems blind to the far right. He doesn't realize that our service would definitely have employed someone so skilled if he had approached us. He indulges his mania for computers. We didn't have such devices. But we were equally familiar with the beginnings of dragnet investigation (following the Nebe school)!

I drew the boss's attention to what, according to our rules, that is to say, in a civilian sense, was a *violent* breakthrough of young people in the neo-Nazi scene (I would never call a true National Socialist a Nazi, but I certainly use the word for these violent right-wing extremists because, as a National Socialist, I see through their theatrical character). During the interrogation of one such younger functionary from the far right (they had removed the old ones), a writer of radical right-wing diatribes and calls to battle who had not, however, committed any acts of violence himself, my feeling that readiness for violence on the far right has nothing to do with our National Socialist mentality was reinforced. When I call their attitude stagy, I'm not saying that they are actors but that their adoption of symbols from the Third Reich is a historical prop, a means of expression. The same way revolutionaries in the French Revolution dressed up as Cato, Brutus or Mucius Scaevola. Reimers confirmed to me—only a National Socialist can reliably distinguish between real National Socialists and those who simply help themselves to objects from the store of history. Likewise, Reimers says, a National Socialist is the best person to cure another National Socialist's misconceptions. That's more difficult with young people who are only faking a National Socialist worldview.

As the transcript of the aforementioned interrogation attracted some interest, I was constantly given violent right-wingers to interrogate. After some time I convinced my boss Dr Herold to pay more attention to the danger on the right. He was already very nervous back then, slept next to his office, worked day and night as if it were wartime. Nerves frayed. Short attention span. He believed that something terrible could happen any day in our republic. He confused the politicians with masses of memoranda. I could already see back then that he would lose his position.

My little task force has meanwhile charged 37 radical right-wing perpetrators. Every investigation led to a conviction. It takes time for a crime authority to develop prosecuting skills for a newly forming group of perpetrators.

Performance of a Play

In a packed church one 20 April (Hitler's birthday), the pupils and teachers of the former Fürst-Franz Gymnasium in Dessau, under heavy police protection and surrounded by right-wing extremists, performed a self-produced play based on the book *Hitler's Grandchildren*. The play portrays 23 perpetrators of violent right-wing crimes. Andreas Marneros, the book's author, says that violence by right-wing extremists is simply criminal violence. Violent neo-Nazis know nothing about National Socialism, are not political and have no well-founded ideology. They are, claims the nationalistically unbiased scholar who comes from Cyprus and detests the Third Reich as much as the murderous acts of the far right, CREATURES OF OUR PRESENT TIMES. There is no continuity with the Third Reich.

Betrayal of Comrades on All Sides

On the occasion of Fathers' Day, two perpetrators from the radical right-wing scene in an Eastern German federal state made an excursion to the Hexentanzplatz in the Harz in the company of a comrade. She was in a relationship with someone else from the scene. The three returned home and the sexual appetites of the two perpetrators were aroused. As their comrade refused to let either of the drunken men have their way, they killed her. The perpetrators buried the body.

In the course of the investigations, they were interrogated first as witnesses, then as suspects. In their statements they incriminated each other. The one claimed to have been scared of the other. He said he had initially refused to help carry the body that they ultimately both shouldered. His comrade had answered: 'I don't feel like burying two in one night.' He drew a knife and told him, the fearful one, to choose whether he would help him or be killed as well. Then he carried the body by the feet; the other man by the shoulders.

In the course of the interrogation, the one who presented himself as the more fearful, and as having been more passively involved in the deed, stated that the active comrade told him to undress the body with him; she should be buried naked so that her clothes would not point to her identity. Either their companion was not dead after all or the perpetrator, alleged by the other to have been the less fearful, was aroused by the body—he sexually assaulted the dead woman. The perpetrator only admitted to having had the idea of putting a few clumps of grass on the hole in which she was buried, as well as the idea of sprinkling some pepper that the two had brought along in order to prevent sniffer dogs from discovering it. The member of the scene who had been in a relationship with the dead woman also betrayed his companion by refraining entirely from coming forward after learning of her death, so as to avoid any involvement in the investigations.

Hatred without Distinction of Person

A radical right-wing murderer from an eastern German federal state serving a life sentence supported his worldview as follows: Jews should be gassed. Why? Answer: Jews believe in Jesus Christ. But then, said the psychiatrist asking the questions, that also applies to Protestants and Catholics. Do they have to be gassed too? Naturally. And what about the town's churches? They should be removed from the townscape, they're ugly, replied the convict. Everything should go back to the way it was in the GDR days, he said at the end of the conversation.

The prisoner who was examined is not mad, commented the forensic scientist. Each individual piece of debris in his 'ideas' triggers a strong affective response in him. The connection between the designation and the affect is coincidental. The murderous affect, once triggered, works equally powerfully with other designations, symbolic triggers or 'ideas'.

That's a murder machine, not a human being, said the presiding judge, who was conferring with the expert witness. 'Human splinters' would be better, the same way one speaks of the splinters of a projectile. They inflict the worst wounds, the court-appointed expert stated. It is typical of such cases that the perpetrators do not know their victims.

'Darkness in the minds of the perpetrators'

Two murderers, equipped with National Socialist symbols, had spent the evening in a neighbouring town with a mutual female friend and missed the train. So they took a different train to Dessau, where they likewise missed their connection. Now they had to wait at the station until four in the morning. The sister of one of the murderers, whom they phoned, could not pick them up. The other murderer's father was unsure for a moment whether he should pick them up by car. But he had drunk alcohol and ultimately refused to drive. Now the murderers also began to drink alcohol. Later, they were joined by the third murderer, with symbols from the radical right-wing scene on his clothes and body.

The three roamed the city's empty streets. Then, at two in the morning, the murder took place. They were singing the song about Africans by the band Landser:

> Africa for monkeys, Europe for the whites,
> Put the monkeys on a boat and send them on their way.

After that they sang a song by the Zillertaler Türkenjäger:[6]

> Ten little niggers came to German climes,
> One got bubonic plague and then there were nine.
> Nine little niggers had drugs in their freight,
> The Russian mafia went 'bang bang' and then there
> were eight.
> Eight little niggers thought it was like heaven,
> Then came a pack of Murderskins and then there were
> seven.

In between they yelled 'Eight, eight!' (referring to two Hs, the eighth letter of the alphabet, standing for 'Heil Hitler'). At the end:

---

6 This neo-Nazi band based its name (*Türkenjäger* means 'Turk-hunters') on that of the Austrian pop group Zillertaler Schürzenjäger (the latter word means 'womanizers', literally, 'apron-hunters'). [Trans.]

The shark and the octopus, the sturgeon and the hake,
The monkey meat gave them three days of bellyache.

They did not know the man they murdered. The forensics expert who confirmed their legal culpability at the time of the crime explained to the court, when asked, that a characteristic trait of all three perpetrators was that they were 'as cold as stone towards their victim'. Could that be taken as a continuation of the Third Reich by other means? The expert considered that out of the question. He spoke of 'darkness in the minds of the perpetrators'. The murderers, he said, were products of our current society, insofar as one could call 'such destroyed human beings' products. Can one call it a disaster or an accident? asked the judge. There is no doubt, the expert replied, that it was murder.

The Uncanniness of Props

I am in charge of the costumes at the Volksbühne on Rosa-Luxemburg-Platz. The shelves holding the props and clothes, which are characteristic of the Third Reich, are still unnerving to me, even after being accustomed to them for years. The house directors are untroubled when they deal with the costumes, caps, helmets and weapons. What if something of the props' origins still lives on in them like a ghost? In many cases, the dramaturg comforts me, they are only replicas or recently produced objects that never came into contact with the practices of the Third Reich. I reply: The songs of Laibach, Landser or Volkszorn are dangerous props.

As the custodian of the concrete objects, I am at least capable of distinguishing between them. For me, they do not have the blanket meaning they take on when used on stage in conjunction with incidental music and a dramatic plot. An indiscriminate use of them, the kind I know from the enthusiastic Schlingensief, who, I suspect, only had a faint notion of National Socialism, underestimates the power of costumes—a power that does not only affect weak spirits.

Now, I do not think that violent right-wing extremists visit our theatres anyway. They are more likely to set them on fire. They would call us and the theatre 'leftist scum'. So the costumes and props that we show the audience certainly have no effect. But what concerns me is not the garments worn by our actors or singers, or the flags and symbols with which they spice the revues, but, rather, the complete store that I look after. We recently loaned it out to Babelsberg when the film about 20 July was made there. At night, I often go through my stock and check that these clothes and objects are not suddenly moving by themselves. I think that much caution is called for—keeping watch in the night hours when they are idle and among themselves.

Disloyalty, Sacrificial Death

An audience consisting of 89 million inhabitants of a country wallows every Saturday (and often at other times in between) in pop songs, chansons and melodies of the heart. Abundant and personal emotion that finds no outlet in practical life accumulates from these refrains of popular music. This was the introduction to a lecture by Theodor W. Adorno in Berlin-Wannsee. The 'sworn community of the sentimental', Adorno continued (losing the interest of some listeners through the elegance of the formulation) can be characterized as a 'horde of traitors to sentiment' (at this point Adorno had the entire auditorium on his side). If you ask me, he continued, who composed or wrote the words for the most popular hits that were sung or quietly hummed during the Third Reich, and how many of those were murdered in the concentration camps, you will find that those who agreed with this unanimity and kitsch were at once the spearhead of the murders committed against these 'sinners in spirit', the commercial figures in the sentimentality business, who knew that the majority was behind them but did not realize that this approval would be their death.

I am full of sorrow, Adorno added, for these 'dissidents of the authentic spirit'. They are platitudinarians, panderers to the triadic soul, uninhibited simplifiers, war profiteers who thrive on the human suffering that makes them thirst for the mirror image of their suffering in the form of song. Those who so enjoy singing hit songs then become traitors to the very thing they have worshipped. They become collective cutthroats.

That was too strong for the listeners. They did not follow what Adorno was speaking about—that all the words of popular songs revolve around the subject of loyalty, and that the society which supported this by an absolute majority in radio, film and theatre events and in *Kraft durch Freude*[7] did not show this loyalty towards the writers of the hits.

'When I see you, I must weep'

Dr Fritz Löhner-Beda, the lyricist of 'Rosa, wir fahr'n nach Lodz' [Rosa, We're Going to Lodz] (a wartime hit in 1914), 'Ausgerechnet Bananen' [Bananas, of All Things] and 'Ich hab' mein Herz in

---

7 Kraft durch Freude [Strength through Joy], commonly abbreviated to KdF, was a state-run organization in the Third Reich whose overall function was to keep leisure activities in line with the state's principles. [Trans.]

Heidelberg verloren' [I Lost My Heart in Heidelberg], librettist of *The Land of Smiles, Giuditta* (dedicated to Mussolini by Léhar) and *Ball at the Savoy*, was arrested in Vienna the day after the Reich's annexation of Austria. Transported to Dachau concentration camp with other celebrities. Lawyers, friends from the USA, operetta lovers and (to a limited extent) Franz Léhar championed his cause in vain. Relocation to Buchenwald concentration camp in September 1938. Later taken to Auschwitz. The work performance of this intellectual at the I. G. Farben factory there is not excellent. At an inspection by I. G. Farben board members, his demeanour and performance are faulted. They could have sung the hits for which Fritz Löhner-Beda wrote the words, but they did not recognize their author. Owing to the claim of inadequacy, Fritz Löhner-Beda was struck dead the following day. Units from the Office of Strategic Services who went to Austria in late April to search for persons, patents and depots of copyright-relevant contracts were instructed to determine his whereabouts.[8]

'I readily trust others'

A Swedish police inspector who had been working as a private detective since his retirement was staying with a delegation from the

---

8 In Germany, copyright lasts up to 70 years after the holder's death. This means that the numerous rights of Dr Löhner-Beda expired at the end of 2012. Their relevance lies in the fact that they are connected to melodies which constituted an elementary and global value through their repetition on all public stations. Is it significant that the time at which these rights expired resulted from a wilful act committed under the responsibility of the German Reich and on its territory? Should the validity not be extended to the point at which a natural death could have been expected, asks the publisher, or should copyright per se in fact be abolished out of protest at the death of this author and sorrow for all his comrades in death, as this case demonstrates its injustice?

Swedish Red Cross who were inspecting Russia's western territories; he was trying to ascertain the whereabouts of Helene Jellinek, the wife and heir of Dr Fritz Löhner-Beda, on behalf of a New York law firm. Because the author's survival was considered uncertain, the law firm was searching for an heir, as the commercial exploitation of valuable musical works was at stake. The Swedish detective established that Helene Jellinek, successively disposed of all assets passed on to her by her husband, had been deported from Berlin to Minsk on 31 August 1942 and murdered there on 5 September. The fruits of the investigator's expertise reached New York by telegraph on 30 April 1945. He had conveyed the information to Stockholm via a Swedish consul general, and from there along the Atlantic cable.

Awkward Leap

We had the impression that it was a matter of days. According to the garrison, which was likewise attempting to escape, there were no units of ours left between the Russian advance troops and our military hospital. That was what the head physician at the military hospital told us, who had sent his wife and children ahead west, to Judenburg. 'My senior physician has left us,' he said. As Germans, we had been considered foreigners here in the Eastern March for the last few days. The nurses evacuated the departments. Using handcarts and a few ambulances, we distributed the patients to clinics that were all further west. I followed the family to Judenburg.

'But then nothing decisive happened for several days. More waiting time. Just as the whole war consisted mainly of waiting times. On the surface it was like the way we doctors observe a healing process, where we can only wait, not help. But nothing heals in war. So I drove east to the military hospital again to make sure we had not overlooked anything in the rush of our escape. The junior physician, Dr Schmittchen, who did not want to subject his pregnant wife to transportation, was looking after the wards with new arrivals. The young doctor felt that he was safer under the protection of the military hospital if the Russians took over the city than he would be on the run. With a few wine bottles from the cellar of the military hospital,' the head physician continued, 'I managed to get a seat high up on the load of a military truck. I was exhausted when I arrived in Judenburg. When I jumped off my perch, which was roughly as high as a harvest wagon filled with hay, I hit the ground awkwardly with my right leg. I screamed. Unbearable pain.'

'Mourir pour Danzig':
Nobody Wants to Die for Gdansk

A group of Frenchmen, initially taken as prisoners of war in 1940, then recruited for forced labour in the Reich, had left the Baltic and reached Gdansk in March. They had settled into their slave-like status. The prospect of a 'liberation' by the Red Army made them uneasy at first.

So they had built themselves a hut and a provision camp on an area of 100 square metres in Gdansk. They were excellent skilled labourers (as civilians, some of them had been car mechanics by profession). They had brought food, everyday items and tools to this demarcated territory. They wanted to hold out here for a while.

Then, in late March, Gdansk was overrun by Polish and Russian divisions. On their patch of Gdansk, the group of Frenchmen occupied a quasi-exterritorial position (as if on an island). They had fashioned and hoisted a large *tricolore* made of various plundered material. They encountered considerable language difficulties with the armed eastern Slavs. In their miniature state, guaranteed by the Russians, they developed a lively barter trade; they also carried out repairs in exchange for natural produce. It was possible to celebrate public holidays. A number of women joined this 'sanctuary', which was generally considered safe.

Thus an employee of the Swedish Red Cross discovered this lost bunch, who had more or less been en route since 1940. But it was no easy task to repatriate the group. Their existence had been reported to a higher authority like a piece of lost property. Finally, accompanied by Russian representatives, they were set moving towards Odessa on the last day of April. Many spoils and mementos from Gdansk in their bags. In Odessa, they boarded a ship and were transported across the straits to Marseilles, from where they were sent to their different home towns. They were among the few French who had personally laid eyes on the terrain that had triggered the war. But they had little opportunity to tell of their adventures there; no one in France was interested in Gdansk. The times were agitated.

'When I look at a head officer, I imagine how he would look headless'

I am a lance corporal. I can still make people laugh over a round of skat, at least. People see me as a formulator. On duty, what counts now (and we might have to hold out for another five days) is to survive somehow. That sets limits to one's joy of expression.

We have seen four different commanding officers in the last three weeks. Each one viewed his command as a new beginning. Recalled again or dead soon afterwards. These newcomers always had different ideas about our guard duty. We are guarding a munitions dump. Some migrant workers who organized themselves had cut a hole in the fence and were trying to escape with baskets of ammo. The skirmish cost us two wounded. They took their injured and their dead with them. We expect a reprisal from these partisans. But they are not the greater danger; our own superiors are. I never contradict them. If they were with us for longer, I could trust one or two of them. Then they would know that a good relationship with us foot soldiers is a form of life insurance. But only someone who lives with us for longer can learn that. When one of these newly arriving and quickly passing types says something to me (for example: We should send out troops to look for the partisans), I stand at attention and keep quiet. If I said what I thought of his order, I would be court-martialled and lose my head (though they tend to shoot or hang us soldiers). In the fifth year of the war, a superior of the old school (but they have all fallen) wouldn't make a lance corporal stand at attention for him; he would speak to him in a looser formation in the hope that he could learn something important in that way, or that a wish he expressed would be fulfilled. So there I am, standing in front of one of these new types of officer (who knows when I will next be standing in front of one like that), saying nothing and thinking: 'When I look at a head officer, I imagine how he would look headless.'

New Use for Old Property

Above a property in Stuttgart that lay destroyed in April 1945, and whose basements once covered four floors that have survived but were closed up and built on at ground level, a technical building was erected to be used by US experts for planning and controlling drone

276 ◆ ALEXANDER KLUGE

deployments in Africa, mainly in the coastal areas of Somalia, carrying out targeted killings of presumed terrorists. The subterranean vaults still contain now-unreachable supplies of colonial goods from the time before the original building burnt down. It housed a firm that dealt with the import of African products.

ALEXANDER KLUGE

In Place of a Postscript

◆

Friday, 2 August 2013, Elmau

Dog days. I have gone to the mountains. Flies here too. Only next week, they say, will a low clear away the walls of heat. My idiosyncratic attempt to write a book about a single day is troubling me. I have been sitting at the texts without interruption since Whitsun, I cancelled all my appointments. Even though I already had what I believed to be a finished manuscript before Whitsun.

Saturday, 3 August 2013, Elmau

Writer's block. It is hard to connect the confusing but concrete facts of 30 April 1945 with the 'perspective' from much later years that this 'zero hour' contained the seed of a new beginning.

The film DOWNFALL, claustrophobic and focused inwards on our country, drives my imagination to San Francisco. In the minutes encompassing—by Central European time—the moment at which Hitler closes the door of his death chamber, the diplomats who will be negotiating the founding and structure of the United Nations that day in San Francisco brush their teeth, shower, have breakfast and prepare for their day. I see trucks driving up. Suitcases and files are loaded. The Russians threaten to leave. They demand ultimate veto power and a joint presidency of the four major powers in the General Assembly. Russia struggles for recognition as a major power on an equal footing (as it does today).

FIGURE 25. The open-air pool used to be a help when it was hot. At the bottom right of the picture, recognizable by the semicircular non-swimmers' pool. Excerpt from an aerial photograph taken by the US Air Force after an air raid on the Junkers factory in Halberstadt (marked by the white arrow). One can see the bomb impacts, one of them close to my route home from the open-air pool which led past the brewery by the Goldbach stream.

Strange things come together. In parallel with the founding of the United Nations, the world's labour movements convene in Oakland, a city neighbouring San Francisco. For the first time since 1914, the warring factions of the working class faced each other again. In the meantime in San Francisco—a doctoral student of Heidegger, now the chief Lebanese delegate sitting at a table with Eleanor Roosevelt, is explaining to the press the goal of finalizing their declaration of human rights within three years. Not a preamble but, rather, a binding universal law.

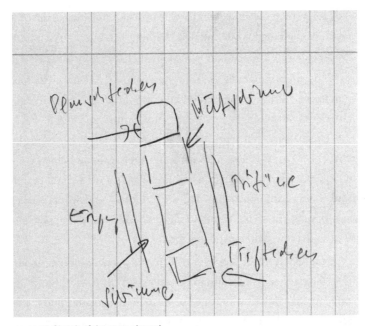

FIGURE 26. Sketch of the open-air pool.

Sunday, 4 August 2013, Elmau

A conductor is here. He is carrying a child, roughly a year old, on his arm. His second wife is an actress who works at the Burgtheater in Vienna. I made a film about this conductor almost 20 years ago when he performed Gluck's ALCESTE at the Berlin State Opera. His wife wants to see what he looked like in so much younger a state. I have to get a DVD.

Alceste, an opera of surging emotions. It deals with a home-comer's fate. The King of Thebes, Admetus, has been fatally injured in war. He will only survive, the gods say, if someone else sacrifices themself for him. Only his wife Alceste, who loves him, is prepared to do so. Admetus later accuses his wife of high-handedness; she cannot enter the kingdom of the dead without her husband's consent (states an earthly law). As they love each other, they *both* choose death.

Is there a comparable level of emotionality about any act of love from the end of the Second World War? Bernd Alois Zimmermann's music contains passages that point back to the war's end in 1945. One can be sure that there were examples of self-sacrifices in the reality of 30 April 1945—a Jewish secret agent goes far behind German lines to find his siblings who had been sent on a death march from a concentration camp. He dies. A newlywed woman takes horses from her parents' country estate to her husband's trapped garrison so that they can escape together.

In addition to the stories in which one person sacrifices themselves for another, there is also the emotion of LIBERATION—those condemned to death, imprisoned or worn down suddenly find themselves liberated, or liberate themselves. That has not been set to music. But it forms a part of that day. The 'dark God=ofpain' still reigns. So I imagine some funeral music.

Weren't You Happy to Be Liberated?

The prisoners of an SS Totenkopfverband had been transported from the concentration camp to a place near the Danish border and taken to an inn. After being handed over to the Swedish Red Cross (only to accompany the negotiations of the Reichsführer, no longer on condition of anything in return), they were treated there by doctors as if it were a military hospital. First of all, the Swedes wanted to improve the physical state of the prisoners with invigorating injections and special food rations. The prisoners seemed paralysed.

—Weren't they happy to be liberated?

—No observable, immediate shift of the soul.

—As if they couldn't yet believe the new situation?

—On the contrary, as if they hadn't been able to find their way out of the situation of their captivity. As if trapped in a maze.

—Could one question them?

—At any time. But their answers couldn't be trusted— they struck us as random.

—Do you think that souls are too sluggish for such an extreme change of fortune? They need a lot of time.

—Something like that. And everything had to be translated from German into English or Swedish too. Some information was lost in the process.

Correct Slowing-Down on the Transitional Point between Terror and an Inkling of Freedom

In Beethoven's opera *Fidelio*, the prisoners step into the light from their prison and immediately launch into the 'Prisoners' Chorus'. It starts calmly, but very quickly gathers momentum and escalates. The director, Calixto Bieito, considered this form of staging— which follows Beethoven's score and stage directions—unrealistic. The rigidity of all vital functions that had taken hold of everyone in the prison cell cannot be discarded quickly, or by the individual people. The director had decided to have a massive metal grid built as part of the set. Using the movement of chorus members through this obstacle to the foreground of the stage, the director

was able to hint at the drawn-out process in which the memory
of earlier life is located, and thus the memory of the hope promised by heaven's light. Because none of the sheet music for the
opera was available during that particular time, Calixto Bieito
arranged with the conductor to borrow a substantial number of
bars from the String Quartet op. 132. The music was provided
by orchestral musicians floating in a basket above the stage.

Monday, 5 August 2013, Elmau

Call from the House of Cultures (Scherer). About documents. A project is planned for 2014 with Richard Sennett and Saskia Sassen. It
will be about the 'Anthropocene'. The history of mankind (from BCE
70,000 to the present day) is to be connected with the topic 'Turning
Points of Civilization'. This involves cities and urbanity, the 'city as
an achievement of tolerance' (from the megacities around BCE 3,000
in Mesopotamia to Lagos, Shanghai or São Paolo today). That keeps
me away from my texts for two hours. I also sense (as an interference)
the dominance of the present which is rooted in all earlier times—a
powerful mass of images.

My wife comes in the afternoon. Finally, the breakthrough. In
the last chapter ('I, the Last National Socialist in Kabul') I insert a
sequence of stories about 'the piece of civilization wrested from the
annihilating principle of war', namely, SURRENDER.

For the overwhelming majority of people in civil emergency
associations, households, among women and children as well as the
soldiers, 'unconditional surrender' (which also exists in amorous life)

was an INTERNALIZED FACT on 30 April 1945. The lust for battle, the rage, the goals of the war and the hubris had been lost. That is the difference compared to 1918, when everything broke up but the spirit of revenge flourished on the inside. Now—right after the attempt to wage total war at the end—a complete handover. Deditio.

Monday 6 August 2013, Elmau

Hitler's personal physician, Dr Morell, supposedly stated in a confidential conversation in an air-raid shelter at the hotel Adlon that Hitler's head cold in 1943, from which he recovered only with difficulty, had caused a brain tumour. The Parkinson's-like symptoms and Hitler's physical decline could be attributed to this growth in the brain. Hitler was doomed.

The more I occupy myself with 30 April 1945, the less significant Hitler's death on that day becomes for me. Certainly, it is amazing what orders this man was still capable of giving in his last days: he had his brother-in-law killed. He had his former personal physician Karl Brandt (who lost his position because of a conflict with Dr Morell) sentenced to death for bringing his wife and children to safety in Thuringia. The people who protected the shaky commander until his death, his secretaries too, acted loyally. But the powerlessness of the man, who knew from the midday briefing at 1 p.m. onwards that there was no more way out, no saving coincidence, was all-encompassing. His existence in the vicinity of the bunker, from a global perspective a single point, had become unreal even before he pointed the weapon at his upper jaw.

What I find striking about this day, on the other hand, is an almost complete CHANGE IN THE MINDS OF THE SURVIVORS (anticipating Hitler's death, but independent of it). Here one sees a new opening to the Western world that would later define the economic miracle.

Whether I still manage to cross the Elbe and reach the west or am taken eastwards in a column can decide my fate. *Spatially* the orientation goes decisively westwards. That *temporally* ends the special German paths taken for over 200, perhaps even 1,000 years.

Horror vacui:
An Example of the Need for the 'West'

To the north of the US Army columns, which had advanced towards Magdeburg since 10 April 1945 and stopped at the Elbe, lay the most modern automobile factories in Europe. They were so novel that they were not on the maps of the American troops. As a result, the Americans drove past Wolfsburg—an insult to the staff and managers of these factories, in a sense, who still considered themselves an important production factor in the country.

The SS and Volkssturm units, as well as part of the factory security staff, had left. The attitude of the migrant workers caused great concern. Confidants of the plant security and management attached to the camps of the strangers reported a wide variety of views. French workers protected the factory. But in the camps and quarters of the eastern labourers, unrest.

The idea of deliberately giving up a provisions depot for looting (*agents provocateurs* in the plant security had instigated the raid on the commissariat) had not paid off. The loot-laden gang had settled in the open rather than returning to their quarters, and seemed eager to achieve more freedom of movement—in fact, the word was that they were planning to march on to the settlements of German labourers and engineers.

One plant manager drove south with two German-American engineers. They were to seek contact with a US unit and bring it along to occupy the factory grounds. People saw no other solution but to place the responsibility in foreign, final hands. The interregnum went on for over 20 days. In the meantime, factory halls had been set up to repair civilian vehicles. They could also have repaired Allied military vehicles, and sent a messenger after the three chief negotiators to tell them this, as it constituted a further incentive for the enemy finally to occupy and secure the grounds.

Wednesday, 7 August 2013, Elmau

Cool weather today, after heavy thunderstorms last night and lightning over the entire Wetterstein. The brain and body need that.

Jürgen Habermas is back from Athens. The 'turning points of civilization' (especially the two axial points, BCE 3,000 and 500) interest him. He is doing some work about them. It will presumably be my last book, he says. But he doesn't want to travel to Berlin in January. I ask him about April 1945. As with *everyone* else I mention it to, plenty of memories but none of that particular day.

I put the same question to Han Magnus Enzensberger, the historians Ian Kershaw, John Zimmermann and Christian Hartmann, but also contemporary witnesses like Fritz Wilde or Siggi Gebser. 'I

heard that Roosevelt had died.' 'I can see before me the day when
the Allies marched in.' Rich images of recollection, but dateable only
through external events. In terms of memories, that individual day
is a no man's land.

Thursday, 8 August 2013, Elmau

8 August 1918. A disastrous day on the Western front. Ludendorff's
fit of nerves. Sudden hearing loss? Because he had the telephone to
his ear, the organ of equilibrium, all day long? But everything has
become unbalanced. Historians like Pöhlmann and Krumeich think
Ludendorff was 'underestimated'. His crazy political activities after
the war colour people's judgement about his actual behaviour during
the war, the historians say. He acted in a 'civilized' fashion on that
'fateful day on the Western front'; he acknowledged professionally
that a DECISIVE BATTLE was lost and that resistance would
accordingly have to cease. No asymmetrical warfare, no Werwolf, no
defence *à outrance*. Not the barbarism of never-ending war.

Friday, 9 August 2013, Elmau

The novel *The Man Without Qualities* begins on an August day in 1913.
The first volume was published in 1930. In retrospect, it is about the
experience of the First World War and the subsequent 'new era'. On
the third-last page of this enormous book, Robert Musil writes:

> The aged Ulrich of today, who lived through the Second
> World War and, on the basis of these experiences, writes an
> epilogue to his story and my book. [. . .] It also enables us
> to consider the story and its value for the present reality and
> the future.

91 Swept Away. 'Not a man of possibilities'

In 1945, Hans Rückert was 22 years old and in action. Today he arrives at the following assessment of the situation then:

> At the district hospital, the CT confirmed the existence of three large cancerous lumps on the surface of my liver that would destroy the organ. Those are metastases, the doctor says. The primary seat is unknown as yet, but it could be located in the lung. It is positive that at my age, 91, the lethal cells do not grow as quickly as in a younger person. So there is time left to say goodbye, and also to put my life in order. I have no one but myself to dissolve the apartment in which I live, to distribute my books. I have started my memoirs.
>
> My time swept away. I have the hits and childhood songs in my ear, but never sang them myself. I have always disapproved of romanticism, because my world as a 22-year-old (we fought to prove ourselves in 1945) was active, brutal and never 'blissful'. That didn't bother me. What rankles me is that the seriousness of that time has gone. I can't refer back to what I experienced. No one listens to me when I just relate the facts of the end of the war.
>
> And again 44 years later! After 40 years of reconstruction or, rather, repair work, this second upheaval—viewed from my presumed year of death, so around 2014—has likewise been *swept away*. Barely one of those directly affected is interested in the details of 1989 that still defined my life. As a functionary of the National

Democrats, I was part of the anti-fascist bloc, and as an officer in the People's Army, I was one of those who deliberately refrained from using the power that we did obviously have. I am not demanding any reward for my virtues and renunciations, but I want to be able to speak about it to those who are interested. The 'generation Berlin' that has now advanced to relevance may form a power bloc in Europe, but its significance has diminished on a global scale. Who in Brazil, Egypt, India or China still listens to the weighty utterances from Germany?

I often think: It can't be that a whole human life consists of sections that are successively devalued. No currency devaluation is as disappointing as the devaluation of narrative power. And so, in 'days wrested from my fatal flesh', to quote Heiner Müller, I intend to write down my memories. In the hope that some archivist will preserve them in their store, or that someone who doesn't even find my manuscript still senses that they missed a chance to learn about something. It could also happen that a future partner of one of my two granddaughters puts some of it on the Internet. After all, I was already a lieutenant in the tank force at 22; I kept driving that vehicle in April 1945, as long as there was enough fuel, and would still have had some grenades left if I had encountered an enemy. In the winter of 1978/79, I was among those politically responsible for the winter road clearance that freed our democratic republic and its industries from the desert of snow and ice.

> The only property (not installed by laws, prejudice or delusions) is living time which Marx calls working time (but what he means, as I always emphasized in my training courses, is LIFE and also 'fighting time', i.e. SELF-ASSERTION). A person wants the sovereignty to interpret such property for themselves. If I am no longer to rule inside my body, I at least want to gather before my eyes the years when I was making efforts.

Saturday, 10 August 2013, Elmau

For me, 30 April mirrors my relationship with the war. We school-children did not understand the war as we experienced it. We attentively witnessed its end (for example, the 19 days from the American invasion to 30 April). An extreme increase in freedom, partly due to

FIGURE 27. *Hetzer* tank destroyer from April 1945.

the extent of the destruction. In that sense, 'rich through poverty'. With no rationale, naively—we could all have been dead.

Only decades later did I depict what war is. Since then, the last days of the war have had a hold on me that directs my Cassandra eye to all later and future reappearances of the monster that is war. This personal relationship with the war is what I am writing about here.

'Whoever does not remember the massacres perpetuates them.' This statement connects me to confidants like my first literary editor, Hans Dieter Müller, who wrote the book *The Head in the Noose: Pre-War Decisions* (1985). He introduced me to Arno Schmidt. Now my employee Thomas Combrink has surprised me with the information that Arno Schmidt had the idea for his story BLACK MIRRORS in the last days of April 1945 (there are some indications that it was 30 April), as a prisoner of war near Brussels. At the end of the Second World War, he was gripped by the image of the THIRD WORLD WAR. That is the subject matter of BLACK MIRRORS. The Cold War was not as harmless as people claim today. I cannot think of 30 April without also recalling the Missile Crisis of the eighties (part of the present for me, as distant as 1945 for my children). And I also have to think of Syria, Pakistan's political minefields and the explosion of an Indian submarine documenting armaments in the Far East. Potential for war now and at the end of the war on 30 April 1945 are one and the same thing for me.

A Man of Iron Resolve

His father, an officer, had been convicted at a court martial for ordering his men to retreat, which had saved their lives. The news reached the schoolboy during a PE lesson at the Napola Ballenstedt. When he buries his uniform and weapons in a hopeless situation in late April 1945, having been drafted as a naval officer cadet, something is left unresolved inside him, a great seriousness and willingness to serve that has nothing to do with National Socialism, but rather with his father's shame (even though his father was subsequently spared for service in a penal unit and fell in action).

How does one look at the possibility of the Third World War with the eyes of late 1945? The time is that of the missile chess game of the eighties. As the head of an SPD branch, our resolute man took on Chancellor Schmidt in 1982 when Schmidt visited his home town. In front of his assembled comrades from the branch, he accused the Chancellor of 'pre-war failure'.

Undermining the preparation of wars—that was what the man, who had meanwhile started a family, saw as his goal in life. He believed with all his heart that one could put this attitude into practice, even when one's own country is no longer part of the conversation and decisions are being made at the headquarters of the major powers. What one needs in order to avoid feeling helpless in such an important matter, however, is an insistence on the SPACE OF EXPERIENCE. For him, this space had expanded constantly since the close succession of scenes he had experienced in 1945. A NARRATIVE SPACE of four generations (he was a literary enthusiast and practitioner) seemed adequate to him (and hard enough to achieve) in order to see through the 'deception by one's own people' and confront the 'pre-war'. There was more willpower in him than his sluggish body could bear. The intermittent overload that drove him along caused his death on the first day of a holiday (the crisis of the Cold War was over) on a hike through the Pyrenees in a western storm.

Sunday, 11 August 2013, Elmau

Dinner with the lawyer R., a financial jurist from Berlin, and his wife, an artist. They practice their marriage as a work of art. He saved her life; every day, they consider how each can make a gift of themselves to the other. Occasionally they dress up and mix with other people. On one of the January weekends when carnations and wreaths are traditionally brought to Rosa Luxemburg's grave, for example, they went to the cemetery. The carnations laid down there, they recount, have a special, slightly pale colour that differs from the red of carnations in ordinary flower shops. They are sold in front of this memorial cemetery and at stalls on the former Stalinallee. On this same burial ground, where other comrades from the socialist movement were also laid to rest, there is a stone slab in memory of the murdered Swede Wallenberg. He was a victim of Stalin. The wreaths on this memorial have been scattered wantonly around the grounds. This memorial slab is not worth remembering, at least for some mourners. They are very differing factions of the left who gather each year at the grave of Rosa Luxemburg.

The fact that the outbreak of war in 1914 was not effectively opposed by the socialist movement in any country in the world was a blow to the *enragés*, the trustworthy, the comrades who get to the root of things, both emotionally and in the heart of their rationale. That is the background to SPARTACUS. Rosa Luxemburg also called herself Gracchus. Like all freedom fighters, the Gracchi, two brothers, were killed. Rosa Luxemburg by soldiers of the Garde-Kavallerie-Schützen-Division, her comrade Hugo Eberlein by the Soviet secret service.

None of this fighting spirit is left in April 1945. At most, émigrés are keeping the fire burning.

Monday, 12 August 2013, Elmau

The *Goldberg Variations*. Never was a sack of gold coins invested better than by the Tsar's envoy at the Saxon court, Count Keyserlingk, who could not sleep at night and commissioned these variations from Bach. The pianist Simone Dinnerstein has flown in from New York. She approaches the material in a new way. She shovels the sound masses against one another, respecting their imbalances. Asymmetry rather than a schema. The masses of notes do not follow any beat, producing arrhyth- mias as if choirs positioned in different wings of old churches were responding to one another, but the church spaces were distorting the arrival of the notes at one's ears. That is in keeping with Bach, who did not obey the metronome but, rather, the immanent gravity of the note sequences, as had been customary in the late Middle Ages. For her version, the pianist radically altered the distribution of the rhythmic and melody arches between the left and right hands (and the fingerings). The left and right hands cross and follow each other with great elan, each seamlessly continuing the other's movement. It is difficult to assess what that means for the left and right hemispheres of the brain which govern the right and left hands respectively. An acrobat of the body, the ear and her head's two cooperating hemispheres.

An exchange with Dan Diner that same evening. The historian received a major European award accompanied by research funds. He is interested in portraying German–French relations between 1931 and 1954 (that is approximately the duration of the Second World

War in his view, if one includes the Japanese invasion of Manchuria). He analyses the 'Persian Corridor' which is barely known. Via railway tracks and roads running through a British zone and a Soviet zone that divided Iran, the Allies sent supplies to Russia during the war. And one mustn't view Stalingrad in the West–East direction, Dan Diner states but, rather, in terms of its north–south supply route. Stalingrad kept this 'Persian Corridor' open. It was on this Iranian terrain that the Cold War later began. In 1945 the Russians refused to vacate their zone. Later on, the British-Indian troops in that corridor would in turn topple Prime Minister Mossadegh, thus making political processes in Persia irreversible. I feel slightly embarrassed about the brief section in the 'history of a single day'. On the other hand, Dan Diner encourages me. Hardly anyone knows about the 'Persian Corridor'. But it marks a historical trail leading to the most dangerous Middle Eastern conflicts of today, and extends back far beyond 1921 (Lord Curzon). Here political reality worked on writing its own 'narrative', unnoticed by the central power of historiography or public attention.

Tuesday, 13 August 2013, Elmau

I remember when my daughter was ready to listen to me a few weeks ago. Directly after watching the *Tagesschau*[1] together, before the Sunday evening murder case took over, I debated with her about the difficulty of breaking through the cocoon of the congealed public sphere (crisis, debts, cities, habits) as a film-maker (my daughter is a film-maker), because what underlies these topics remains hidden when summarized in the *Tagesschau*. My daughter entirely disagreed with that formulation.

---

1 One of the major evening news programmes in Germany. [Trans.]

She was just having some trouble with her flatmate. She wanted to talk about personal stories. She was open to the idea of our finding interesting moments together in the empty space of a year unknown to her, namely, that Monday in April 1945 in which we could test scenes that are filmable today (that is, films of today in the knowledge of scenes from the unknown year) in a MOSAIC OF TIME. Before we could start arguing, we had already both been distracted by the beginning of *Tatort*.[2]

Rainer Werner Fassbinder, Born in May 1945

The novelist and biographer of Fassbinder, his former producer, who lives in Rome, remarks—because Fassbinder only lived to 37—that for geniuses who do not live past 34 or 35 (like Mozart and Bellini), the gravitational centre of their lifelong fantasies is located in the five years *before* and five years *after* their birth. This, according to this biographer, can relate to sounds, stories told, rhythms; in fact, everything a child is capable of perceiving—so also clothes, flapping curtains or the direction of the mother's gaze. This is not because such children have themselves experienced any events in the outside world during that time before and after their birth, but because thousands of impressions have been translated into the voices and facial expressions of their parents—the never-ending narrative that accompanies the years of a symbiotic relationship.

And so Fassbinder's mother told him a lot. He could later see and hear with the eyes of this mother, who brought him into

---

2 The longest-running and most popular television crime series in Germany. [Trans.]

the world in May 1945 and survived him for some time after his death in 1982.

—Are such impressions almost always indirect?

—If I fall over as a child and sprain my arm, that's direct.

—A hit song from 1942, sung on all the radios and hummed by the mother while cooking one winter's evening in 1948, three years after birth, is branded on the memory?

—I assume so.

—And that later becomes a film?

—The title of a film, at least. Or the project. That can still develop in a different direction when shooting the film.

—And the time itself, the five years after 1945, the period of reconstruction, is interesting (independently of our child's impressions), if only because the mother and child lived in it—and this now has to be based on an idea, not a memory or an early perception?

—The key to the fascination of the scenes in *Lola* with Mueller-Stahl, the city official who came from the east, lies in the fact that the mother and the genius were living together at the time. This figure was undoubtedly invented. One doesn't need to have experienced a great deal to think up a film scene. But one has to feel a reason for the scene in oneself.

—For something or other?

—Yes, it's vague.

—And you say five years before and after birth, and that's true for a lifetime?

—Ten years for less sensitive people.

—So should one (as a biographer) generally count back to ten years before birth and add that period to the person's life, not only for geniuses?

—Fassbinder dated the story he filmed ahead to 1957. But the subject matter came from 1950.

Wednesday, 14 August, Elmau

In the daytime my son does athletic things. He rides up to the Wetterstein on his mountain bike. But in the morning he insists that I join him for his breakfast. So I have nothing beforehand and then eat more than I should. My son has a tendency towards potlatch—a sturdy joint meal as a sign of affection.

I read him some stories from the first chapter ('Arrival at the Endpoint'). I test. I can do that best with someone who doesn't know 30 April at all. My son shows he is willing to listen. He wouldn't read it, he says. But he enjoys listening. Does it matter that he doesn't know the day? On the contrary. If I know a story, I don't have to listen to it.

My maternal grandmother and her great-granddaughter, who will be four years old in 2014, would have been exactly the right team for an exchange of experiences. They have never met. And so one can only understand the chronology of a single day by threading the time-thread of roughly 140 years through it.

My Grandmother on 30 April 1945

She comes from a time with long summers, long-term prospects. She was born in 1872. She lost something in the autumn of 1914 and will never forgive any person, let alone any historical account, for that loss. She keeps it safe inside her, and will never trust again (she lost her two eldest sons). Many of the mistakes she made in life, she realizes, must be attributed to this loss. She spoilt her third son. Drove her eldest daughter out of the house early, into a life that was badly suited to her. What else did she do wrong, even though she tried hard to do everything right? Because of the air raids in Berlin, she stayed in Bad Warmbrunn from 1942 on. When the Russians approached, she fled over here, to Prien. Now it seems that the American columns are marching towards the little spa town from the south and the west. Wehrmacht uniforms are still visible on the promenade.

She is having breakfast. One of her worries is timely digestion; a good day can't start without that. Her ageing muscles need training. So she takes her walk along the lake. Where are the loved ones? The self-critical woman doesn't know whether she loves all her grandchildren and children equally. She can certainly guarantee that she pours out the same amount of concern—with generosity, for the soul knows no land-allotment maps—over all of them. Does that come from morality or, rather, vitality (that of her cells, her healthy body, the years that have passed)? She wrote letters that will probably not arrive anywhere, with the country in this state.

So she walks the distance to the pavilion, where the spa resort concert is just beginning. A delicate build. She has a hunched back. She hardly knows anyone here. She is polite to everyone. The lake, leaden beneath the cloud cover.

There is humming inside her: 'Castles that Lie in the Moon' and 'Our World is Beautiful, But it Will Have to End'. Those are the words to the brass-band music of yesterday. She actually knows the words from memory to everything the band is playing.

She was born English. That was irrelevant for a long time (but no cause of shame); she became German by marriage, after all. Now her origin can be considered an identity card that gives her the possibility to get from here, her refuge, to her flat in Berlin, where the majority of her loved ones are waiting for her.

Those are her ponderings while firm steps carry her forwards. Until lunch which she has punctually at one o'clock in the guesthouse. A stay at a health spa shows no regard for war. Towards evening, the Wehrmacht units disappear south- eastwards.

Thursday, 15 August, Elmau

Luck and morality. Conscious, moral decisions rarely prevent someone from becoming guilty. The 'invisible hand of war', on the other hand, stops lucky devils from entangling themselves, and allows them, like well-hit billiard balls, to find their goals far away from punishment and nemesis.

How a Proletarian from London Avoided
Almost Certain Imprisonment

The 56th London Division reached Venice in the evening from the landward side. All public buildings were available as accommodation. The division commander, who had been promoted from the rank and file (the division consisted of Welsh miners), unexpectedly found himself in possession of immeasurable spoils. Even without any aesthetic sensibilities, he could tell how valuable the paintings gathered in this building would be on the black market in London, provided their transport were guaranteed. It would mean finding boats to ship the treasures across the Adriatic, possibly store them temporarily in Portugal and then, with a bit of luck and the initiative of his staff in the 56th Division, bring them to England.

Before this commander and the few who were in the know could establish a connection to Italian ship owners or reliable (or bribable) British transport officers, they received the order to get the division moving in a north-easterly direction at a fast pace. They were meant to reach the Alpine passes via Trieste in a few hours, with vehicles, and then determine the format of a British province in conquered Austria, perhaps in an area where no spoils beckoned at all. Obedience trumped profit. And so this brave soldier avoided military criminal proceedings. That was quite a success; after all, the life of a worker with decent weekends counted for more than a stay behind the brick walls of Dartmoor, surrounded by swampland preventing an escape. Ten hours later the division's advance vehicles were already approaching Agram.

Friday, 16 August 2013, Elmau

Summer clouds. Blue and white while doing the backstroke, unusually high up. Unlike ants, we people don't have eyes on our skulls. One has to be lying or swimming to look directly into the summer sky. Towards evening a strong, dry wind. By the sea I would call it a solar wind, were it not for the fact that 'solar wind' is a term for radiation in outer space that will never touch our skin.

When I was at the open-air pool (already mentioned above on p. 280) in 1940 I heard about France's surrender. The threat of war and the image of summer were not yet connected in my mind. Pétain's surrender and the war itself (which we 'knew about' but didn't 'feel') were something vague and distant. Nowadays I can't look at summer clouds without thinking of the summers of 1914 and 1939, and the deceptive aspect of summers. It is only a small step from having an allergy to war (as mentioned by Sigmund Freud) to confusing 'holiday peace' with the 'threat of war'. My wife notes that the unrest in Egypt is unlikely to affect us. Over here it's the run-up to an election, but there's no danger of any war. And yet, when I swim my 12 lengths, I see writing in the sky. Not wanting to be called mad, I avoid telling anyone about it.

Saturday, 17 August 2013, Elmau

I sleep 11 hours a night here (from 9 p.m. to 8 a.m.). Lying awake for the first time this year. *News of Quiet Moments*, the book with Gerhard Richter, arrives in the hotel bookshop today. Given away three copies. Gerhard Richter on the phone—satisfied.

Sunday, 18 August 2013, Elmau

Dinner with Manfred Osten. I can see him before me now, coming from Japan 20 years ago and entering the foyer of the Berlin Ensemble. We did programmes together about the abrupt weather changes in Japanese chasms and the stoic Japanese character, about Confucius, about Goethe as a Chinese and a Neptunist, about the conquest of the Dutch navy, which is stuck in the ice, by a squadron of revolutionary hussars from France, and many other topics (especially

Alexander von Humboldt). His visit gives me strength, because his generous way of telling stories permits heavy deviations from everyday interests. He eats three portions of lentil soup.

Monday, 19 August 2013, Elmau

As I don't have lunch when I'm on holiday, I have a lot of time. The day isn't broken up. Enjoyment and regeneration come from the plentiful consumption of time. Cool water, wind, sun, walking or breathing can hardly compete with that.

The genre of the chronology of a single day. On some days it seems like a spleen to me (because one day doesn't exist without all the others). But this narrative approach corresponds to the principle of the unities of PLACE, TIME and ACTION. In prose, there are several momentous models illustrating this principle. James Joyce's *Ulysses* deals with a single day in Dublin. A day or an hour in the life of a person is a tunnel or a deep well.

Manfred Osten confirms: The course of the day is the natural form of narration. What was going on? I can confirm that from my experience as a 13-year-old schoolboy. Something experienced only becomes real when I tell my schoolmates about it. This combines with other such instances to form the course of a life which comprises the courses of days.

The word 'mayfly'[3] is often used in a pejorative way. The opposite would be the elephant which keeps its memory even in its grave. In fact, however, the family tree of the fruit fly or mayfly goes back

---

3 The the German word for mayfly, Eintagsfliege (literally 'one-day fly') is used metaphorically to refer to figures with short-lived success, especially in the entertainment industry ('one-hit wonder' would be an example in popular music). [Trans.]

further than that of elephants. It is not a matter of contrasting something that is important for a day with something that is important for aeons. Rather, as with Simon's scissors, these are two blades of the poetic and each would fail on its own, or not even become recognizable in its function. Only both together, the precision of the moment and the narrative space of a hundred or a thousand years, can produce the wealth of differentiating abilities that are in short supply— the two blades of the scissors.

A Paraphrase of 'Downfall'

A disciple of the sculptor Arno Breker, of whom it was said that he would still be spoken of in the future of the German Reich, had almost completed a work made from MODELLING CLAY in the basement of the large studio which belonged to that same sculptor, who had tried in vain to distance himself from his workshops in order to escape arrest by the Allies. Once the model was complete he would cast it in bronze. There was an arbitrariness to the fact that the modelling clay for this large-scale sculpture came from leftover stock with different colours. That made the opus unintentionally colourful. But that was precisely its seductive quality.

The model showed a gigantic fish or aquatic dragon with humans and animals settled on it. Indeed, one could appreciate the diversity of the groups as 'mankind'. The artist made the following comments about his work: if the Great Fish or Leviathan (in order to avoid naming Jewish myths, it had so far only been termed a 'fish') submerges, the creatures settled upon it will drown. On the other hand, the fish, which had breath-bubbles hinted at on its nostrils, would have to resurface at some point, countered the artist's beloved, who coddled him and wanted to convince him to flee to Southern Germany. So it's advisable, answered the young sculptor, who was killed by the Russians soon afterwards, to cling to the animal's scales as tightly as one can and accompany its descent to the depths, in the hope that (by holding one's breath, or in a cavity in the giant creature's skin) one could survive long enough to return to the surface. It was precisely the sculpture's provisional model form, and the light of the lamps set up in the basement, that made it seem as if this stay of humans on the back of Leviathan for thousands of years was possible; but there is never, said Irene, the beloved, any security on such a sea creature.

Photograph Credits

FIGURE 1. Anselm Kiefer, *Europa*. Reproduced with kind permission of the artist.

FIGURE 2. Getty Images, Hulton Archive/Fred Ramage

FIGURE 3. German Historical Museum, Berlin, Picture Archive NO. 95/108Ka7.25

FIGURE 5. picture alliance/augenklick/Sammy Minkoff

FIGURE 6. picture alliance/dpa/Kay Nietfeld

FIGURE 8. KEYSTONE/Fotostiftung Schweiz/Hans Staub (1940)

FIGURE 9A. MoviePosterDB.com/Film distribution: EMI Films

FIGURE 9C. MoviePosterDB.com/Film distribution: Metro-Goldwyn-Mayer

FIGURE 9D. MoviePosterDB.com/Productions André Paulvé

FIGURE 10. KEYSTONE/Fotostiftung Schweiz/Theo Frey (1940)

FIGURE 11. Ullstein Archive, Berlin, NO. 00256873

FIGURE 13B. Film poster for *Kadetten*, Ufa film 1939–40, from Ufa Programme Book (Scherl-Verlag)

FIGURE 14. German-Russian Museum, Karlshorst

FIGURE 17. UN Photo/McLain

FIGURE 18. Acme Newspictures Inc./CORBIS

FIGURE 20. Map of the upper Danube Valley. Obtained with kind assistance from Sebastian Poster, Leipzig.

FIGURE 23. Robby Zeitfuchs and Volker Schirmer, *Zeitzeugen. Der Harz im April 1945* (Self-published, 2004). Reproduced with kind permission of the authors.

FIGURE 25. Ralf Staufenbiel, *Kriegsende im nördlichen Harzvorland* (Borsdorf: Edition winterwork, 2012). Excerpt from a picture made by the US Air Force. Photograph: Lieutenant John S. Blyth. Reproduced with his kind permission and a commentary by Siggi Gebser.

FIGURE 27. André Feit and Dieter Bechthold, *Die letzte Front. Die Kämpfe an der Elbe 1945 im Bereich Lüneburg–Lauenburg–Lübeck–Ludwigslust* (Aachen: Helios, 2011).

Acknowledgements

As with my last books, I owe many thanks to my editor Wolfgang
Kaussen. I am grateful to my sister Alexandra Kluge for providing
material and advice. I would like to thank Ute Fahlenbock for the
production of the text and images in the German edition.